I0600138

Between the

Powers

By Sister Salacious

Sister Salacious
BETWEEN THE POWERS

Sister Salacious
BETWEEN THE POWERS

To everyone who had ever fantasized about mysterious older men, magic, and the taboo~

Thank you to my beautiful beta readers and friends who put up with me as I wrote this. And for waiting by my side as I write the second!

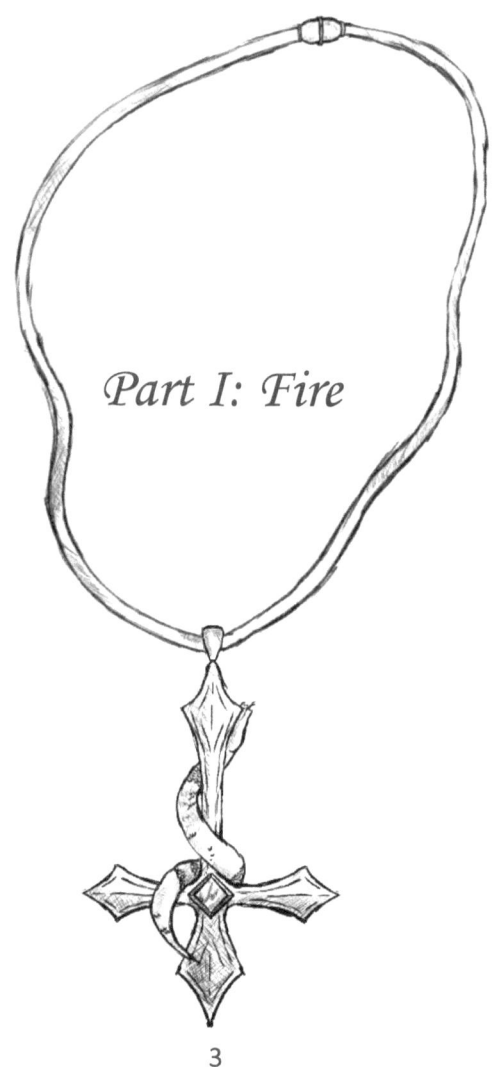

Part I: Fire

Halloween Ritual

I woke up to the clanging of church bells, the ringing echoing through the halls of the abbey, signaling to all the sisters that it was time to get up. I prop myself up, letting my eyes adjust to the brazen morning light that greeted my hungover body; my little room was flooded with it. Everything ached as I slid out of my hard twin bed, the cold floor beneath my feet waking me up more than the sun could. I started my routine, gathering my robes and toiletries before wandering down the hall to the communal bathrooms.

Other sisters emerged from their rooms, some naked and others wearing the bare minimum, as we made our journey to get ready. Today is the annual Halloween celebration and the start of the festivity season, so each of us has to make sure that we have the appropriate clothes on.

BETWEEN THE POWERS

Us younger sisters, the first through fourth years, need to have our hair pulled back away from our faces, done up in messy buns, seductive makeup, and our robes need to be clipped up so that our legs show underneath. Why? Something about it being a preference of some of the Papas. None of us were allowed undergarments in case we were selected to be this year's offerings so we each styled our robes accordingly to be revealing but to keep us covered. The older sisters, who were more established, were able to style their robes how they preferred as long as they could do their jobs in them. Some older women wore their robes long like a nun habit since they worked in the kitchen or gardens. Those in the libraries and studies would have them off their shoulders or pulled tight like a corset. The sisters who did not have a set job usually pulled them up in a fashion similar to that of newer sisters, but they changed their makeup or accessorized to make them seem more desirable.

It baffled me during my first year here that there were frequent parties and rituals like this where we were allowed to, for lack of a better word, fraternize with the heads of the organization.

As we all finished getting dressed, we shuffled out towards our tasks for the day. I was only charged with waiting on the Papa's today as they would be busy preparing for this evening. I saunter through the stone halls of the abbey to the senior

5

clergy's wing, making my way up the staircase to their rooms. Each one of the Papa's had their own personal kitchens, and bathrooms attached to their rooms so they could keep to themselves. It seemed to isolate them so that they were not disturbed while away from work. I make my way to the first of the doors, knocking briefly as I await my instructions. Behind the door, the sounds of cluttering and a few voices chattering arose before the door was pulled open by an older Sister whose hair and make-up looked disheveled.

"I got Arthur today, don't worry about it." Her voice was silky and smooth as she told me off. A smile crept across her face as she slid the door shut. I sighed softly and shuffled down the next door, where the audible sounds of someone being fucked to oblivion could be heard through the wooden door. Every moan was punctuated with a grunt and audible bed squeaking. It had taken me a moment to move on from his door, a twinge of jealousy arousing in my stomach as I wished I could be so 'passionately' rode into a mattress. But I did not look forward to the touch of a man in power.

I proceeded to the last of the three doors on this floor and rapped my knuckles against its darkened grain. A soft pinging of bottles being knocked around and a bed creaking were then soon followed by the door opening. Before me stood Alessandro, his sheets pulled around his body and his face crinkled up with mild displeasure. He was the youngest of ruling three and, to many, the most attractive. He wasn't the last of the Satanic popes, with at least three cardinals below him, but he was the most important. The most successful, charismatic, and attractive... or so they say.

"Ah... Sister Wenstrom... good morning. I am not in the least bit ready, but come in." His voice was raspy as he invited me into his chambers. As I stepped inside, he slowly shut the door behind me before shuffling back to what looked like a bed for eight. I stand at the foot of the bed looking expectantly towards him, waiting for any instructions on how to help him with the day. Instead, he flops back into bed and curls up with his mountain of pillows leaving me there. I look around the room, the royal blue walls soaked in any light that filtered through his two open windows. His closet door was open, and each suit that hung inside looked neat and pressed, his papal robes spilling out past the suits.

They were an interesting change from charcoal black jackets and matching slacks, the silk of their sleeves catching the low light with a gentle shimmer. What started as a slope of black rose jacquard satin from the velvet hanger, followed down to a cuff of lavender silk. Brushing over the cool fabric as I tugged it from the hold, I was greeted with the detail of a matching ribbon that would run down his spine. The front of the vestments plainly wore an embroidered pentagram of golden thread, something which was usually covered by his matching gold and white scarf that wore the

7

inverted cross with a snake laced up its center. Feeling it in my hand, a moment of envy washed through my mind, knowing that I would never own something so expensive with my position within the monastery.

Minutes drag past before I walk over and pull out his robes for the day, setting them on a nearby crimson settee. I then went to his kitchen and looked for anything he might enjoy. Since he was most likely hungover, I settled on brewing some coffee. Setting up the maker, I can hear him shuffling around in bed, starting the pot. I then make my way back out to his bedroom. He has changed from a curled-up ball to a spread-eagle position on his massive bed. The sheet that had wrapped his body was now contained to his ankles and shins, leaving the rest of him exposed. He was a well-built little man for being in his fifties; grey hairs graced his chest, leading neatly to the nest of hair that surrounded his groin. His skin was a pale olive that was kissed with freckles and sun spots, and his face was lightly wrinkled. As I gazed upon his form with my hands clasped behind my back, I noticed he was staring at me. His gaze was sharp, one blue iris the other a haunting white in his black sclera, it didn't take long before I turned my head embarrassed.

"You don't have to be afraid of me Cara Mia, I do not mind a little staring." He chuckled softly and rolled over, propping himself up on one elbow and staring me down. If he was ill from the party last night, he certainly did not show it now; the youngest of the Belladonna boys was a favorite with us younger sisters, so he often used that to his advantage. He patted the space next to him on the bed, inviting me up. I step back and slip back into the kitchen instead as I hear the coffee pot sputter. I can hear him sigh and flop back over in the other room. I grab a coffee mug from his cabinet and snort at the words painted on the side "Doing Hoe Shit." Pouring a cup, I then saunter back out to his room with it in hand and set it down on his nightstand next to him.

I watch with my hands behind my back as Alessandro sits up again to grab the coffee. He takes a small sip of the boiling bean water and frowns ever so slightly. A free hand dives into the crack between his headboard and mattress to pull out a small halfway-empty bottle of amaretto, adding as much as he can to the cup without overfilling it. Taking another sip, he seemed pleased with his addition and puts the bottle away.

"Care to join me, sister? I am much more pleasant than my brothers." He cocks an eyebrow and focuses his mismatched eyes on me, patting the bed in front of him.

I sigh and walk over, carefully sitting at the foot, observing his every move. I know it wasn't uncommon for the brothers three to sleep with us; it was just something I had managed to avoid in my first year here and I did not want to start my second year with it unless it was at a ritual. Most of them had

9

overlooked me this far, but Alessandro had been busy fronting the Shadows' project for these last few years, so he didn't have the chance to spot me. He continues to sip on his morning coffee as silence overtakes the room, the day seems calm at this point no surprises or mishaps yet. And even with this being my first time waiting on one of the three, I don't seem to be fucking it up just yet.

"Ehm, so... uh Papa how has the tour been going?"

"Hm?" He drawls in a dazed, hungover tone.

"For your new album? You were gone for almost a year...?"

"Oh, yeah that's been going pretty great lately though coming home after months was a much-needed break. I managed to dance a hole in my shoe!"

"That's good... uhm... I am so sorry I have yet to be in this position. What exactly is my job here for you...?"

"To wait on my every need and whim no matter how obscene, lest you do not consent though. Satanas knows we do not want to be like those god-fearing monsters."

I stifle a small laugh and smile just a little relaxing as we converse. "Mhmm, okay then..." A shy 'hah' leaves me as I chew

10

my lip for a moment. Another question came bubbling to the front of my mind.

"Are you three really brothers? Like related?" I asked as I needed clarification. Many of the rituals I have seen here have involved some sexual aspect, and well… Incest isn't exactly something that people are pleased to take part in.

"Eh?" Alessandro looks me over for a moment as if trying to gauge the seriousness of my question. "No no, we just call each other brother, it is a title thing like the um..." The words seemed to slip him briefly before he waived it off. "…the Christians. When Father Cassian found each of us with the eye, he took us in and trained us. Though I can't say, we were all born with the gift… some are lucky to have it bestowed."

He paused again. As if he was searching his mind, he sighed for a moment as he relaxed once more. "We are close, family-like. No relation though. We are not even from the same country!" he said with pleased triumph. "Arthur is from the UK, Caesar was born stateside, and I from Rome."

Cassian must have been searching for decades to find them all with how spread out they were. The whole hierarchy of The Ministry was interesting, mimicking the larger churches in the world. If something isn't broken, though, why bother fixing it? I nodded for a moment, maybe I pushed too much. That felt like information that I should have already known or maybe that I didn't need to know. I was here to keep him company and do chores for him today.

"Do you think you have been pretty successful in bringing in new members?"

"Ha! When have I NOT been successful eh? I bring in the black sheep in droves; brothers' old songs make it easy, though." He smiles victoriously at me before finishing off his coffee, setting the mug on his nightstand, and sliding out of bed. The sheet followed with and fell to the floor once both feet were planted firmly on the ground. Alessandro looks back over his shoulder at me for a moment before walking over to his vanity. He stands there before turning to face me. I blush and look away; it wasn't like I hadn't seen it all before. After all, he was a Cardinal before this, and as next in line, you get to participate in the rituals. I can hear Alessandro laugh softly before his footsteps lead away again. When I raised my head, I caught him walking into the bathroom with a door following shut behind. The sound of the shower replaces the silence, and I relax a bit more, knowing I don't need to expect anything. The bed I had been sitting on felt so soft that I couldn't help but lay down and sprawl out on its black sheet.

My mind wanders as I listen to the shower run, I don't know if I want to be picked for tonight. The idea made me squirm. Imagine being the star for the biggest holiday of the year and having all three 'brothers' and the cardinal use you. I feel agonizing worry creep into my chest, when I was a part of the church I was used. Would I be safe here if I wanted to participate? What if I need to back out? Minutes drag by as I lay sprawled out there, Alessandro taking his sweet time in the shower and ensuring he is also ready for this evening's ritual.

Forever seemed to dance by, but the shower finally shut off, and I could hear him singing before he stepped out, a towel now wrapped around him. He made his way back to the bed and looked at me.

"So, I see you are enjoying my bed, no? It is much better than the beds we have down in the abbey; they have to keep us boys happy, I suppose." He shrugs and wanders to his vanity, sitting on the little chair. He turns on the lights that frame the mirror, highlighting his face and creating a new warm glow in the room. I sit up to watch him; it feels like watching a well-oiled machine as he goes through his face paints and brushes, applying his iconic black and white pattern. Once the lines were clean and the black and white so vibrant that it looked fake, he stood up, stretching, letting the towel fall to the floor. I throw myself back down on the bed, avoiding my gaze upon his body; I can hear him shuffle across the hardwood floor and the rustle of cloth. Curiously, I sit up and look around again; now he is sitting in his recliner that sat near the fireplace, dressed fully in his robes. His

13

mitre sat in front of him, and he leaned forward with his hands pressed together tentatively.

"You are coming with me, no?"

"Yes, sorry, I um, is there anything I need to do?"

"Well, no amore. Just join me, and maybe I will give you tonight's honor, huh?" The man leaned forward as he picked up the black mitre that was covered in a thin spider's web of gold lace, the front of which wore the same inverted cross. Placing it on his head, he adjusted the wide onyx ribbons lined with thin bands of wisteria purple till they lay comfortably flat.

I look down, blushing profusely, before shimmying from his luxurious bed. Quickly, I fix my robes, making sure they lay as they should, and walk over to where he sat. He held out a hand as he stood up. The black leather glove was adorned with golden talons that were cold to the touch, and I took his hand. He tucks my hand in his arm and we leave the room, as his door opens the smell of burning wood and cinnamon wafts through the hallways. Alessandro leads us to the staircase down into the abbey where behind us Arthur and Caesar fall in line with their ladies in waiting in tow. Our little procession walks down the large stone staircase and turns down the path towards the ritual temple.

The eyes of stragglers turned to us, a glimmer of awe on their faces though many of them had seen this very scene dozens of times. Arthur was in the same smooth black satin robes with a sangria lining and warm ivory accents as he had been for the last few decades. His ivory miter sat back on his head as his white hair now blended with the white and silver ribbons that cascaded down his back. Caesar still bore his air of arrogance in his obsidian chasuble with lining of emerald green and accents of silver venetian lace, staring down his nose at those he didn't wear on his arm tonight. Opulence was the name of the game, and yet the woman, myself included, who walked next to them were dressed in nothing more than our habits.

The scents in the air began to grow heavier as we near the building, my heartbeat starts pounding in my chest as the realization of being chosen starts to become more and more realistic. This would be my second Halloween ritual and I could potentially be the star of the whole show this evening.

Alessandro tugs on my hand as he changes paths, going through the clergy entrance to the temple, leading us essentially backstage. We are followed by the other brothers and as we enter, I can see a little man sitting in a bright red cassock. He stands and faces us, his makeup the most plain I have seen on any of them. The blackness around his eyes made him look meek and scared, yet in his eyes, you could see a lust for power that all head cardinals have. His jaw was tight as he looked at the older Belladonna men, and yet his face softened at the sight of Papa and

BETWEEN THE POWERS

I. He bows to Alessandro and I before offering his hand to me. Alessandro let go, and I took his hand.

"Hello, Sister Wenstrom; I see you are one of our newer candidates for this evening. My name is Judas." He winks at me and pulls on my hand to lead me to a set of risers where the other two have positioned themselves.

The three brothers leave the room for a moment as the Cardinal stands by us, his hands clasped in front of his chest. Not long after the three disappeared from the room, six more women made their way into the room, only one or two of them dressed like me. I crinkle my nose as I look around; I wasn't one in three; I was one of nine that they get to pick from, and now I feel as if my chances were dwindling. I am not sure why I want this; I have been avoiding any intimate interactions with anyone; why would I want my first one to be with four older men and in front of the entire congregation nonetheless? It feels as if time starts to drag slowly, as we can hear them in the other room discussing whom they want to offer the spot of honor to for the night. After a while longer, Alessandro emerges and grabs a hold of my hand, leading me into the room where the other Belladonna men sat. I can hear groans from the other sisters and the sounds of them shuffling out of the room. I turn my head to catch a glimpse of the Cardinal ushering them out before he quickly shuffles in to join us.

"So, Sister, you do understand what this would include for the evening, correct?"

I nod slightly as I stare at Arthur, his face wrinkled with time his skeletal makeup greyed and smudged. Caesar doesn't even bother to look over at me as he sits with his arms crossed; Alessandro looks down at me expectantly as if I need to say something.

"I um… I think I do?"

"Well, you would be… used… in a ritual where the four of us will get to make a display of devotion to our dark father."

"The four… of you?" I ask, feigning ignorance even though I have witnessed this once before. However, in my first official ritual, Alessandro was still on tour, so we did not get to witness the full ceremony. Arthur nods and pulls out a rolled-up paper from his sleeves and a pen, sliding it across the table to me.

"Yes, if you understand what this entails, I need you to sign this paper. We need written consent from everyone here for the records. Your signature though will be the most important, sweetheart."

I can feel an overwhelming wave of emotions, lust, fear, and excitement, come crashing down onto me. When I served the church, I had to stay pure and pray away these thoughts even after

I was taken advantage of, but here they are asking me if I want to participate. I sign my consent and watch as the others add theirs to the document. We sit in the room for a few hours discussing what will most likely happen and any safety precautions in place to not create the next in line. The sunlight outside wanes as we near the hour and I can feel myself getting increasingly nervous. With the sun gone now and the echoing voices of singing erupting from the temple next door, Alessandro, and the others stand up. Judas guides me to stand behind the three brothers and he falls in line behind me. The door in front of us swings open and we make our way out into the temple. The usual soft marble walls and stained-glass windows were taken over with garlands of blackened roses and dying leaves, red candles sat in each of the wall sconces. Upon the main stage, where every couple of weeks we have a sermon from the Papas, sat a large cliché ritual table, black candles lit up the space, and Jack-o-lanterns lined the stairs and stage.

As all eyes flip to us, we make our way to center stage. Alessandro stops and addresses the crowd, his words pulling in the attention of everyone in attendance. Judas guides me to the table and helps me up; I sit on the edge and close my eyes, trying to ignore the feeling of dread that came creeping in. It flooded my mind with a dense fog of unease, condensing into a sheen of fear as the moment drew near. I feel soft leather cuffs get attached to my wrists and ankles, my robe softly pulled apart, and suddenly, someone's hand on my cheek. I open my eyes and it is Judas looking at me with concern.

"If you do not want to do this we can stop now, I know your past amore this is a huge thing for you no?" He murmured; his tone flat but there was more behind those eyes. I couldn't place my finger on it, but it was comforting.

Fuck...

I sigh softly and place my hand on his, listening to Alessandro working the crowd. I let the thoughts run through my mind for a moment before taking a deep breath.

"I want to try this one since it is finally my say... thank you though."

The world around me seemed to get warmer, I felt a nervous heat pooling in the pits of my stomach. The cold stone of the ritual table was the only other thing grounding me to the moment. Judas's hands continued to busy themselves as he helped me get bound, the warmth of his fingers radiated through his fine leather gloves. Before too long, my hands and ankles were bound to the table, and I was lying down with my face to the sky. My robes were splayed out around my form and Judas carefully tightened the binds that held me in place. As he finished, I could hear Alessandro's voice dissipate and the eerie silence of the crowd draw in for a moment as we awaited the arrival of the ghouls.

BETWEEN THE POWERS

Suddenly, the chapel roared with the sound of a pipe organ bellowing out a fugue. I close my eyes tightly and take a deep breath as I feel the men gather around me. The chapel space fills with an energy I have never felt before, like lust in its most raw form has flooded the room.

My eyes slide open to see the four men gathered around me. They all take turns bowing to kiss my cheek, though Alessandro leans in just a bit further to kiss my lips softly. As he did so, I breathed in his scent; it was musky and tainted with alcohol and a distinct wisp of almonds. His painted lips left behind black smudges on my face and he smiled at me giving a small wink before leaning in again. The nerves that had lingered before started to melt off as I could feel myself getting drunk off of his kisses. Just as I could feel myself leaning into it, he slipped down and pulled my robes back just a bit more to get at my awaiting neck and collarbones.

It was almost enough to distract me from the hands I felt just further below. It was warm and rough, slithering up my thigh and tracing every curve in my flesh. This was the hand of a much older man, careful but steady in his actions. Arthur teased at my skin as Alessandro kissed my neck, it wasn't too long before another joined in. This time, the hands had crept over my breast, leaving the thin fabric that sat between my skin and theirs in place. It seemed more tentative and harsh. As if the plump breast in his

20

hands had offended him and he would shape them how he saw fit. That had to be Caesar, I doubt I was his first choice when the Sister he was with earlier was an option. Her perky breasts rivaled my own as they often splayed or sagged with their weight, though it meant nothing at this moment as I had all three of the figureheads paying me special attention.

It wasn't long till Caesar and Arthur concluded their interest in me, though I could not tell if they had finished or feigned it for the clergy. As they stepped back, they took their spots in their usual seats calling up a few women to relax with them as Alessandro and Judas continued. Alessandro seemed more interested with his brothers out of the way. He let his warm leather gloves wander my body, taking his time to admire my form laid out for him. His breath was warm and shaky as he rested his head on my shoulder, a free hand of his taking off his mitre, setting it on the floor below. While Alessandro took his time, I could feel this building wanton desire in my chest. The nerves were gone now; I was being worshipped on this stone table. Alessandro's hand slipped into my robe gently splaying it open further to reveal my soft breasts. My nipples hardened to points as he carefully stroked and teased them, the golden talons grazing my skin ever so slightly. Judas on the other hand was down by my legs his hands anxious in their actions as they caressed my calves and thighs. His warm lips left soft kisses up and down my skin as he gave me all his attention. My mind sinks into a place of bliss as my skin prickles with every touch, the music ringing in the background being cut by the gentle groans of the two men playing with me.

Judas was the first to be brave enough to join me on the slab, his hands sliding up under my remaining robes and under my shoulders holding my body closer to him. Alessandro lets out a disgruntled gasp as he readjusts his position to continue his tender worship. Judas's red cassock furls out around us and cascades down his body like a river, he sits upright and looks down upon me with a burning desire I had not seen before. His hand makes its way to my throat and pins me flat. I gasp softly as he takes full control of my breath, his free hand snakes down my body again as he adjusts his position grinding into my leg. Under his cassock, it felt as if he was wearing tight latex or leather pants that clung to his body. I could feel his cock as it throbbed painfully against the fabric, he dared not take it out though as he was using the friction to get him closer. I could hear Alessandro chuckle softly as he leaned in closer to my ear.

"Mmmmm, once he is done, I will show the temple how to truly defile a flower such as yourself."

A shiver ran down my spine as I knew he had more planned for me. Judas continues his mission, soft whimpering moans escaping his lips as he defiles himself on me. His grip on my throat loosens just a bit more as his thrusts become ever so slightly erratic, his face blushes a deep red as I can hear his whimper turn into an achy moan. His jaw tightens up as I feel him push against me just a little harder. His eyes flutter for a moment and his head rocks back before he carefully dismounts and takes a few wobbly steps towards my head. Judas leans down to kiss my forehead and steps back allowing Alessandro to have me completely to himself. The man who had sat idly worshiping my neck and shoulder now pushes himself up and makes his way to my legs. Alessandro turns to face the crowd and drops his robes, revealing his bare body underneath. The chapel echoes with the gentle roar of applause that silents itself quickly as he turns back to me. He stood over me bare; his member erects as he stared down at my defiled body. His black hair falls in his face as he climbs up on the table with me, slithering his body along mine, his warm skin against mine feels inviting, and yet as I feel my lust build inside me, I can't help but feel anxious. His face meets mine and time stops for a moment, my heart beats in my chest and I cannot help but whisper our safe word. Alessandro's face, once filled with lust, stops dead and looks at me with concern, panic even.

"Are you okay...? Do I need to get off?" he whispers in my ear trying to continue the show for those in the audience. I could hear them murmuring as if the older ones knew something was wrong.

"I-I can't do this... the others were impersonal with this, but I do not think I can withstand this..."

"Okay… my dear, I am going to move off, be still, and I will have the cardinal come over and get you down."

Alessandro sits back up on his knees and makes a showful gesture towards the crowd as if to say he was done. The crowd roared with laughter and playful chants, chiding him for bursting too soon. As he made his way back down, Judas rushed over, quickly undoing my bindings and sitting me up. My robes fell off my shoulders, and I froze. Anxiety seeps into every ounce of my being as I no longer feel confident as I had before. My hands tremble and I feel myself choking on each breath, the world around me feels as if it is going black. My vision was in pinholes as all I could see was black and red; the sounds around me roared as if amplified a thousand times. I felt hot, yet frozen as the fear creeps into me. I was unsafe, my brain screaming that they were going to harm me. That just like those that came before I was going to be used, that my choice my will was going to be taken away from me.

I shoot up from my sat position glancing around as the Belladonna brothers stare at me, the cardinal nervously on his knees in front of me. Pulling on my black robes I make a wobbly dash to the back rooms. Bursting through the door I collapse on the floor as I start to hyperventilate, panic eating through me as the walls I kept up fell around me. It had been years since I had felt this way, since I felt truly unsafe. I hear the door creak open, my whole body flipping to face the doorway at my would-be attacker.

But it wasn't someone dangerous, I knew this man, I joined this church under him, I was just under him he wasn't going to hurt me but he is a man in power... he could if he wanted to. Alessandro stands in the doorway staring down at me, his eyebrows knit together in concern. Hesitantly he saunters my way, the panic in my chest swelling for a moment until his warm hand touches my cheek.

"Sweetheart, what is going on...?" His voice was cooling, and soft like falling snow.

"I-I... I couldn't ... I-I'm so sorry I wanted to... I wanted to but something didn't feel safe... I didn't feel safe."

"Oh, my dear... you are safe here. These halls are safe for you; Satan will protect you... I will protect you..."

I stare back into his face, his white eye sending a chill down my spine as it stares at me with intent. The panic recedes as I sit there, he does not move, frozen as I take the time to process. I scooch back and push my shaken body up off the floor, standing above Alessandro as he sits there perched something burns inside me. Only for a moment though as the sudden appearance of Judas through the cracked door startles us. His face was puzzled, anxious even. That melts away though as he sees me standing over Alessandro, the concern devolves into curiosity.

"Sister Wenstrom, do you need any help…?" Judas cocks his head as he gazes at me waiting for a response.

Alessandro stands up ruffling his robes for a moment, preening as if there was someone there to impress. Turning around he walks towards Judas and out the door, Judas scrabbles towards me and offers a hand to lead me back out to the chapel. His grip was strong but the softness of his Italian leather gloves offered an enriching calmness as I am led back through the halls of the abbey, the sound of a party echo towards us. Judas pulls me along for a moment, the music growing louder, before he hesitates and stops. Whipping around, his red cassock fluttering as he did so, he looks down at me concern returning to his face. I stop and turn my face to his, my cheeks flushing red as I do so. Judas wasn't an unattractive man with his messy blonde hair and well-maintained sideburns. His plump lips sat parted as if he was waiting for a word to volunteer its self-up to be spoken.

"I am sorry sister; the ritual did not go as planned. I do hope that we can help you work through the past. If I may though… You are very… attractive." His free hand drifts up towards my face to brush the hair from my cheek.

I could feel my muscles tense for a moment, I felt as if I needed to run but why should I run? He wasn't the same man who took advantage of me when I attended church in town. He never hurt me; Alessandro didn't either, but… the power they hold scared me. It was the same power that those pigs held, yet they did not seem interested in using it against us. I feel myself take a step back, and the hand that sat warmly on my cheek retracted quickly.

"My apologies, sister. Let us continue to the party, right? I am sure there are some interested parties waiting for me." He winked at me before turning back around and pulling me along through the halls till we reached the large recreation hall.

Many of the sisters were clumped together with drinks in their hands, each one talking and giggling with each other. They all sat close together to hear one another over the music; those who weren't chittering were dancing to the music that boomed over us. I scan the crowd, looking for any of the sisters I know personally when I spot Alessandro standing with a champagne flute in hand, dancing about in the crowds of women. He had shed his robes in favor of his tight-fitting suit, allowing him to move through the crowds, getting as close as possible with them. His black pants hid very little as we could all see him sporting a very erect member that seemed to strain against the confines of the fabric.

Judas lets go of my hand and brushes his across the top of my head before shuffling into the party, his cassock of red not allowing him to vanish within the crowds of black and white. I stand there for a moment in the archway, unease roiling in the pit of my stomach. Taking a deep breath, I let my feet lead the way, my head on a swivel as I take in the sights of a full ritual party.

27

BETWEEN THE POWERS

With Alessandro home, he was able to set up the party how he wanted, last year's streamers and pumpkins were traded out for strobe lights and fog machines. Cassian tried to make the event enjoyable but he did not connect with the crowd of us as much as his third son did. Thankfully this year he stayed at the head table with Sister Lucille, they were accompanied by Arthur and Caesar who sat conversing with each other, adoring older sisters practically hanging off their arms. Before I knew it, I found myself in the center of the dance floor, everyone else was enjoying themselves yet I couldn't help but feel unease. I close my eyes and stand there letting the music engulf me, the driving bass lines pounding in my ears.

The nerves slowly break away and I open my eyes again taking in the flashing lights only to be startled by a soft grip on my shoulder. My whole-body tenses as I whip around being met with the piercing gaze of mismatched eyes. Alessandro laughed softly and removed his hand from my shoulder, offering me one of the wine glasses that sat in his hand. I take it and stare down at what I can only assume be white wine, it swirled in the glass innocently as if it was nothing more than harmless water. Lifting the glass to my lips I let the bitter-sweet liquid splash over my tongue, and pool in my stomach. My eagerness to finish the glass sparked Alessandro to down his as if it was nothing more than a shot. A mischievous smile crosses his face as the music changes and he starts dancing at me, like a bird trying to woo a potential mate. I couldn't help but laugh softly at his attempt, though it certainly wouldn't be enticing enough for me. Rolling my eyes, I twirled the stem between my fingers and shook my head.

Alessandro danced about slowly drifting back into the crowd as if he hadn't just come to dance with me for the moment. I felt something swell in my chest and I sighed shuffling to the bar to set down my glass. This party really wasn't for me; I couldn't sit through the ritual so why should I stay for the after-celebration? Making my way back towards the archway and towards the abbey again I feel two sets of eyes digging into my back. I carry on though, finding my way through the now darkened candle-lit hallways to my room in the women's wing. The smell of cinnamon from earlier had burned itself into the walls again, just like last year the scent mixed with the old wood and stone brought an unearthly feel to the abbey again. I swing open the door to my little one-window room and stare at the hard bed I was to return to, it was seemingly disappointing now that I had sat on one more lush earlier today. Rolling my eyes, I step in and shut the door behind me to begin my bedtime ritual by slipping off my soft cotton robe. I kick it to the side along with my flats from the day. A cool breeze snuck in through my cracked window and rushed across my body sending a chill down my spine. Quickly I shoved myself into the pile of blankets I left strewn about on the bed this morning. Sleep tugged at me, dragging me into blissful unconsciousness, away from the panic and roller-coaster of today.

A Missed Summoning

The ringing of bells awakens the abbey again, just as it has every other day; I lay there counting the chimes, contemplating today's ritual. Today was the first of November; for some people, it was the day of the dead; for us here, it was a summoning day. They would summon a new ghoul to the abbey and retire the oldest one, allowing them to go back to hell. I sit up and swing my legs over the bed, again the cold floor biting into the bottom of my feet as it did every morning. Standing up, a twinge of pain sinks into my joints, my knees popping as I walk to my closet and pull out my new dress for the day. With that in hand, I make my way out into the hallway, joining the sea of naked women in our march to the communal showers. Today, while being a special day, we didn't need to dress up in any particular style so I opted for the usual.

BETWEEN THE POWERS

After bathing and drying off I pull my hair back into a messy bun and wrap myself up in my robes and pull the belt tight.

We all make our way out to the abbey and to our assigned jobs for the day. Before I head towards my usual job in the library, I make a quick stop by my room needing to grab my phone that I had left abandoned in my nightstand. Opening the door, I am greeted with a made bed, a singular white rose, and a letter sealed with wax embossed with Alessandro's personal stamp. Hesitantly I step further into my room and look around, there weren't a lot of places for someone to hide if there was someone even here. Everything else didn't look disturbed, not my closet with all my robes, or my small oak desk in the corner for personal studies. Just my bed. The one thing I always leave a mess, the one comfort item I never change was made. I grab the letter that lay on my bed and crack open the wax seal to get at the contents inside. I am greeted with a few words followed with what looks like an official order.

Sister Wenstrom,

I apologize for the uncomfortableness of yesterday's ordeal and hope that you can forgive me for it. I am making a formal order though for you to be reassigned as my personal assistant. If this displeases you then I ask you to tell me today rather than in the future.

Alessandro Belladonna

BETWEEN THE POWERS

Sure, enough at the bottom of the page was an official signed order requesting my presence as Alessandro's official assistant, his lady-in-waiting. I feel my mouth go dry at the thought that I would have to work around him more... consistently. Though I am not sure why, I wanted him, I wanted nothing more than to slither into bed with him. Yet his power, his position, they unnerved me. Was that what I was afraid of? I shake off the thought and set the letter on my desk alongside the rose. I didn't need it to be there when I returned to my room's safety this evening. The bells chime again; shit, I was late. I scurry out of my room and through the halls, leaving my device behind once again. My feet carry me in a flurry as I fly up the stone staircase to Alessandro's room, rapping my knuckles against the solid door. Once again, a clattering of bottles whispers through the door, followed by a groggy old man. Alessandro stood in the doorway, one eye closed, wrapped in a sheet. His soft black hair was ruffled and there was remnants of his face paint smudged on his neck.

"Ah, Sister I am so glad you could join me today! I was wondering if the cardinal was able to deliver my note." His voice was raspy, and his breath was laden with alcohol, but even as miserable as he looked, he cracked a smile at me and winked before stepping to the side, allowing me in.

The door shuts behind me and he shuffles back to his bed, flopping down in the mess of pillows and blankets. The room was still dark, the curtains that were opened yesterday were shut so tightly that not even a sliver of sunlight peeked through. The only light source was a desk lamp that provided a glow to his room. His floor was littered with shooters and empty wine glasses, his room smelled as if a bar was dumped onto the floor. I crinkle my nose and make my way to the windows, drawing open the curtains and letting the room flood with crisp daylight. Behind me, I could hear a very disgruntled Alessandro roll over pulling at whatever blankets were nearby to cover his head. Sliding open the window I poke my head outside and glance around. Below Alessandro's window sat the garden that Arthur tended to every day, the few late blossoms give a final wave as the growing season has come to a close. The aspen trees that littered the grounds were shades of decaying orange, and the occasional sister walked past as she tended to the groundskeeping. A cool breeze rushes past my face carrying around the few baby hairs that did not stay put in the bun. Stepping back from the window I turn around to see Alessandro's face poking out from the mountain of blankets he was under.

For a man who held power over an entire church, he sure liked to act childish sometimes. He was looking up at me, an almost puppy dog look in his eyes as if begging me to come closer. I take a deep breath and walk past him, going into the kitchen to make his coffee for today. Yesterday given me a rough idea of how this role should be played, and today I was determined to show him that I was unphased by yesterday's events. The coffee maker

33

sputtered as it finished draining into the large black mug I pulled out today and I carefully picked it up, the steam wafting into my face as I did so. As steady as I could I brought the mug around to where Alessandro sat sequestered in his blankets, a grin slowly spreading on his face as he saw the coffee mug in my hand. Placing the mug gently on the nightstand next to his bed I take a few steps back, as if I were a zookeeper feeding a ravenous animal. Just the same as yesterday, Alessandro reached for the mug, took a sip, and pulled out a bottle from the head of his bed, adding just enough to make it perfect.

"You know sister, I like this more confident you. But I uh- I did not call you here to be my permanent servant just to make you serve. The cardinal suggested to help you be more okay with, well, me to have you exposed to me more often." He chuckles taking another sip of the piping hot liquid, his eyes focusing on the dark bean water that sat in his mug. "I don't know if that is how it works, but eh, well I do not mind so much."

"Yesterday was… a big day for everyone. You were home to do the ritual with us and I guess I let nerves get the best of me."

"Nerves?"

"Yes… nerves, now is there anything in particular that I need to assist with today or am I to just accompany you in your work till later tonight?"

"Ooooh sister, no need to be so uh, spicy. I just wanted you to join me through the day if that is all right by you." He again laughs and shakes his head, loosening the messy black bangs that were tucked neatly behind his ears. Taking a deep sigh Alessandro throws off his blankets and slides towards the edge of the bed planting his feet firmly on the floor. I turn my head to the floor to avoid staring at his naked form, it didn't feel right to gaze upon him after failing him last night. I could feel his gaze burning into me, he stared for a moment then walked away. The sound of his bathroom door clicking shut and the shower turning on gave me a chance to look back up. I looked around the room once more, the deep blue of the walls felt otherworldly when lit up with sunlight. The fresh light revealed a fur de lis pattern painted into the walls, it stuck out more in the light as they were painted in a gloss finish rather than the matte. His room felt as if it was crafted for someone of royalty, the intricate painting on the wall, a vanity with depictions of hell fire carved into the legs, a floor that looked as if it were made of cherry wood, and this bed. This bed that was so large it could fit a small family in comfortably with all their pets. Though I cannot imagine any family wanting to lay in a bed that had each post carved into the shape of a nude woman.

I stand up and walk over to Alessandro's closet pulling out a clean suit for the day, this was one of the few rituals during the year where we didn't have to see the Papa's in their embroidered robes. I lay it out on his chair and find his shoes to

35

place on the floor next to it. I look back towards the bed, my eyes tracing the form of each woman that adorned his posts. It was difficult to get a great look at them when he typically had this room shrouded in darkness. Each one faced away from the center of the bed, their breasts out and their hands held in the Baphomet pose. My mind wanders for a moment as my feet drag me closer to the bed once again. I can't help but sit down on the plush bedding, sighing as I lay back as I had before, gazing up at the spider's lace canopy that covered the top. Alessandro's voice carried out from the room as he was singing to himself again, he seemed to be enjoying his shower for the most part. I didn't care all too much as I sank myself deeper into the plush of his bed. Closing my eyes I let myself linger there, I felt safe and warm. The bed was far better quality than anything I had previously slept in or on.

"Sister! Come on it is time to accompany me on my stroll!" I felt a hand shaking me awake and I startled. Every muscle in my body threw me upright, and I looked around frantically to see a fully painted Alessandro, dressed and polished, giggling at me. "I see someone enjoys my bed, no? Maybe if you'd like I can get you to sleep here all the time."

I crinkled my nose at him as I quickly flattened out my habit, how embarrassing of me to have fallen asleep in his bed on my second day working in here. I wonder if previous sisters ever had that problem. Alessandro holds out his hand for me to take, placing my hand in the crook of his arm and leading us out of his room. We walked past his brothers' rooms and back down the staircase, heading towards the doors that let out to the garden. His shoes clicked innocuously on the stone tiling beneath our feet as he strides toward the door. The walls were decorated with little garlands much like the ones in the temple yesterday; each one swayed ever so softly as a breeze ruffled through the halls. Slowly, we made our way to the doors that opened to the gardens. A silent stroll with Alessandro felt intimidating, my mind flashed back to the times I would be paraded through the halls being shamed for my impurity. A chill rolled down my spine as all I could feel at that moment was shame. The church had taken my chance to sleep with a powerful man without fear and now I could not even walk comfortably through the halls with him. I felt my head sink for a moment before the brassy tone of Judas's voice rang out in greeting.

"Hello, Papa! A beautiful autumn day for a stroll, yes?"

"Ah Cardinal, what a pleasant surprise. Would you care to join us on our little walk?"

"Sure thing, as long as it is okay with the sister you have in tow."

I look up to see the cardinal adorned in his black cassock staring patiently at me. Quickly, I nod my head and look back up to

37

BETWEEN THE POWERS

Alessandro who smiles softly and nods at the Cardinal. Judas makes his way to my other side standing so close I could feel the air that came off of his cassock as we made our way outside. The two of them talked above me, about the plans for the ritual tonight and about the goings on inside the upper clergy. I let my mind shut them out momentarily as I took in the sight of the garden during the fall. Most of Arthur's flowers had died off since they were summer and spring blooms but the spaces were taken over by a cornucopia of fall crops that my fellow sisters had been tending to all year. The ground was covered in the orange windblown leaves of the nearby aspen forest. Many of the senior Sisters tending to the groundwork came over to greet Alessandro and Judas, joining in on their conversations. I felt as if I was only there to be the doe-eyed girl on Alessandro's arm. I didn't know how to join in on these conversations, I was barely a sister, a member of the church. It wasn't my place to join in on this conversation, I was just here as arm candy. A breeze finds its way to us, disturbing the quiet peace and ruffling the skirts of all of us sisters. A few continue to chatter as we walk through the garden pathways and I can feel Alessandro's grip tighten ever so slightly on my hand. One of the sisters had casually mentioned the failed ritual from last night. She had noticed that Alessandro did not get to complete his part and that I was the reason for that.

"Well, Sister Mayweather I do not think that is any of your business. Satanas, Lucifer surely knows the devotion we all hold, and he knows we uphold the comfortability of our vessels. I do not think he minded that we respected her wishes. Now if you will excuse us, I don't feel like I should entertain this any longer." The senior sister wrought her face in disappointment at Alessandro as we walked off, grunting in disbelief before returning to her task. Alessandro led us away from the garden and more towards the summoning temple, the old wooden church was once used for Christ-friendly activities was now converted into a hall for summoning and trading Ghouls. Its white paint was chipped and aged as no one had felt the need to keep up the appearance of purity. The once-standing symbol of humanity's belief in a sky man was allowed to wilt an age into the perfect setting for tonight's ritual.

We walk up to the church, our footsteps making the old wooden stairs creak ever so slightly as we do so. Judas steps forward to open the door for Alessandro and I before following again, falling right in line with our steps. Alessandro lets out a relaxed sigh and leans down kissing my cheek suddenly before letting go of my hand. Now free he casually steps into the large nave clasping his hands across his chest.

"Ah! Don't you feel it you two? This space will be teaming with *his* presence tonight!" Alessandro excitedly traced the large pentagram that had been carved into the floor with his footsteps and turns to face Judas and I who stood there in the narthex. Judas looked pleased with himself, standing with his hips cocked at an angle letting his eyes dance across the lightly disturbed cobwebs and dilapidated Christian relics. The pews were all pushed off to the side, making room for the ritual to take place tonight since only a handful of the clergy would attend this evening. I take a few steps forward, inhaling the scent of well-aged wood and dust. The building felt like a little church my family had belonged to since before the first incident. It was well-loved and taken care of in its years of service but had now been taken over by a different keeper—one who was not as gentle with its age.

"Papa, if I may, who is in line to go home this year?"

"Ah, Quintessence gets to return this year. If I am right, we should be getting their counterpart Cosmic in return."

"So, wait, each year you trade out your ghouls? Is it just for the band or for the whole church?" Alessandro and Judas both turn and look at me quizzically. "I-I haven't exactly gotten to it in my library work…"

"Yes, we do. Every year the eldest ghoul in our ranks returns home as they are not made to be here their whole lives…" Judas's voice was smooth, reassuring just as if he was speaking to one of the younger members of the flock. "…And this year it sounds like the last of Arthur 's band gets to, hmm, retire?"

"Oh… okay, who all is going to be here tonight? Last year they did first come first serve for the witnesses."

"Well! This year since I am home, I have already chosen my witnesses. You are invited to join me tonight again Sister. That is if you don't have any plans."

Me? I hadn't seen this one yet so I was unsure of what to expect.

"Um… sure, I can come since you have me no longer sorting books that is."

"Perfecta!"

Alessandro pulls Judas to the side leaving me to stand there by myself, they were discussing more on the ritual tonight I know that much. I make my way over to one of the way-sided pews and sit down. The old wood groaned as I relaxed, my hands sat folded in my lap and I let my eyes wander. I imagined this church used to have life; a little preacher man would sit at the front reading to his sheep. Maybe a small child ran around in the back to burn off some energy while the rest of the family would be focused in on the hymnal. The candle wax build-up from years of burning created gnarled pillars of white that adorned the main stage. Every spider's web that came to exist in this church created their own supernatural lace across the ceiling hiding much of the damage from age and the weather.

Sister Salacious
BETWEEN THE POWERS

It was in its own way still very cozy, and yet I could not
shake the feeling of discomfort that came from it. My first time
was in a church much like this one, though it wasn't something I
had wanted to be a part of. It was an older classmate who attended
the same church as my family and I did. After the sermon that day,
he had found me in the bathroom. A quiet, harmless tween who
was just trying to wash her hands. It was odd, the little pink ruffled
gown my mother picked out for me was 'too sexual' for a child to
wear. After it had happened, I tried to tell mom what he did. I even
talk to the pastor. Well, apparently, I was too impure and he had to
cleanse me. He cleansed me every Sunday for a year… I never
went back to that church.

I felt my mind go numb as I let my surroundings walk me
back to the nightmares I had experienced before. The classmate,
the pastor, the shame. It was a different kind of shame and pain
when it was something that happened to you and not because of
something you did. My hands moved to the edge of the pew,
gripping tightly as I stare off at the stained-glass windows. What
those men did to me still caused pain all these years later, even
after months of therapy. And yet, now here I was. In one of the
biggest temples of sin, as a member who in my own twisted
fantasies would gladly let any one of the men here rail me. I would
even let the bitter, harsh Caesar use me for a night if it meant I got
to enjoy my own body. But even now as I let those ideas seep into
my brain, I felt guilt rise as well. Shame was a stupidly powerful

42

tool, and after being exposed to it for most of my life it became an ingrained battle for me. My heart longed for me to cut loose, to do the things that would make God turn a blind eye. But my mind fears what would happen. It fears being reprimanded, abused, and shouted at.

Maybe I should have left the church sooner. I had separated myself from my family and the religion I was raised in at the age of 21. That year I had attempted to find myself and had instead appeared in the bottom of a bottle. I should consider myself lucky though. Because at the bottom of that bottle, was a kind older man who wanted nothing more than to talk. Now I didn't know Alessandro was a Satanic Pope when we met, he just seemed to be a rather energetic person with a silver tongue. At 22 I joined the Ministry and officially cut myself off from my family. They would lose their minds if they could see the antics I got up to here, even if I was tame in comparison to many of the other sisters. I just wish I could experience lust without guilt eating away at me now.

Coming back from zoning out, I look back towards where Judas and Alessandro were to see them still very much in the middle of their conversation before Alessandro straightens up more and glances at me. There was something wrong, a twinge of worry? Maybe even regret? I couldn't be sure but as I soon as I had noticed his look he turned away and made his way out of the church. Judas stood there alone, his eyes focused on the old

43

stained-glass windows, hands folded behind his back. He turned to face me, walking over slowly as if I were a wild animal he was trying not to spook.

"Where did Papa have to go? I-I feel like I should be with him if I am supposed to be his assistant, right?"

"He um, well he has some paperwork he needs to attend to real quick. I was asked to keep an eye on you." He holds out his hand, and I take it. Warmth radiated out from its leather confines, it was soft and comforting as he gave me a gentle squeeze. "I will take you around on the rest of this walk if you don't mind."

"N-Not at all, thank you."

He pulls me up from my spot on the ancient pew, my robes picking up dust and detritus that I quickly brush off with my free hand. We make our way back out of the church, Judas holding my hand, our fingers barely intertwined. It felt scandalous to be holding hands with him this way, he was a senior clergy member, he had importance and I was just a second-year sister. Yet we were holding hands and walking about the temple grounds as if we were high school sweethearts. I could feel the envious eyes of the others digging into my skin and I couldn't help but feel embarrassed. My eyes wandered up Judas's body as we made our way around, his dirty blonde hair peeked out from his biretta as it sat perched on his head. Out here in the open-air Judas didn't look as dark and foreboding as I had thought when I first joined. And he most certainly didn't look the same as he did the night before. His features were softer as if age had been changing him with a light feather brush. I could feel my heart skip a beat as I admired him, not noticing that the entire time he had been glancing at me ever so often.

We made our way back to the doors of the church, Judas pushing them open again this time to lock them open. I went in further and sat down on one of the pews crossing my arms and leaning back against the old splintering wood. He made his way over to me and sat down as well removing the biretta that had covered up his hair before, now letting it fall softly into his eyes.

"So, would you like to stay here while I set up for this evening?"

"Um… Sure I can stay here."

"Alright let me know if you need anything okay?"

He stands up placing his hat next to me and peels off his gloves handing them to me. Unbuttoning his cassock, he reveals underneath a white T-shirt and a pair of tight jeans, the cassock then gets slid off and set on my other side. Judas typically wasn't seen in casual clothing, the cassocks he usually wore covered up any distinguishing features of his body. It had made him a floating figure that always appeared neat. He had a light belly that poked out his shirt ever so slightly and his arms were built strong, like someone who worked in carpentry for a living. His little mustache betrayed the fact that in reality he seemed to be a bit fuzzier, unlike Alessandro who was tidy with his body hair. Judas looked like the little old Italian man you would expect to talk you off your feet in New York. I sat there in awe with the view as he went to work pulling out large candelabras and transforming the space from a slightly abandoned church to a haunting ritual site.

I must have fallen asleep at some point as I now startle awake back inside my little one window room. *Damn it.* I wanted to go see that ritual this year, but who took me back to my room? I slip out of bed still wearing my full robe from today, and look around hoping for a note or something to tell me what happened. Instead on my floor lay the black cassock that I can only imagine Judas was wearing earlier, it must have fallen off me when I was brought back to my room. Bending down I pick up the cassock, the fabric being deceptively heavy as I bring it to my chest. With a mild hesitation I bury my face in its soft folds taking a deep breath, Judas's scent floods my senses. It was oaky and warm; it smelled as if he walked through the smoke of a small campfire and sprinkled then with only the finest of whiskeys. There was an underlying sweetness that I could not put my finger on, but I was hooked. I flop back into my bed with his cassock wrapped up in my arms allowing myself to fall asleep again this time my face buried in the most sinfully sweet scents I was allowed.

A Lost Sensation

The weeks seemingly passed uneventfully, Alessandro found ways to make my mornings interesting and would pass me off to the cardinal in the afternoons. I wasn't entirely sure why though; did they have some sort of agreement I wasn't in on? I am not one to complain, I get to spend time with two of the most sought-after men in the church. The cassock that was left with me has yet to be returned to Judas and I hoped he forgot about it for now. I keep it tucked beneath my bed when I am not in my room, but every night I pull it out and wrap it around myself. Its thick fabric adding an extra warmth in the ever-freezing nights, if I could get my hands on one of Alessandro's coats it would make my lonely nights better.

Christmas is this week, specifically this Friday. The clergy has been busy arranging the festivities to Alessandro's specifications this year. The halls have been lined carefully with holly and pine garlands; the occasional mistletoe sat in the doorways of each of the important clergy members. All except for Sister Lucille that is, she is making sure there is no reason for Cassian to be in her doorway all the time. Unlike the previous year we were told to refrain from presents, there had been rumors that the clergy has a surprise for us. The members have been keeping tight lipped about the celebrations this year.

I make my way down the main hall to the temple's cafeteria; Alessandro had requested I pick up lunch today for us and the Cardinal. The stained-glass windows that sat sunken into the old stone were frosted over, the depictions of hell each wearing a lace of ice. It was a bit chilly as I made my way towards the warm glow of the lunch room. I made my way through the archway and rows of tables to the kitchen window. A soft ring of the bell brings a sister to the window; a small scowl crosses her face as she looks me up and down.

"Well, if it isn't the little pet, enjoying the easy life?"

"I-I, it certainly is not easy, Alessandro can be demanding! That and he seems to never leave without his cardinal, so I am taking care of both of them at this point." I look down into my hands wringing them ever so slightly. "Look, I am here to collect lunch for them can we please just make this easy."

BETWEEN THE POWERS

The sister scoffed and went towards the back, presumably to grab the lunches as I requested. Many of the new sisters that had joined the same time I did have become bitter that I was permanently assigned to work for Alessandro as if it was my choice to take care of the man who thrills and terrifies me all the time. She returns to the window with a tray with three small cloches covering the tops of the plates and hands it to me, promptly leaving the window. I take the tray and make my way back through the halls admiring the stained glass. As I near the stairways the stained glass turns to depictions of the Papas each one posed as if they were a renaissance angel. The tray felt heavy in my hands and my arms ached ever so slightly as I carried it up the stairway. As I passed by the doors of the other two Belladonna men, Arthur emerged from his dressed in his usual papal robes, sans hat of course.

"Ah, Sister Wenstrom! It is so good to see you are still busily working for my little brother. Is he still trying to woo you?"

"Woo me? I am just here as his maid your unholiness nothing more. Though he and the cardinal seem to have taken interest in using me as that."

"It is amusing to see him pick someone to fawn over, especially at his age. By the time I had control I already had my life partner picked out. She may not be with us now but she would be happy to see he has picked someone." With that he turns and disappears down the stairs, leaving that shred of sentiment to linger in the air around me. I vaguely knew about his lost partner, everyone did, but no one had ever heard the old man bring her up organically.

I grumble a little and make my way over to Alessandro's door, knocking with my heel. It takes them a moment but the door opens and I make my way inside setting the tray down on the foot of the bed. Alessandro sit's up from his position on the bed, with a smile on his face. It was odd not seeing him with his face paint this late in the day, but it wasn't unusual if he wasn't planning on going out. Judas made his way over from the door, his makeup crisp as if it was just done moments before I entered the room. He crawls on the bed from the other side making his way over awkwardly across the plush top of the bed. The two of them scooch in sitting cross legged, it was as if they were two teenage boys getting settled for a picnic. I stay on the edge of the bed and wait as they sort through the lunches.

It was odd watching them interact together in what feels like an intimate setting. Judas, while the lesser of the two powers, would take more charge in setting out the food and Alessandro would let him, it felt like an unshared order had been passed to the lesser. I keep a wary eye on both of them; it may have been a few weeks since my last incident but I couldn't shake the feeling that there was something was in the works. We commenced our lunch,

Alessandro being more than eager to scarf down his lunch only to chase it with a swig of his "behind the bed" special. As we finished, I took the tray and set it just outside the door. I would have to take it down later when Alessandro decides he is finished with me today. Heading back to the bed I stop short as I watch the two of them lean in closer to each other. They were talking in a hushed voice as if they were plotting something. I clear my voice and step closer.

"So, um Papa- "

"Alessandro, cara mia you have been working in here long enough." He corrected with a cheeky smirk.

"Right, Alessandro… Are there any other tasks you need me to do today? I do believe all dishes have been taken care of and the weather outside is a bit to nasty for a walk around the promenade."

"Hmm I suppose I could part ways with you today; Cardinal is there anything you needed?"

Judas cocks his head thoughtfully for a moment before setting his gaze intently on me, the mismatched gaze sending an unnerving chill up my spine.

BETWEEN THE POWERS

"I request that you be available later this evening, I will stop by your room if that is alright. I need a hand with a few of my tasks."

I nod and look back over to Alessandro who glowered at Judas for a moment before then also shooting a look over at me, a softer one thankfully.

"One more question principessa. Who would you see being on top in a threesome, Judas, or me?" My breath fell short as I gawk at them for a second before looking down, I can feel my face getting warm and I fidget with my hands near my chest for a moment. The question came out of left field, but I'll be damned if it didn't cross my mind once or twice before.

"I- er I think you would be sir." With that I turn and quickly make my way out of the room hearing the two of them giggling behind me like a bunch of school girls. They were as juvenile as two older men could get, I would say it was endearing if it wasn't for the fact that I was the center point for their behaviors. I kind of liked being the middle of their trouble making and misbehaving.

As I get outside of the room, I grab the tray and hustle back through the halls to the cafeteria dropping it off at the window. In my hurry to get back to my room I did not see one of the brothers heading my way. We crashed into each other and I can hear the disgruntled murmurings from him as he picks himself back up. I look up at him and can feel myself shrink back as his eyes find their way down to me with a searing disgust.

"Watch where you are going sister, not all of us can afford to be so careless." He hissed; his gaze locked on my mildly frightened face.

"I didn't see you; it happens I-I was just trying to get back to my room."

"Fucking watch it. You are a pet, don't think that you will get special treatment from the rest of us because you are being passed around like cheap jack." His words stung; my face dropped as I immediately turned my gaze to the floor. "Know your place skank."

I wanted to ball up my firsts right there and throw the first hit, in reality, if I did so I would be punished by Sister Lucille. She was the enforcer and essentially the Abbess of The Ministry, so anything we sisters or brothers did she knew about. And she loved to keep a tight leash on us sisters so that we kept up the mask of delicate and helpless women. It was a stupid rule of hers that pissed off most of us as it felt like she was trying to force us all into some form of subservience.

I crinkle my nose at him apologizing profusely, a move to appease the brother before I continue scuttling down the hall to my room. I had no clue what Judas needed my help with tonight but I can at least take this time to nap and possibly journal. Bursting into my room I go to my desk and pull out a little journal and a ballpoint pen jotting down my activities of the week. Breakfast with Alessandro, mending his suits, listening to him rant about clergy problems, and then lunch with the two of them. It wasn't as much as I usually did but it felt as if he had been making my workload a bit lighter here and there as we drew near Christmas. He might be running me into the dirt soon.

I scrawl in the journal for a bit more, marking down any passing thoughts before shutting the little blue fabric-bound journal and stuffing it in a drawer. If I am right, I can get in a small nap before Judas comes to collect me. Making sure my door is shut I reach under my bed and pull out the tightly wrapped cassock. It no longer held the heavy musk of Judas's cologne but if I was lucky there were still a few spots that were fragrant. Taking the bundled-up cassock, I hold it close to my face and fall into my stiff bed allowing myself to drift off hoping the knock will be enough to wake me later.

Later came though and there was no knock on the door, I found myself waking up in the darkness of my room the ticking of my small desk clock the only sound I could hear. I get up and find the lights, flicking them on makes my eyes sting as they adjust. I don't remember turning them off before my nap but it is possible I could have. I rub them for a moment and peer at my desk clock, *1 am*, did Judas not need me after all? Maybe not, walking back to my little bed I sit down and look about wondering what to do with myself. Maybe if I am lucky, I can sneak down to the kitchen and snag a light snack or attend a witch's hour confessional with Arthur. I just hope that no one is in the kitchen if I go down there. Standing up I flatten out my robes and pick up the Cassock that I had been sleeping with. Just then behind me, there was the sound of someone clearing their throat, I nearly jumped out of my skin as I turned around. There behind me stood Judas neatly posed in the door frame of my closet, his arms crossed and a grin across his face. On instinct I chucked the cassock at my door as if I were throwing it into the closet, he laughed and stepped out walking to the pile of fabric picking it up, and draping it over his arm.

"Ah sister, I was wondering if I was ever going to get this back from you. It is very nice, no?"

I feel my face flush red and I look away with a guilty pout on my face. "It is... though I wish the scent on it would last longer. HEY! *How long* have you been sitting there?"

"Meh only the last 20 minutes or so, I was going to come see if you would be willing to join me tonight for a bit of ceremony and devotion but seeing you tangled up in my cassock was too cute." He flashes me a toothy smile and bows his head towards me. "But I do get how that can be a bit creepy."

55

BETWEEN THE POWERS

"20! 20 whole minutes you watched me sleep and you didn't think to wake me! TWENTY! And at one in the fucking morning no less!"

"Hush sister, the rest of the abbey around you is asleep." I turn my head and huff slightly before facing Judas again trying to hide the embarrassment on my face.

"Sir, what did you need my help with this evening?"

"Oooh so curt now, temper temper. I was going to see if you would join me for some light satanic duties and sinning, but I can see you are not in the mood." He teased at me, crinkling his nose, and smiling.

"Well, I am awake now... what is it that we need to do?"

"Why don't you come join me in my chambers and I will show you?"

I sigh and open my bedroom door letting Judas out then following close behind him. His Red cassock billowed as he hastily walked through the hall, he had a mission of that I couldn't be sure but I had my suspicions. He was the only one at the ritual who had gotten a chance to lay with me before I panicked. My mind flashes back to him grinding against me as his hands were wrapped softly around my throat. I watched as he whimpered and moaned, the leather pants that he had were helping bind his hardened cock as he dug his hips into mine. I can only imagine the cum running down his leg afterward, his body shook as he climbed off of me. I secretly wish it was me that was filled with his seed. I am snapped back to reality as I walk into him, we had stopped in front of an unlabeled wooden door. Judas snickered softly as he flipped through the keys on his belt ring unlocking the door with a simple skeleton key. The door swung open revealing a quaint little room, the walls were an eggshell white and he had a queen-sized bed nuzzled up into the corner with a messy arrangement of blankets and pillows. A single nightstand held a lamp and a small stack of books and unopened juice boxes, across the room sat a Tv stand with a myriad of game consoles and a single TV. Compared to Alessandro's room Judas's was that of a rowdy college boy, he may have been a higher member of the clergy but he certainly did not get the same luxuries.

"I know it is very how do you say… lackluster? Mother refuses to use her status to give me the room I would like but I just have to wait till Alessandro steps down."

I look over at him mildly perplexed, the room didn't even look like it belonged as a part of this building. Mine at least had the stone walls and dungeon-esk feel of a room in an ancient church. His looks like it was recently renovated and slid into place. I watch as Judas shuffles about his room stripping off his red cassock and tossing it haphazardly into the closet alongside his stolen black cassock. Beneath he was wearing tight leather pants that clung to his body as if it were a second skin, leaving practically nothing to the imagination. His loose black T-shirt barely covering the bulge in his pants.

"So, sister I wanted to see if we could try something. Even I can see that you are getting more comfortable around Alessandro but that's not the only point I wanted to help you with. During the ritual you were okay being touched, but once it came to being... *penetrated* well you had it come to a full stop."

"I never minded the touching... it was when they went further against my will. They had made me impure and took away everything that I believed when they climbed on top of me over and over again. When Papa... Alessandro had climbed atop me I felt thrilled yet something in my head said that I was not safe. That my no's were going to be the tune that I was raped too again."

"Oh, my dear, he was never going to hurt you. Those men that did those things to you, they are scum... worse than that they do not deserve the sweet relief of life that is death." He walks over and shuts the door behind me; my nerves tense up as I keep my eye on his every move. "I would never let another hurt you again, you are too perfect."

Judas steps in close to me, his cologne pulls me in further and I find myself resting my head on his chest. I couldn't help but

58

melt as his strong arms wrapped around me and held me there. Against my wishes tears well up in my eyes as I sink into one of the few kind gestures I have felt in a long time. I had tried for so long to avoid connection; I joined the Satanic church to run from the Catholics. I was considered dirty and impure but here I was accepted, no one questioned where I came from and the sisters had helped me accept my body for what it was. I may have slowly worked towards accepting myself again but accepting others, and accepting intimacy was an uphill battle. As tears run down my cheeks I break down, my knees go weak and I sink to the floor, Judas joining me as he rocks my back and forth.

"I know, let it out. You are safe here; you are not alone in this."

I sniffle and bring my knees closer to my chest as the tears keep rolling down my face. Letting someone hold me brought warmth into my chest, one that I had not felt since before the church. He was so warm, so gentle. I felt myself sink into him more until I couldn't go further. Judas cooed at me softly as he gave me a reassuring squeeze.

"You know Sister, it took me years to feel like myself again. When Lucille told Cassian I was not his bastard I was effectively beaten within an inch of my life by that bag of bones. Any time he looked at me after then I felt like a whelp, a useless dog tossed to the side. I still had my place in the line of succession, stuck behind three who were not of blood, but I was effectively disowned by the single most important figure in my small life." He takes a deep breath as he loosens his grip ever so slightly. "It is nothing compared to what you had gone through but, I too lost my faith in humanity. I felt disgusted by myself as if my mother's choices had deliberately put me in harm's way. I cannot blame her though, with the relationship Alessandro and I have the sooner she told him the better."

"W-what do you mean by that...?"

"Well," he takes a moment and sighs, "Alessandro and I have always been close, he has brought me up alongside him in rank as far as he could. But we had... a special relationship as young men. Let's just say that we got to explore each other as far as we possibly could at that age. But that is beside the point, I want you to trust us. It has been a while, no? You deserve to feel safe."

Ah, that's why they always seem joined at the hip, passing glances between each other like filthy notes in the hall.

I nodded and scooched gently out of his arms sitting in front of him, I felt small. He was perched on his knees looking down at me, his usually cared-for blonde hair was lightly ruffled and the look he was giving me made me blush. I couldn't tell what it was, but was he...in love with me? His gaze was soft, those mismatched eyes were pools that I could see myself lost in, and the more I stared back at him the more I could feel it. It didn't matter that he had endless black around his eyes, I could still see every crease in his skin, every little scar and blemish that decorated his face. Yet his eyes told me stories I could only hope to fully understand. He had always been in the background running the church, attending to paperwork, working endlessly to ensure smooth transitions throughout the day. He helped bring in the new lambs and place them where they needed to be. A shepherd in the field, guiding us before the dogs got to us.

Judas stood up and stretched before offering me a hand. I took it and stood with him; his other hand came to my cheek and wiped away the tears that still stained my skin. Pulling me towards the center of the room as if I were being given a choice, he bit the inside of his lip before speaking.

"I will not push my luck and ask if you would like to join me here tonight. But my door is always open to you Alessandro's is too but he is more reluctant to tell you so. He has an image to keep of being the aloof playboy ya know?"

"Can I stay…? My room gets cold sometimes in the winter." I look down at my hands trying to avoid the hot red blush I can feel spreading across my cheeks.

"Of course, Principessa. Anything for you." He smiled softly at me, moving to the bed where he adjusted the many pillows and blankets to allow for company. Carefully he then leads me back over to his bed helping me sit down and get situated in a way that feels comfortable. Turning off the light, I can hear him shimmying out of his tight leather pants. He slid in behind me one arm is draped over my hip as he kept our lower halves separated by both a blanket and pillow. His warmth radiates through making this cold evening all the more relaxing.

"You won't do anything will you…?" I ask hesitantly as we both lay there in silence. His original intention for bringing me into his room felt like he wanted to screw me, perhaps my crying threw him off.

"No no, while your beauty and spirit may cause me to stir, I care too much about your safety to do that to you. When you are ready you are ready, and until then I will take every sweet moment I can get with you."

"I don't know if I can show that same care for you and Papa…" I murmured feeling guilty. I couldn't lie that the month of being close and working between the two of them had definitely brewed some feelings. But I couldn't tell if they were the kind that I could act on long term, or if it was just infatuation with attractive men.

"That's fine too, he and I have each other… and I hope we always will. But there is room for you if you feel like you belong." He purred. "I pray perhaps you see something more in two old farts like us…" This was moving fast, wasn't it? It is barely December and yet I can't help but long to be in their beds. Wrapped in their arms. Perhaps I was being naïve, 23 was nothing compared to the lives they have led. I was but a glimmer in my mother's eye when they were beginning to change the world. My heart seemed to pound in my chest as I lay there, anxiety creeping in as I listened to the voices in my head. Each one calls out to put down the other. Maybe I was putting myself in danger, falling for another fairytale trope. Wait… they have each other? What did he mean by that? As my mind raced I could hear him singing behind me. His voice was tired, yet it was warm and filled with a welcoming vibrato. My skin prickled as each sung word passed my ear, quieting the voices as it became the only thing I could hear. I feel myself drifting off as his voice softly carries out a tune, it was unfamiliar to me but felt as if it was written to be my lullaby.

The Days Before Christmas

The next morning, I woke up with a startle, I did not hear the church bells ringing this morning and when my eyes opened, I was not in the safety that was my room. It wasn't a dream then last night, being brought here, being held, and falling asleep next to someone who I had begun to admire. I sit up and look around, the room was flooded with light from a skylight I had failed to notice the night before. A small alarm clock on the nightstand read *12:16*. Not only did I fail by missing my morning shower, and waking up in my own room, I was about 3 hours late for my usual morning tasks. I throw myself out of bed and rush to the door, greeted with a clean set of robes and a white rose with a note pinned to the hem.

I told Alessandro you will be a little late today and took care of getting him up, take your time my bathroom is across the hall so feel free to get ready there.

64

I pull the robe down from the hanger it was on and was pleasantly surprised by the addition of a few towels behind it as well as a length of ribbon with two keys on it. One looked much like the skeleton key that Judas used to open his door last night, the other I can only assume was for his personal bathroom. I cracked open the door and shot across to the adjacent door fiddling with the keys until I got it open. Shutting it behind me I take a deep breath and take a glance around. This bathroom was much nicer than the group bathrooms we shared in the sinners wing. Instead of an inground hot tub to bathe in there was a porcelain claw foot tub nestled neatly along the back wall, and instead of a freestanding shower with multiple heads there was a singular shower blocked off with ornate stained-glass walls and a door depicting a siren. The toilet sat a few feet away from the tub and was across from a large counter with a glass bowl sink. Various toiletries scattered the counter and the large mirror was lined with sticky notes with messages of self-love scrawled across them. Gingerly I strip out of my old clothes letting them fall to the floor where I stood and made my way over the bathtub. Along the side was a shelf that held various body washes and bubble bath solutions. I hadn't had a proper bubble bath in so long that seeing the bottles there tempted me just enough. He did say to take my time after all.

I turned on the faucet and let the water warm before plugging the drain and pouring in two caps full of the most fragrant bubble bath there was available. As the tub filled with bubbles and water, I slipped myself in letting the warmth bring me back to the safe place I was last night. Once it was comfortably full enough, I shut off the water and sank into the bath breathing in the heavy scents of bergamot and citrus. It felt as if I had my own slice of paradise in that moment and I shut my eyes contemplating my activities for the next few days.

I am sure another hour had passed as the water started to cool significantly and the bubbles were dying down. I pushed myself into an upright position just in time to hear voices, a set of keys jingling and the door flying open. I quickly sank myself back into the water and watched over the lip of the tub as Judas comes dashing in followed by Alessandro. The two of them were busy entertaining each other, Judas's eyes were filled with a lust I had never seen before as he shoved Alessandro up against the bathroom door. He sunk his teeth into Alessandro's partially exposed collar hungrily kissing and sucking at him while his hands undid the white buttons holding Alessandro's suit closed. Alessandro's hands were frantically undoing Judas's cassock sliding the heavy black fabric off his shoulders the two of them were ravenous for each other. As if they were two lovers who had not touched each other's flesh in many nights, the both of them were getting undressed quickly. As Judas's pants were undone Alessandro shoved him back and sunk to his knees looking up at the younger man, his face paint smudged to hell from where Judas's hands were. His hands deftly pull out the throbbing cock that was being held back by a tight pair of grey boxers. Alessandro, smiles as he keeps his mismatched eyes on the face of his lover, slowly running his tongue along the girthy shaft leaving black lipstick marks along the side before taking the head in his mouth. Judas moaned deeply as Alessandro goes to work bobbing and swirling his hardened member, ever so often panting as Alessandro's free hands would stroke the shaft and lightly caress his sack. I watched eagerly from the tub trying to be careful as to not make a sound, practically holding my breath as I watched the most powerful man in the church pleasure his underling. Judas's hands search for counter to brace himself against as Alessandro drags him closer to the edge, his voice was shaky as he panted.

"*F-fuck me,* you sure know how to use that mouth of yours don't you."

Alessandro smiled and laughed softly as he worked the length of Judas's cock, carefully standing back up, he appears to be a few inches shorter than Judas. Judas looked down at Alessandro biting his lip as he continues to stroke his cock. Carefully he slides his hand down Alessandro's pants and tugs at his member as well. Freeing up a hand he pulls off Alessandro's pants and I can't help but gasp as his fully erect member was longer yet slimmer than Judas's. The two of them freeze as they hear my gasp and both sets of mismatched eyes shoot my way. On instinct I sink further into the water hoping they did not see me nor heard the water slosh about as I did so. I can hear Judas whine as Alessandro makes his way closer to where I was hiding, hesitantly I look up and am met with a very messy Alessandro. His eyes were wide and if it wasn't for the heavy paint that covered his skin, I would say he was blushing.

"Erm... hello sister. I see you are awake now... that's *good*." He turns his head back to Judas and narrows his eyes. "I thought you said we would be alone."

"I honestly thought she had gone... I am so sorry Sister we did not mean to interrupt your bath."

"N-No by all means... please continue. I don't mind." My eyes scan their reactions, Alessandro seemed eager to get back to it but Judas on the other hand hesitated a moment before looking back over to me.

"I think we will have to continue this in the room Papa, our little lamb is getting ahead of herself."

I huff in protest as the two of them roughly throw their clothes back on before shuffling out the door. I can hear the other door slam across the hall as I stand up in the tub. That was the first time in months that I wanted to see more... hell I even wanted to participate if they would let me. Pulling the plug, I shuffle to the shower to finish washing up and rinse off. I take my time drying off until I hear the door close again and mine suddenly opens with a messy faced Judas slinking in, his neck and collarbones littered with hickeys and white, grey, and black splotches everywhere. He smiles at me awkwardly as I sat half naked in the bathroom getting myself ready for the rest of the day. Judas makes his way over to the sink to wash off the makeup and to apply a fresh coat.

"My apologies Sister, I did not realize you were still getting ready. I assumed because my door had been left cracked that you were no longer in either or were at least in my room getting ready to leave." He sheepishly laughs as he combs his hair back into place. "That is one way to find out the depth of the relationship I have with him no?"

"Do you two frequently um… play with each other?"

"As of late no, if I am being entirely honest with you dear, he… we have been more focused on trying to get to know you more."

I blush and look down as I finish getting dressed and pinning a small lace veil in my hair. "I didn't mean to interrupt your sex life…"

"You did nothing wrong sweetheart; you just have us each on little hooks waiting to see who you will choose… well that is if you choose to pursue one of us in that manner."

"Would I really have to choose if I *did* decide I wanted to be with you?"

"I suppose not, though not everyone gets the chance to sleep with a Papa and a Cardinal. You would let us know though, right? If you wanted either of us...?"

"I think I would..." I step closer to Judas and place my hand on his cheek, my heart racing in my chest as I leave a soft kiss on his shoulder before turning to leave. He stands there silently as I slip from the bathroom and make my way through the stone halls once again to Alessandro's room. I passed the occasional sister who turned to me with a small glare, though a few seemed to soften their looks at me as I made my way through. Climbing the staircase I was passed by Caesar who was busier with straightening his suit than he was walking down the stairs. He would stop every few steps and find something new to reposition. But by the time he had made it down to the bottom I had been standing there for a moment watching. He looks back up at me and gives me a small nod acknowledging my existence but that was it. So I saunter over to Alessandro's door. As I arrive, I knock loudly on the hard wood, the door flies open and Alessandro stands there, his face bare and his hair a mess. He ushers me into the room quickly and shuts the door eyeing me cautiously for a moment.

"You won't share this with that hell bitch, right? She CAN NOT know that Judas and I are still fraternizing with each other. If she finds out she will have him moved back to Italy and I am afraid I will never see him again."

I stare at Alessandro wide eyed for a moment before shaking my head. By hell bitch I assumed he meant the Abbess of the ministry. She had a tendency to behave like there was a stick up her ass. "It isn't my place to tell her, so I am not sure why I would."

"Good so you understand, I am so sorry cara mia that that is how you found out we are in touch with each other. Must be odd seeing me with another man's cock in my mouth." He chuckles before walking towards his personal bathroom. "I just have to fix up my hair at the very least before going back out to do my jobs for the day. Do you mind hanging out here till I return?" My stomach growls loudly and I am reminded that I had effectively skipped two meals as it feels like a pit opens up inside me.

"Is it possible I return later...? My stomach..."

"If you need lunch just use my kitchen, I heard through my Ghouls that some of the siblings are getting... bitchy with you."

"O-Oh okay then... thank you." I shuffle towards his kitchen and rummage around for a moment throwing together a light lunch for me. I stand in the kitchen as I scarf it down catching a glimpse of Alessandro as he dashes out of the room and out his door. I was unsure of where he was going but he did ask that I stayed here. Technically that was an order so I wandered around his suite for a moment before finding myself atop his bed again. This time instead of staying at the foot of the bed I crawled up towards the head where he would be most of the time and buried myself in the pillows that littered the bed. I took a deep breath in and my senses were flooded with the scent that could only be Alessandro's. It was harsh, littered with alcohol and fire but there was a more subtle scent that lay underneath. It was gentle and floral as if the other scents were used to cover up a sweeter side to him. I catch a soft moan in my throat as I can't help but bury my face further, I could feel myself getting drunk off his scent alone, or potentially spilled spots of liquor. I wrap my arms around the pillows and prop myself up relaxing as I lay there in his bed. I let my mind go blank as time slips by me, I felt utterly useless but each time I got up to look for a chore or task to do everything was done, my phone was always tucked away in my room and we had no other entertainment in the church unless it was music or the rare television. After a few hours I poke around through Alessandro's items and find a record player and a few records, I picked up the oldest one that had a psychedelic cover and manage to get the music playing. Smiling I recognize Cassian's old music from before the Shadows' project was halted temporarily. I take a moment steal myself away from where I was and danced to the music enjoying the freedom and space I had in that moment.

Time goes by and I switch the albums a few times till I reached Meglio. By this point it was almost midnight and Alessandro had been missing the better part of the day. Granted I didn't exactly show up to work on time today so I couldn't expect him to be back on time as he usually is. The next song starts up just in time for Alessandro to reenter the room, he looked a little disheveled but not as bad as he was earlier today and I could smell the fragrant liquor radiating off of him. He steps in and smiles as he hears his song, shutting the door behind him he starts singing along his eyes focused on me as he does so. Alessandro steps towards me holding out a hand hesitantly, I took it, the soft white satin warm to the touch. With one smooth movement he pulls me to him and places his other hand in the small of my back.

In the limited space he leads me in a waltz to his song, singing it to me, at me. Waltzing to a rock song was not something I had anticipated in my life, and yet here we were. We twirl about the space for a moment longer, my heart beating in my throat as I feel myself pressed up tightly against his body. My heart races and my breath gets caught in my throat; I could not tear my gaze away from his. It was like the room filled with a magic and energy that I could not see. Like the song had cast its spell on the two of us and I could swear his white eye was glowing. As the song ended, he swings us into a dip, our faces just inches away from each other. Like two magnets we draw closer until the light fades from his eyes, he smiles at me and stands us up rubbing my cheek and stepping away to go shut off the record player.

"W-Why did you stop?"

"It isn't right to you, I left you here all day by mistake and got drunk. I do not deserve the sweet reward of your kiss for all of my patience and penance."

"But…" I stop myself. He had said no, wishing to punish himself for his own bad habits. "I'm sorry sir, is there anything you need me to do tonight or shall I head back to my room?"

"If you go, may I join you there? Such a big bed gets awfully lonely with no one to share it with."

I bow my head and smile laughing softly. "I don't know why the two of you suddenly want to sleep with me. Didn't I fail your rituals twice? And surely, I have not been that great of a housekeeper for you. Don't even get me started on the incident at Thanksgiving."

"Well… I cannot speak for the Cardinal but as for me, I can say that you have enchanted me. You are so… diligent and quiet and kind. You have done nothing but work for me and put up with our shenanigans for the last few months. As odd as it is to say this as an older man… I have developed a crush… so to speak. And I am very jealous the Cardinal got to you first."

"You hardly know me though…"

"I know you were taken advantage of; I know that's why you were, are afraid of me. I know the other Siblings have taken a disliking to you because you have caught both of our eyes. I know you like to hum little tunes while working and that you always come in smelling like sweet strawberries and green apples… I know the cardinal… Judas has been trying to help you through something I will never understand. For Satan's sake I was handed my new life on a silver platter, I had no need to fear those in power around me." He walks back towards me stopping just short. "I know I could have anyone here in this stone castle and yet I am chasing you and that hopeless cardinal." He laughs and shakes his head. "My apologies Sister… It must be the Vodka in me but I think I must go to bed… you are free to go for the evening."

With that he disappears to the bathroom returning a few minutes later mostly naked. He slips into his massive bed and buries himself in the blankets. I cannot help but feel as if I must stay, like he needed me for some reason. So, I quietly open and shut the door before sneaking over to his chairs that sit by the fireplace and made myself comfortable. I allow myself to drift off to sleep, at least tomorrow I will be at work on time.

The next morning, I find myself being shaken awake by Alessandro who had a half worried look on his face. I was on the floor apparently; the cold hard wood was not exactly the best place to sleep. I sit up my joint's aching as I do so. Alessandro lets out a relaxed breath of air and stands up walking away for a moment before coming over to help me back up. His hair was stuck up in different directions and the his hickies from yesterday were darker and more pronounced across his body. For being in his 50's he still had that boyish charm that made him all the more attractive.

"Satanas, what the hell are you doing here! If you were going to stay you should have joined me."

"I wanted to but... you seemed upset last night and I didn't want to get myself in trouble."

He sighs and steps closer me suddenly pulling me up from the floor and in for a hug, squeezing me tightly leaving a soft kiss on my forehead. "Ah, you are silly girl... You would not get in trouble here we do not punish for such behavior." I laugh softly and wrap my arms around him as well, but only for a second. For the first time in months I felt something other than lust as I stood this close to him. We stand there together for a moment before I pull off to go start my job for the day, but Alessandro catches my wrist and stops me.

"No need, I wanted to ask something of you... I know this seems like a silly formality, and I fully understand if you were to reject the notion but, would you like to become my partner...? I guess they would call you a girlfriend if you were to say yes." My

76

face flushes at the question and I can feel all my muscles taught as if I needed to run from the situation. But ignoring my instinct I nod slightly and look up to see Alessandro's face light up gleefully.

"Perfect! I suppose though I would have to stop my "meetings" with the cardinal... but you have no idea how happy this makes me."

"Y-You don't have to stop... I like the cardinal as well. Could we not... be all together?" Really they had been together before I had ever appeared in the picture, it would be wrong of me to demand him to leave. That and I didn't mind at all the thought of all three of us together.

He cocks an eyebrow and thinks for a moment, "I think we could work that out if it is what you wished. But we will eventually have to bring it up to the rest of the Belladonna line to let them know as well."

"Well... that day will come when it does." I murmur, trying to let my mind process the new implications of my position. House maid, Satanic nun, official girlfriend to the Satanic pope... woof.

"Come come! I want you to actually join me in this bed for once, you do not need to sit at the foot like a meek little creature."

BETWEEN THE POWERS

Like a giddy kid, Alessandro dives into his bed and with open arms invites me to join him. I slip off my shoes and join him on top of his plush bedding, sinking into the nest of blankets and pillows that surround us. I hesitantly nuzzled in close to him taking in his scent, the alcohol faded off from the night before and he now smelled more like orchids and roses. We lay there together for a little while, it felt as if I was unable to move, that is until the Cardinal burst into the room. His brows furrowed before he spotted us. Judas's jaw dropped as he saw us sitting there together and all he could do was quietly back out of the room shutting the door behind him. The two of us laugh together before Alessandro lets out a deep sigh.

"Maybe he had something to say to us…?" I offer in excuse, half expecting Judas to reappear in the room.

"Eh perhaps, but I can talk to him later. I do have a job to do today though my sweet, if you like you can go to the cardinal or stay here. I suppose you can go to your room but what is the fun in that." Before I get a chance to answer he winks at me and leans in leaving a small kiss on my cheek before taking off on his morning routine getting fully dressed, his skeleton like face paint included before slipping out the door. I sit in the bed for a few more minutes before sliding out and shuffling to the bathroom so that I myself can get ready as well. As I enter Alessandro's bathroom, I am greeted with a much nicer one than Judas's though it looks the same in most aspects the tub was changed out for a jacuzzi and there was a lack of self-love sticky notes everywhere. As much as I would have loved to try out the facilities here, I took a quick shower and tried to find something for me to cover up with so I could run to my room and get my clothes. I dug around in a few drawers hoping Alessandro had maybe a loose shirt or something that would cover me just enough to go running through the halls in the cold but I came up emptyhanded. I poked my head out of Alessandro's door and saw the coast was clear. With that I ran through the halls naked with nothing more than Judas's keys around my neck, hoping and praying to Satan that I was not caught by anyone as I returned to my room. But as I get to my room, I notice the door cracked and even in all my nudeness I hesitated to dash right in. Instead, I slid along the wall ever so slightly so that I could listen to what was going on in my room if someone was in there.

I could hear voices, people talking. They were familiar, though one seemed to continue to mock the other. Leaning in closer to listen better, my peeping was interrupted by an older sister who gasped. She stared at me, mouth open as I stood covering my nudeness with my hands. Shaking my head, I pleaded silently with her to stay quiet. But she began to open her mouth, chest swelling as she prepared to shout at me for being naked outside of our usual morning parade. I groaned in frustration and dashed into my room despite the voices to avoid listening to her.

79

BETWEEN THE POWERS

Though as the door slammed shut behind me, I heard a resounding 'NO!'.

I turn around and freeze hoping I didn't accidently find myself in the wrong room. Instead of being in the wrong room I see both Alessandro and Judas standing there frozen behind me. They stood side by side as if trying to hide something, the two of them trying their damnedest to keep straight faces.

"What in the Hell are you doing here! I told you, Judas's or my room!"

"I-I needed clean clothes, what are you two doing in here!"

Judas rolls his eyes, "close your eyes and I will grab you something then go to my room, I at least have video games to keep someone occupied with." I did as I was told and shut my eyes tightly as the sounds of Judas rummaging around were then followed quickly by my robes hitting my face with a light thud. "There, now get dressed and scram."

I quickly pull on my robes and flee back out of my door, coming face to face with the sister once more. Her scowl grew but she opted to stalk off instead of shouting. I had no idea that both of them were going to be in my room, what were they hiding? My stomach growled at me and I change course from Judas's room to the cafeteria. Hopefully my absence went un-noticed and I can get food without being hazed. I sauntered through the tables and made my way up to the window where I was greeted with a scowl.

"Oh look guys it's the pet, you know, they can go missing from their duties but no one bats an eye." The Brother who mocked me leaned against the window and leered at me. "What do you need?" his voice was gruff and grating as he stared down his nose at me.

"I was just coming to see if I could score some… breakfast?"

He snorts and laughs at me before turning his back towards me and walks off into the warm kitchen. "Make it yourself pet, after all your boss has a kitchen doesn't, he?" I stand there embarrassed as the rest of the kitchen talks in hushed voices occasionally throwing a spiteful glance in my direction. I feel anger building in my chest for a second, it was unfair that they were being dickheads just because I work for Alessandro. They couldn't even get the privilege to do so, so why should I care what they think. I storm off out of the cafeteria and towards the wing where the Papa's rooms were. Flying up the stairs I made my way down the row to Alessandro's room when there was a soft click of someone's door closing and footsteps being made in my direction.

"Sister! So glad I caught you, the Cardinal said you were under the weather last night I hope everything is well now?"

"Arthur hi, um yeah I am doing okay now, just coming to make breakfast is all I prefer to make it myself and he um Alessandro said I could use his kitchen."

"Ah, have they decided that you can no longer take part in meal time at the cafeteria? They did that to my Mona before I married her. Except they didn't tell her that at first, they just gave her bad food that made her very sick every few days. It will pass, it always does!" I paused, my hand on the handle as I stare at him. This was twice now that he mentioned her, adding her story to my know lore but only in pieces.

"Arthur, I always heard the others talking about your wife what happened to her…?"

His face weakens a little, the usual mirth that he wore on his face replaced with a twinge of sorrow and a creasing of frown lines. He takes a deep breath before speaking again. "She, well she's gone, but I am sure you knew that. May I invite you inside for some tea? This is something best shared over a warm drink." I nod slightly as this was something I had wanted to know for a while. He smiled at me painfully before turning back to his room, gesturing for me to follow him in. Inside was a brightly lit little habitat for the eldest brother. His walls were painted with a soft sage green and were littered with floral wall sconces that lit up the room. Next to his fire place were two long tables covered with a variety of green plants, some crawling up the walls, others

82

branching out like wild hair. On his nightstand sat a pot with white poinsettias that had photos of a woman nestled next to them. His bed was much smaller than Alessandro's giving way to making the room much larger, it felt as if it had a woman's touch to it. That the space was loved and well taken care of even if it was just Arthur most days. I felt myself drawn to the large painting of a woman that sat over the fireplace, her face was soft and rounded, cheeks a rosy pink with the brightest smile to match. Her eyes seem were a deep green, and her brunette curls fell playfully on either side of her shoulders. Around her neck was a Satanic Cross, an inverted crucifix with a snake up the middle, hanging low onto her breasts and her hands were painted in a clasped position in front of her as if someone managed to catch the moment, she got a joke. There was an inscription carved into a bronze plate at the bottom of the frame "*Mona Lucile Belladonna.*"

"Wasn't she beautiful?" He mused as he followed my gaze to the painting.

"She looks so happy…" I say softly. "Is that…. Is that her?" He gave a nod as he looked away.

"Well she was, that was painted the week we found out we were with child, there was going to be a little bouncing baby Belladonna to take up the mantel someday." Arthur says as he scuttles about getting together a small tea set before setting up a small place setting for the two of us by the fire place. He comes over and removes his off-white cardigan and sits down gesturing his hand to me to join him. "She loved to garden and spend time with me while I was just a Cardinal, often she would drag me out to see her flowers when I had my head stuck in books for too long. It wasn't uncommon for her to be laughing; she brought a certain gleefulness to these walls that feels long gone now."

"I'm so sorry, what happened to her…? If you don't mind me asking that is."

"She um…" his voice gets caught in his throat for a moment so he grabs his tea cup and take a quick sip of the fresh tea he poured. "She passed away in child birth due to some complications. Even the best of our doctors and midwives could not help her… We lost the little girl as well." He looks down at his tea and sighs, his face contorted as he tried to not let a tear roll down his cheek. "I felt so lost after losing my Mona, she was always a little ray of sunshine even when she was being harassed, even in death."

I sit there for a moment stunned and in silence as the words left his mouth. He kept his face down for a moment longer before attempting to compose himself. Arthur sits up and lightly dabs at the tears that were forming in the corners of his eyes attempting to not smudge his carefully done up paints. The silence between us stagnated for a moment before Arthur cleared his throat and took another sip of tea. This man, who months ago had traced his hands across my bare body in a ritual, now sat before me with a piece of his broken heart resting in the air between us.

"You know, I believe you would make a perfect wife for my brother. He already seems to be stuck on you as is." Arthur said, sipping on his tea once more as he shifted gears quickly. "I knew he would be quite the spitfire when Cassian brought him home, finding a partner would have been hard."

"Me? I don't think I could... Hell, I don't even want children honestly so I would be useless for bringing an heir to the family."

"You don't need to bring an heir, as much as Cassian and Lucille insist on it there are still many more in line for the power. But you have made my brother very happy these last few weeks, even with you just being around."

I nod and take a sip of my tea, a light blush creeping across my cheeks. Arthur and I sat and chatted for a while longer. He would reminisce about how his wife would tend to flower gardens all day and teach him how to tend to them as well for days she was busy. That she would insist on getting him out of the building to go on an outing as just Mona and Arthur, not the Papa and his Prima del madre. Just the two of them. After she had passed on, he said he found himself tending to her gardens as to not lose the few things she had left behind. He came down from being the cocky strung-up Cardinal and Papa like his father was and mellowed out. If it wasn't for Mona, he was unsure if the Shadows' project would have ever been brought back, she loved to listen to him sing and pressured Lucille to let the project move forward. Mona had been important in many decisions, from the band to changing how the Ministry conducted itself in the public eye. After a while Arthur slowed down as something came to mind, finishing off his tea he stood up and shuffled off to his bathroom returning with a small yellow box. He sat back down as he held it close to his chest for a moment before handing it to me.

"I have kept this here for so long, hoping I could pass it off to the next Mrs. Belladonna be it mine or my brothers. I think you should wear it; Mona would have loved to meet you had she gotten the chance."

He reaches out and hands me the small yellow box. As carefully as I could I shook it open. Inside was a Satanic Cross necklace, adorned with small diamonds set in its golden frame. In the center was a deep red ruby that brought the piece together. I look up at Arthur not sure what to say.

"Take it and wear it with pride dear, I think you will make Alessandro very happy if you choose to stay with him." He stands up and cleans up his tea set before coming back out. "I do have to go check the frost on my garden beds and roses my dear. I never bothered to learn your actual name by the way, I was told to just refer to you as Sister Wenstrom. What may I call you dear?"

I stand up and straighten out my robes, "Thank you Arthur I appreciate this... and my name is Gale."

"Ah well, Sister Gale, be careful out there alright?" With that, we shuffle out of Arthur's room and I carefully place the little box in my pocket before going into Alessandro's room. It started to feel like home entering Alessandro's room every day, its blue walls feeling more comfortable than my stone walls that I called home. The room was always warm, and there was almost always someone waiting for me who seemed happy to see me in the space. I go to the kitchen and throw together a rough French toast breakfast making an extra two servings in case both of them decided to come up here. The vanilla and cinnamon lent a hand to the space making it smell warm and inviting, I open a few windows to let the fresh frosted air roll through and carry the smell outside. Taking my late breakfast, I sit next to the fire that seemingly never stopped and enjoyed this moment of peace that I have created for myself. The French toast was some of the sweetest I had enjoyed in months; warm and fluffy they were the perfect breakfast.

After I had finished up, I took the time to clean up the kitchen organizing the various dishes that were littered through the cabinets. By the time I was done it was close to lunchtime and I started to wonder where they were. As if my thoughts had summoned them, the two of them strolled back into the room chatting about the plans for Christmas tomorrow. Both of their mismatched gazes met mine and they stopped talking for a second.

"So sister, I heard from Arthur that you two had a little chat. Is everything alright?"

"Yeah, we were just talking, he told me about his wife and we shared some tea. Nothing too major."

The two of them exchange knowing looks with each other. "Yes, and you shared something else. Why didn't you tell us your first name?"

I laugh softly and shake my head, "Well I didn't know if I was going to be in the church long enough for anyone to get to know me."

"Your name is beautiful Gale, don't try to hide that."

"She probably has her reasons for not wanting to share that with everyone Alessandro."

Alessandro shakes his head and laughs as if the reason was beyond him. He didn't care though, at that moment he was just happy to know my name. "Well Gale, I am glad to know you further than just 'Sister Wenstrom' finally." He says relieved before walking over to his bed and shimmying out of his suit jacket.

"We have a surprise for you actually, that's why we do not want you to go into your room again tonight. Is it possible for us to ask if you could stay with one of us tonight?"

"Why can't we all share a bed...? Alessandro's is plenty big for all three of us." I ask lightheartedly hoping that they will agree. Judas's face shifts into a gentle frown.

"You know that if I get caught with Alessandro, I will be sent away..."

"But-"

"No ifs no ands no buts my dear Gale but since it is the night before Christmas, I will keep you company until I have to go to bed, yes?"

I nodded and accepted the compromise; it wasn't what I wanted, so I still had to choose whether to stay with Alessandro or Judas. We settled down for the day, since it was a holiday there was not much for them to do and if they did not have a job for me there was not much for me to do either. Through the rest of the afternoon and into the evening we talked and shared drinks, Alessandro had been sharing from one of his many stashes and the three of us were good and drunk when it came time for Judas to head back to his room, none of us wanted to be split apart. I managed to beg him to stay for a few more minutes, those few more minutes turned into an hour and was long enough for

Alessandro to pass out in bed, the little man wrapped himself up in most of his blankets and became a sleeping lump on the bed. The room grew colder as the fire started to die down and Judas and I crawled into bed together with Alessandro, though he was not too interested in sharing his warm fortress. Judas stripped off his cassock and unfurled as much as he could, pulling me in close to him. I let my hands come to rest in his lap naturally and we slowly dozed off together, as my eyes shut for the night the fire went out in the room, and all went cold.

Our Christmas Sin

The bells chimed out loud and clear rousting the three of us from our slumber, their brassy voices echoing all around us as the abbey came to life again. It was Christmas morning, though instead of us running to a cathedral to pray for a little baby we had gifts to find and some mischief to get after. Judas slinks out of the room quickly as he has to change into a more festive outfit for today and rather than taking his sweet time, Alessandro rolls out of bed to do the same. I on the other hand do not have many options so I take a small shower as Alessandro gets ready and throw on my robes again, pulling the hemline in the front up to my hips to create a different skirt shape and tightening the belt to give me a cinched waistline. The veil that I occasionally put in my hair was rolled up and used to tie a bow as I let my locks hang down as a ponytail rather than a bun. I looked at myself in the mirror, while cute it felt as if something was missing. Pulling out the necklace that Arthur gave me I slide it around my neck and close the clasp in the back. In my chest a warmth grows, I couldn't help but smile at the woman staring back at me in the mirror. She had soft amber eyes and dark blonde hair that swooped neatly into the ponytail, her tawny skin that was sprinkled with freckles across her cheeks and shoulders. She was beautiful and she was me.

I step out of the bathroom with a smile on my face and a fire in my heart not expecting what I saw when I came out. Alessandro was standing with his arms folded across his chest, a light furrow on his brow as he looked at Judas who was, by all means, tied up like a Christmas present himself. He was in what looked to be a blue blazer and black trousers with his Cardinal makeup down crisply. A big red bow was tied around his neck and tied off the intricate body bindings that wrapped around him. Judas smiled and was very proud of himself showing off his festive outfit for the day since he was allowed to break from his usual form. Alessandro on the other hand was wearing a tight pair of black jeans that flared out at the ankle and a loose-fitting button-up adorned with an embroidered pentacle in the back. He had his hair slicked back being held together by a mini-Santa hat hair clip. I had never noticed before but Alessandro's ears were slightly pointed to a tip at the end much like that of an elf or vampire, he had small diamond clip-ons and a tinge of red lipstick. They carried on back and forth about their outfit choices and what the plan was for today. Many of the older sisters will be joining Arthur later this afternoon for a social affair with hot beverages and sharing their favorite memories of the past. Lucille and Cassian were going to be with Caesar as they went out to bring gifts to the members who were less fortunate than the rest and the young sisters were going to be out with their families outside of these stone walls.

"Why don't we join Arthur today? I have nowhere to be and unless you two have plans we have nothing to do."

"Sure we can join Fratello later, but for now I do want us to show you what we were putting together yesterday."

Alessandro saunters over and stands above me leaning down to plant a small kiss on my forehead. Softly he grabs my hand and leads me out of the room, Judas close behind us as we made our walk to my room in the Sisters wing. Along the way, the occasional bitter woman would shoot us a sideways glance always to be thwarted by a stern look from either Alessandro or Judas. When we arrived at my room, my door was adorned with a small wreath and a little letter tucked into the door jam. I pulled it out and tucked it away under my breast as Alessandro opened my door my room sparkled with the light of a thousand stars. I quickly slip past to see what could possibly be making all that light when I notice that my bed was no longer that thin uncomfortable mattress on an old wooden frame but rather a much thicker pillow top much like Alessandro's. Even the sheet set was different, I would almost say that it was satin or silk with how it glimmered. My floor was covered with a plush fuzzy rug that was littered with sparkling threads that caught the morning sunlight and on my small writing desk sat a neatly wrapped package.

"That one is from me" Judas's voice was soft as he cooed at me to open it. Picking up the box, I gently peel apart the glistening wrapping paper to be met with a large bundle of fabric that was concealing something deeper. My hands ran across the fabric it felt familiar, worn, and soft smelling of Judas's vibrant musk. I unfurl the fabric to see it was one of his cassocks, hemmed and mended to be closer to my size. Altered to look like a jacket or maybe even a house robe. In one of the pockets I reached in, I pulled out a small glass bottle that had Eau de Judas written across its make-shift label. I couldn't help but laugh as I looked up at the two of them.

"You seemed happy being wrapped up in that old thing so I thought I could give it to you, along with your own personal bottle of me for whenever I am busy and you need a pick me up." In the other pocket, I pulled out a similar bottle that was labeled as Alessandro's instead of Judas's.

"I know I tend to smell like a mini bar most nights but Judas mentioned how you seem to enjoy people's signature scents. I don't get it but if it makes you happy then so be it."

94

The three of us stayed there in my room for a little while longer, I sitting on my new bed while Alessandro sat on the floor his head in my lap and Judas against the door chatting about our Christmases past. Alessandro used to get new bottles of booze to add to his collection and the occasional boob cup to match. His mentor never approved but when she passed on Cassian kept up the tradition as a way to try and bond with his last heir. Judas was often given a new game or two and then was put to work reading and translating books in the collection. Lucille insisted that he did not partake in many of the festivities unless specifically invited to and so year after year he didn't. That was until he got promoted to head cardinal and next in line should anything happen to Cassian's acknowledged line of succession. I wanted to share my memories but every time I tried to think back on them memories came flooding back of my abuse. It seemed as if every good time had to be interrupted by the invasive memories of those heinous men. Judas seemingly caught on and changed the subject insisting we walk around the temple for a bit before we joined Arthur.

"I don't think I have enjoyed a day off as much as today, being papa is a lot of work. A figurehead, a lead singer, a leader. Usually, I am being carted off to deal with some lousy task like signing papers I do not get time to explore like I did as a younger man."

"Oh Alessandro, you, and I both know why they don't let you 'explore' anymore," Judas said leaning closer to the slightly smaller man. Alessandro whips his head around and catches Judas by the throat softly squeezing as he pushes him towards the stone wall.

"E-easy there Papa, Lucille could catch us." Judas chokes out, his face turning a bright red as he is flattened against the wall.

"You and I both know that she is out of the house with the bag of bones in tow."

"You can't do shit out here in the hallway, to open too many could happen across us." Judas whimpered, a shit-eating grin across his face as he wriggled against Alessandro's hand. My own heart was set a flutter as I watched the two, almost jealous that it wasn't me under his grip.

"Hmm right indeed but not if I do this!" Alessandro grabs our hands and drags us down the hall a bit more to a hidden stairwell where the three of us fit snuggly underneath completely out of sight. Alessandro's eyes were glazed over with lust as he stared at the cardinal seemingly forgetting I was in the space with them. Whenever those two started to interact, the whole world disappeared from them. With a single hand Alessandro pulls at the ribbon around Judas's neck, the bow tumbling apart. As if on instinct Judas sinks to his knees gazing up at Alessandro, their white irises trained on each other not breaking contact.

Alessandro's hand goes for Judas's throat again and a soft whimper escapes the man's lips. He tilts his face up towards him, Judas's lips parting in anticipation as Alessandro drew near. He too sinks onto one knee drawing closer, their lips meet and I can hear one of them let out a sigh as if that was the one release they were waiting for. They did not separate unless it was for air, Alessandro's free hand found its way to his cheek holding him there as if they were lost lovers and this may be their last moment together.

Judas let his hands wander up Alessandro's lithe body, a hand coming to rest with a fist full of hair the other on the small of his back, the two intertwined with only each other. I shrank back into the corner as much as I could wanting nothing more than to join in but it felt wrong. This was their moment; their space and I was just a visitor. Their voices join in a duet of lust as they moan between breaths. Alessandro was the first to break sitting up straight, a hand still firmly on Judas's throat, his eyes rise to meet mine and a smile creeps across his face. Judas whimpers again as Alessandro's attention is momentarily on me. The cardinal began to push himself up causing Alessandro to pin the man to the ground. Judas's legs shoot out from under him and he lays sprawled out on the ground, his cock throbbing against the

97

confines of his suit pants, begging to be released. Even with the dim lighting under the stairs, it was obvious they had a burning desire for each other.

Alessandro snakes his way up the Cardinal's body stopping only when their cocks met. He released the throat hold he had and ran his hands down Judas's body pulling out the shirt that was neatly tucked into the waistline of the suit pants then unbuttoning the shirt entirely. I could feel myself growing more aroused by the second as he took his time with him. Kissing, licking, biting, and sucking, he makes his way down Judas's body to the bulge in his pants taking a moment to stroke the shaft with his palm. He moans softly and bites his lip thrusting his hips slowly into Alessandro's hand. It felt wrong. Me being here. I was an insert, a cover-up. A beard even. Perhaps these months had been a ruse so that they could find excuses to be with each other, a scapegoat for the random hickies and bite marks. But even with that budding idea, I couldn't help but be enraptured by their lust.

Judas rolls his head back and catches me staring at them intently, his chest rose and fell with shaky breath as he waved me over. Alessandro watched from his position straddling one of Judas's legs, carefully pulling out his cock to run his tongue along the length of it. I crawl over on my hands and knees unsure of what to do, Judas lured me in and pulled me down to him so he could whisper in my ear.

"You know my sweet… you are allowed to join if it so pleases you."

I nod slightly shifting back into a sitting position, taking one hand I run it through Judas's messy blonde strands the other on his closest hand as it makes its way to my inner thighs. Suddenly his mouth falls open letting out a gasp, Alessandro had taken his cock fully in his mouth and was teasing Judas by just playing with the head. I stared in awe as I watched him lick and suck at the girthy member, paying special attention to just under the head. Alessandro's free hand was busy just further south as he was stroking his cock. I wanted to join in so badly. Carefully I make my way down to where Alessandro was, Judas's hand finding its way to my ass squeezing it firmly and rubbing it before I sit back down. I whimper at Alessandro to pull his attention to me and he sits up his gaze piercing my soul for a moment as he moves his hand from Judas's shaft to my chin. I crinkle my nose slightly as he grabs hold and pulls me closer.

"Do you really want to play this time *maiala*?" His voice was smooth as he drew me near. Like a dog on a leash, I followed his movements until I was face to-face with him. He pressed his warm lips to mine and swiped his tongue begging entrance into my mouth. My lips part and he slips his tongue against mine, his hands pulled at my hips daring me to come closer. Drawn like a moth to a flame I made my way closer, swinging my leg over Judas's hips his cock sitting just inches below my dripping cunt. Judas's hands slithered up my legs and gripped my thighs holding me in place, he squeezed tightly rubbing his thumbs across my skin. Alessandro pulls back and smiles at me, carefully placing one hand on my shoulder and the other snaking up my robes to rub between my legs. As he touches me his smile turns into a smirk, feeling that I have no panties he pushes me down closer to Judas's cock.

I suck in a breath and look at him with worry in my eyes and he stops for a moment, concern in his face until my gaze softens. This man wasn't going to hurt me, just play with me so I bend willingly to the pressure and feel the tip press against my lips, Judas again whimpers behind me, he wants to play too but Alessandro shoots him a withering glare before turning his attention back towards me. He helps guide the other man's cock into me as I sink down more, with a cautious rhythm I start to ride, hearing the gentle moans behind me as I keep my eyes on Alessandro who sits back on his knees, his cock poking out of his trousers. I motion for him to come closer and as he sits up more, I slide my hand down his chest and to his pants popping open the top button allowing for more freedom. I then wrap my hand around his member and start to stroke his cock, slowly at first until he was closer to me. Something had taken over, my mind relinquishing the usual hesitation and anxiety as I followed instinct.

Our chests were practically touching, face to face as I rode Judas. Judas's hands were still firmly on my thighs as if he was guiding my every move. I could hear him panting behind me, broken words falling from his mouth as he rolled his hips into me. Alessandro leaned in leaving kisses along my neck one hand on my cheek, the other on my hand guiding my movements. His teeth graze my throat and a dark growl escapes past his lips, I can't help but whimper myself, I wanted him to pin me down and take me too. The greedy thought of being fucked raw by both of them set my nerves on fire. The lust builds in my chest and I let my other hand slip down between my legs feeling Judas's cock as it slips in and out with ease. I tease my clit ever so softly, a deep wanting ache builds ever in my core. Alessandro suddenly wraps an arm around me and pulls me off of Judas, a startled but giggly yelp leaving me as he lays me down. Judas moves quickly out of Papa's way; my head being placed in his lap as he settles behind me.

The Cardinal strokes his cock as he watches Alessandro position himself in front of me. I look up into his eyes as he stares longingly at me, a free hand stroking his cock as the other comes down to rest on my chin. Alessandro slithers up my body parting my robe and exposing my bare body beneath, his nails dragging down my chest as he grips my hips and pushes himself against me. He moans deeply as he starts to fuck my slick slit, moving one hand from my hips to toy with my clit. My eyes flit back and forth between Alessandro and Judas as the two of them pleasure

101

themselves with me. Judas's hand slips from my chin down my chest to play with my breast, I bite my lip and close my eyes for a moment as they both pay attention to me. Alessandro fucks me carefully as he continues playing with my clit, the sensation building deep inside me. I pant quietly as he kisses my body, dragging the tip of his tongue up my sensitive skin. The three of us in union create a small choir of pleasure, each of us moaning as we enjoy each other's flesh. I can feel a pull in my core like someone is stretching a rope tight.

I watch as Judas's head lulls back his breathing shaky he picks up the pace. His voice comes out in a whimper, a panting moan. Alessandro sits up and watches him, pushing his hips down onto me as he still used his thumb to rub my clit. Judas's breath hitches in his throat as he pushes his hips forward, falling apart as he shoots across my chest. Alessandro laughs softly as he pulls me closer to him by my hips. My eyes stay trained on Judas as he sits behind me panting, he rocks back on his ankles placing his hands behind him. I can't help but moan as Alessandro pushes me closer and closer, the rope being pulled was at its limit as it starts to fray. My hands find his wrist and I grab a hold as the rope snaps and the sun bursts inside me. I tighten my jaw to stiffen the noises from my chest, my eyes fluttering for a moment as I finish under his hand. As if that was his cue, he pins my shoulders as he takes longer strokes, groaning as he uses me as a sex toy. His breathing slowly became ragged and in the blink of an eye, he had pulled back as he shot his load across my body. He closes his eyes and keeps his head down for a moment as his cock pulses, semen dripping from his tip. Taking a deep breath, he sits up and looks over to Judas who has adjusted his position and tucked himself away.

"Clean her up won't you Cardinal? She has been such a good girl." Alessandro murmured between pants, looking pleased with himself as he checked me over.

Judas scooches me into his lap more and pulls out a hidden cloth that was neatly folded to wipe the cum from my chest and neck. After I was all cleaned up, he leaned down and placed a kiss on my cheek, I turned my head to try and catch his lips but he pulled away before I could. The three of us take our time collecting ourselves and getting dressed again, hoping that no one has walked by us in our little game. Not like it would have been the first time someone got caught screwing in the halls.

Judas snaked out first followed by Alessandro who helped me up and pulled me out into the light. Their makeup was a bit smudged and I had black and grey streaks all over my neck and face. I blush at them as they carefully wipe away the paint, the lust that was there replaced with something sweeter and warm. Maybe I was a tool, a toy, a game… but fuck was it a fun one. I could get used to being their plaything though in my heart I felt a twinge.

"Come on you two, we are going to miss the hot chocolate with Arthur if we stay here any longer." Judas grabs my hand and I grab Alessandro's as we make our way through the halls to the library where Arthur was set up with many of the sisters sprawled across the massive library.

The New Year

I made my way down the darkened halls back to my room; the New Year's Eve party was wrapping up and many of us were stumbling around to get to bed. Some sisters helped each other hobble down to their rooms and others crawled, the whole Ministry smelled of booze and regret. There were only a small handful of us that didn't partake in Alessandro's homemade jungle juice. Judas had taken it upon himself to drag Alessandro back to his room and for the sake of our morning selves we agreed to stay in our own rooms tonight. With my head spinning I shuffle my way along the wall to my room. Grabbing for the handle I noticed my door was already open, and without thinking I slipped inside. Maybe I had left it open by accident, it wasn't impossible since today has been nothing but busy. As I stumbled in, I was hit with an unfamiliar scent, the curated tango of Judas and Alessandro was being masked by something much heavier and more floral. It permeated the airspace around me, my head felt heavy and nausea built in my stomach. Quickly searching the wall for my switch, I flip on the blinding light and are greeted with the one woman you dread to see alone.

Sister Lucille, the abbess, stood in front of me her arms folded as she held a note, a length of ribbon, and a small clip-on diamond earring. She looked like the old school teacher who would rap your knuckles with a ruler if she decided you were in the wrong. Her dress suit was perfectly pleated and her hair was brushed back, she stood above me as a statue of matriarchal power. Her claws tightened their grip on the items as she looked down at me, her face contorted in a disgusted scowl. I couldn't help but feel myself shrink back away from her, but I had nowhere I could go that she wouldn't find me.

"I see Cardinal did not heed my warning about messing around with Alessandro. I just didn't think they roped a woman to be in between them." She hissed, white teeth practically grinding as she offered a withering smile.

"I-I can explain it's not-"

"It's not what? Not what it looks like? You DON'T have both of their colognes in your room, you HAVEN'T slept with them both in the same room? You were the only sister who just "happened" to not leave their Christmas letter on their door during room checks? I am not as dumb as they have led you to believe." I can feel my stomach doing summersaults as she corners me, it was never against the rules to sleep with them. Or at least I thought it wasn't frowned upon.

"You know, you are assigned to work for Papa. You are his housemaid, his whore, and only his. The fact that you have managed to get my little J wrapped up in his juvenile behavior again is abhorrent. And you know exactly what's going to happen don't you."

"Don't send him away please, we weren't doing anything wrong!" I protested, though my voice sounded weak with all the booze in my system. I felt weak.

"You know not of what you speak, Judas is destined for something far greater than the lead singer of a silly little band." Lucille hissed before a disapproving laugh slipped from her maw.

"Please, I-I need him to stay I-I think I love him... them. I need them and they..." I squeak out as the world around me blurred. "They belong here, you haven't seen how much they need each other..."

She scoffs as she shakes her head and she throws the incriminating items on the floor. "If you love him so much then you must choose. I will deal with whoever is left, and I will deal with them in the way I see fit. Not that I need to explain myself to you, whelp, and if you breathe a word of this to anyone…" She leans in close to me, her wrinkled face mere inches from mine, "I will make sure that you will find yourself back in that snake pit we saved you from."

With that, she stomps on the pile of evidence shattering the earring. She leaves my room, her fog of flowers following close behind as I am left in the wake. How come she knew? What else did she know about me? About Judas and Alessandro? Was she watching us…?

Standing there, my heart racing in my chest, sober and terrified I shut my door and fell to my knees. There was a weight on me, my breath was unable to leave my throat and tears started to stream down my face. What did she mean by deal with? Did she really have the power to send me back? The world became small, strict, and dark. I couldn't breathe, I couldn't move all I could do was curl up in a ball on the ground. Fear sat in my chest and for the rest of the night, I could not sleep.

Daylight crept in through my window, greeting my deflated form on the floor. My body ached all over and the words from last night rattled around my brain like a moth in a jar. How was I going to let them know that we were found out? Could I even show up to do my work today without Lucille taking that as my choice? I slowly pulled myself up off of the floor as the bell chimed to rouse the abbey. As unsuspecting as I could I slipped in with the rest of the sisters for our plod to the showers. Many of them kept their heads low, some sick and others embarrassed but not even one would walk close to me. It was like they knew that I was trouble.

As quick as I possibly could I took a shower and changed my clothes before sneaking off towards Judas's wing. My eyes scanned the halls back and forth for any sign of Lucille before I dashed towards Judas's door. The key I wore around my neck lets me slip into his room quietly to be greeted by a very much still asleep Judas. He was sprawled out in bed, a controller on the floor and his TV faintly humming game over music from whatever he had been playing before falling asleep. I stand there, my heart thrumming against my rib cage, it felt as if it was beating so hard that it could have awaken him. Judas's body shifts as he groans and readjusts a pillow before flattening back out. I clasp my hands together wanting to wake him but fearing that it would be the wrong choice. Against all better judgment, I slip out of his room and make my way to Alessandro's room. He was going to be easier to tell off, but I doubt he would take it lightly. Not after everything we did, not after Christmas…

#

"I am sorry sir, but I need to be transferred jobs. I enjoyed working as your… assistant but something has come up and I no longer feel comfortable working here." I say, lying through my teeth as I held back tears knowing that this resignation was forced for his protection.

"I am so sorry amore, is there something that I did to make you feel such a way?" Alessandro asked, his brows knitting together as he was trying to decipher my face for his crime. "Whatever it is let me pay for it ten fold I well and truly did not mean to hurt you."

"N-No I… I just no longer feel like this is where I should be. M-my time would be better spent back in the library… with the books."

"Are you sure this is what you want? I do not mind letting you change jobs cara mia, I just ask that you come see me before the end of each day." He murmured, almost dejected that I was running from this cushy position.

"I-I am not sure that I… that I can come to see you, sir." I squeaked as I squeezed my hands together, praying he would just leave it alone.

"What is with this whole "sir" act? Why won't you come see me my sweet?" He was making this harder than it needed to be.

"I just can't I am sorry; may I leave Papa?"

"No you may not, what is going on?" he starts to walk towards me, his loose-fitting pajama pants hanging effortlessly off his hips. I turn my eyes to the floor and step back as he approaches, I couldn't let him distract me… this was for our safety. His safety… Perhaps I could convince Lucille to leave them alone if I picked Judas.

"Sir, I must insist. It is what I feel is best for everyone… for me."

"It's not what you want though, is it? Who put you up to this? We were doing so well… I thought you trusted me more…" I winced. Of course, I trusted him. That was the problem though, wasn't it? I craved him, desired him. Perhaps even could go so far as to say I loved him, but Lucille scared me more. She knew things, and she had power that was outside of Alessandro's reach.

"I-I do" the words catch in my throat before spilling out a hopeless lie, "I just, I can't be here anymore and feel like an active member of the mission. Really, my time is better spent elsewhere."

"Hah, is this really about being important to 'world domination'? Come on diavolina being here with me is more than enough. I can make you one of the most important women for it if you so wish. I could burn the world to the ground, just for you to smile." Tears burn in my eyes as I close them tightly taking another step away from him.

"Please… I need to go…"

Alessandro's eyes search me for an answer before letting out a defeated huff as he waves me off in dismissal. I quickly turn to leave as I feel tears welling up in my eyes, and as the door clicks behind me a wave crashes over my heart. Before the tears could fall, I ran down the stairs and ducked beneath them collapsing again onto the floor. My eyes stung as tears streamed down my face and I choked back heavy sobs. I didn't want to leave him, but I couldn't let Judas be separated from him either. There is nothing she can do to Alessandro without upsetting the rest of the clergy anyway, right? I was drowning in my tears as it felt as if a hole was ripped open inside my chest. A hollow, empty void that consumed the love I had felt towards Alessandro, the longing and desire. I longed to crawl back up his stairs and into his arms while apologizing for being some stupid girl. To cuddle up close to him again and be held tightly through the cold night. I wanted to walk into the room to see him sprawled out butt naked as I had so many days before, I shake my head trying to clear the thoughts that clouded my brain. The want I had for him pulled at my heart but I couldn't. He had to just be Papa now, for Judas's sake… for mine.

After I felt as if I had cried out all that I could, I sat up and tried to shake the dust off of my robes. I needed to see Judas before word got around to him that I had to abandon Alessandro… Papa. I stand up and shake the rest of the dust out of the rest of my robes and start to make my way towards his wing again. Sister should have no problem with me going to see him now, right? Maybe she will see I made a choice and just drop it. I shuffle through the halls, my eyes searching the frosted windows for any spark, for a glimmer. I needed a reason to smile, to act as if all was fine. If Judas figured out his mother came to speak with me hell would break loose, where was it in her right to intimidate the sisters for sleeping around as they pleased? Slut shaming was well and truly frowned upon here, but then again it now felt as if any activities I did were strictly forbidden again.

The stone halls felt cold, not in the way that ice is cold, but in the way a corpse is cold. They felt lifeless and empty, and the spark I had was in danger of being snuffed out completely. I find myself in front of his door, staring down at my hands unsure of how I should enter the room. I grip the door handle and slide the key in, hesitating to turn it the door suddenly is pulled open and I am hit with a floral mist. It enveloped my senses and sent panic straight through my core. I pull my key from the door and fold my hands in front of me feigning innocence. Lucille steps out and bumps into me, she looks down, and a snarl slides onto her face.

"Good, you made the right choice. I won't have to make his life hell." Her voice rumbled in hushed tones.

"Is everything alright Mother?" Judas comes to the door and opens it up, his face cracks into a large smile as he sees me standing there. "Ah! Gale, come in I wasn't expecting you until later!"

"We will speak more later J; I have to let the rest of the Clergy know." With that Lucille shoves past, taking her cloud of death with her. I step inside Judas's room and as the door clicks shut, I can feel tears spill down my cheeks. The breath leaves my chest and I turn to face Judas whose smile dropped as he gazed upon my face. He quickly comes to me, his hands on my cheeks trying to wipe away the tears his brow furrowed and his already concerned cardinal paint now cartoonishly contorted in worry.

"Ah no, splendore why the tears?" He says resting his forehead against mine. "Did something happen on your way here?"

"I-I can no longer see Alessandro... I told him already I cannot work as his assistant but how do I tell him I can't ..I cannot see him anymore."

His brow furrows again as he pulls back and looks into my face, his eyes darting back and forth looking for any clue to my predicament. "Fiore mio, did he harm you? Do I need to go kick his ass for you?"

"N-no... I cannot tell you why please do not make a big thing about it... I do not wish to hurt either of you."

"You cannot hurt me, Gale, Alessandro he may be a bit more delicato but…Do I need to be the bearer of bad news for our lover? Do you no longer love him?"

My lip shakes as I try to halt sobs from taking over my words, everything catches in my throat and I cannot speak. Tears continue to roll down my face and all I can do is bury my face in his warm cassock. I could not tell him that it was his mother's fault I was a mess. Nor that she had threatened them, Satan knows what she has planned for them. But she couldn't do much to Alessandro without backlash from the church and Judas is her own baby boy, sending him away is about as far as she would be willing to go. I threw my arms around Judas and held on tightly as my knees grew weak.

"Oh, my sweet, come now. I will talk to him tomorrow for now come sit." He carefully wraps his arms around me and walks us towards his bed. He flops back and pulls me on top of him, gently rubbing my back and singing to me in a hushed voice. My heart breaks inside my chest as I rack my brain for any way to tell him that I still love Alessandro but cannot be with them both. After a little while I slid off to the side and he lets out a slight groan and stretches out before sitting up. His face turns to me and his white and green gaze sends a chill down my spine.

"I…I need you to tell Alessandro that as much as I love him… I cannot see him anymore… for his sake."

"Did someone threaten you?" his voice was flat, cold, devoid of all life. He was serious as his gaze hardened and he no longer felt safe.

"y-yes... a sister... threatened me and she can hurt us all if I do not comply..."

"Who is it then?!" He questioned, practically shouting.

"I cannot tell you that...she said if anyone found out that... that she would get me removed and sent back to... them..."

"You cannot be serious, I have more power, Alessandro has more power! We can protect you!" Though his voice shook with outrage, it would break if he knew it was his own mother who threatened me.

"No. You can't... please just... please." I whimper, defeated as I felt required to withhold any incriminating information.

He crinkles his nose at me and scowls at me for a moment more before letting his face relax. A sigh escapes his lips and he looks defeated. "I will let him know... but this will break his heart amoruccia."

"I know, okay? I get that... but I have to."

"It is okay, just breathe. If you need you can stay here tonight, I have duties to attend to so I must leave but I will come

116

back later." With that, he stands and leans down leaving a kiss on my forehead then turns to make his way out of the room. Hesitating at the door he turned to look at me again he looked hurt, but that didn't stop him as he walked out to attend to what he had to do. I sit there on his bed, softly pulling at his blankets to cover myself up and trying to not cry again today. His room felt so plain, so devoid of character that it didn't truly feel like his, like a hotel room is made to appease the public but not the one who stays in the room. The white walls reflected the harsh light of the lamps making it feel sterile. His bedside table that once held books was now covered with a few juice boxes and a letter. Its wax seal had been broken but was still neatly tucked away as if read quickly and then left. Hesitantly I reach over and snatch it up inspecting the seal. It was a small white and gold stamping of the Satanic Cross with no embellishment aside from the 666 above and on the sides of the Satanic Cross. It was the seal of Cassian, the oldest living Belladonna, and the 'father' of Alessandro and his brothers. Curiosity tugged at my heart strings and I carefully pull out the letter trying to ensure nothing tore.

Cardinal Judas Belladonna,

You are summoned to the chambers of Cassian and Lucille to discuss your new role in Project Shadows.' You must not share with the clergy that Alessandro has been removed from power and that we are without a leader. It is requested you bring

117

*your first list of songs for a proposed new album and to select your
Ghouls for tour and recording dates.*

*You are expected to not be as big of a
disappointment as the last time you came.*

*-The Guards
of Cassian*

What? Alessandro wasn't in power any longer? Is that
why he was back early for the ritual season? Alessandro was no
longer the one in charge so who was?

I reread the letter a few times trying to see if I had
possibly misread it at any point. Judas was the next in line, and he
was now in charge of the Shadows' project. That meant he held the
power...or did he? I scan the room for any other documents that
looked important but aside from a few more books and his
collection of video games scattered across the shelves of his tv
stand there was nothing. Sliding off the bed I proceed to look
underneath snooping for anything that holds more information.
Underneath aside from the occasional bunched-up blanket, and
cassock were random dolls and figurines. Many of them dressed up
and neatly tucked away as if they were collector's items. I huff and
sit up trying to think of anywhere he would hide something
personal. In a last-ditch attempt, I shoved my hand between the
mattress and bed frame hoping that there was something just

tucked away much like I would tuck away my own diary. Alas there was nothing except for a pink bullet vibe and a baggy of silicon strokers. I carefully tuck his toys back in place and crawl back up on the bed pulling the blankets over my head. Maybe Judas could tell me something when he returns, until then I need to take a nap.

#

Judas slinks back into his room around midnight and walks over to me curled up in his bed. I had the letter in my hands and blankets covering my entire body except for my toes. He gingerly takes the letter out and walks away with it, as he does so I shoot my head out from the covers.

"What is going on? Why did you have to go see them? Why is Alessandro not in charge anymore?"

"Shhh stellina, please too many questions I promise everything will be explained. We are just currently in the process of planning, that is all I know. Alessandro was removed from stage during his last performance and the main church has decided he is far too pompous... no aloof to be leading the 'mission' any further." He whispered, guilt written across his face.

"What does that mean for you then?"

119

"I guess we will see, but I am not Papa. At least I won't be for quite some time until everything else is dealt with…"

"Does Alessandro know?"

"I don't think he fully does yet, though from my understanding they weren't going to tell him until April so that I had time to have songs ready and Ghouls at my ready." Pursing his lips, he opened to speak again but no sound followed as his eyes drifted off to the side.

"But what about his fans…? Didn't he draw in quite a crowd?" My questions brought on a sigh as he chewed on his lip.

"They are hoping I can do the same, after all, that is the way of Shadows.' They pass it on to the next even if they are not ready to let go."

I shake my head as I try to fully process this. Alessandro does not know; he does not know that he is no longer the all-powerful. And yet Judas knows, now I know. How was that fair that they could depose him without letting him know?

I look back up at Judas who shifted to the other side of the room. He was stripping down for the evening removing the red cassock he was wearing today. Beneath he was wearing a black button up that was tucked into a very tight pair of ripped black jeans. I watched with mild eagerness as he undid every button and slid the shirt off of his shoulders. Against my better judgment, I watched. Biting my lip I scooched closer to the edge of the bed as he begins to undo his jeans. He pulls them down and I couldn't help but laugh softly as his supple ass pops out of the tight cotton that bound them. A new question appeared to distract from before.

"Hey! How come you wear normal clothes under your clerical uniforms?"

"I just like to; they don't tell me no and it allows me to dress how I want. That and I get to go off property grounds quite frequently so normal clothing lets me blend in a bit more."

"You get to leave? Why what do you do all day?" What did he do all day? I caught most of his tasks when I saw him around ministry grounds but there were times he did up and vanish.

"Now now, can't share all my secrets tonight. Though one of these days... if you would like I could take you out with me."

"I would like that very much; it has been a hot minute since I left this place."

He chuckles and walks over towards me, his boxers clinging to every curve of his body leaving very little to the imagination. I blush and look up at him from my position on the bed. As I lay there with my head and arms hanging off, he climbs up next to me and swings a leg over as he sits on my legs. I let out an 'oof' and try to push myself up to look back at him but he quickly pins me by my shoulders. He was trying to distract me from the other thousands of questions I had in my mind.

His warm rough hands were firm on my shoulders as he begins to massage my body. I let out a groan and melt in his touch as he worked my body softly. It was quiet for a moment as we sit there, and then he starts to hum a familiar tune. Though soon after words start to follow closely behind as he slides his hands down my sides, squeezing my rib cage ever so slightly. He had the voice for ballads, one that was rich and sorrowful.

I can feel myself starting to fall asleep again as his siren song lulls me into a safe space. It wasn't too much longer before I fully passed out hoping that today's choices do not come back to haunt me in my dreams.

A Warning and Change

"You know… It is interesting watching you humans running around. Your drama, your morals, the choices you have to make just to keep someone happy. It seems tiring, I don't envy a single one of you."

"Who's speaking? Who's there?" I sit up in darkness, the space around me pitch black and seemingly endless. The ground beneath me was hard and hot to the touch, yet it did not burn me.

"I mean you could take an educated guess considering you live in one of my few temples but, then again you were one of Gods before coming here so I understand you aren't used to someone answering your prayers." The voice rumbled around me, echoing in the space as its phonics enveloped me.

123

"But... I don't pray; I barely even participate in the occasional sermon when someone is giving one."

"You don't have to say anything for me to come to you, ugh, that is beside the point. Look I am here now, I offer comfort and knowledge if you so seek it."

"Where are you? How do I know this isn't some stupid joke or someone trying to trick me..."

"Oh you humans..." The black abyss transforms as fire takes over the empty space as far as the eye can see. The ground beneath me shimmered as it reflected the fire's blaze. The walls of flame form a room, and from the other end stood a man. He was tall and lanky with a large set of blackened wings spread on either side of his body. As the fire completes the room behind him, he makes his way towards me, his figure becoming clearer to me. He walked with a large staff wrapped in the skeleton of a snake; his figure was fully naked. His body was lean and muscular with skin that shifted between all the colors of humanity like a kaleidoscope or ever-changing tie-dye. Raven's black hair hung down past his shoulders and swayed with each step. He was beautiful, more beautiful than any one person on earth that I had seen and yet he seemingly represented the sin within all of us. Towering above me he looks down and raises a warm clawed hand to my cheek, the small almond-shaped nails sharp yet gentle as they graze my skin.

124

My eyes rise to meet his gaze to be met with two stark white irises in a sea of black much like that of the Belladonna family.

"I promise, I am more real and more attentive than God is in his little throne. Now my sweet child why did your heart call out to me hm?"

"I-I don't know...Today has been a shit day if I am to be honest your eminence..." My heart thrummed against my ribs as I stared up at the fallen angel.

"Tut tut, you don't have to use titles with me, I am here for you."

"I'm sorry... I just, for the sake of the two I love I had to choose one in order to protect them both. And yet I cannot shake the feeling as if I have picked wrong... I wish I didn't have to pick."

"Why would you have to pick? Alessandro and Judas are fine men, though they are a bit older than you are and have been *very* exclusive to each other. Their paths I have set in stone, I know near everything that will happen to them and I promise by staying with them both you won't get either of them sent away." Those words felt like lies as they came from his lips, but my unease lifted like cold being warmed from my bones.

"But Lucille-"

"She cannot do anything until the end of April of this year; go to your loves it will not affect their fates. Take this bit of knowledge with you though. Three great men will fall when the fourth rises, Death will come scythe in hand and no one can stop the reaper."

"Someone's going to die...?" Who? Should I ask who?

"Everyone dies eventually my sweet, but you have time to enjoy before things get turned upside down. So go, and do not be alarmed when you awake, I have left with you a gift one that only a few have received and shared through time. Should you ever need me, I am always here for you just ask for me. Now go, someone is worried about you." His hand drifted to my shoulder, rubbing down my arm before the world around me had vanished.

With that, I snap upright where I was the night before, except this time both Judas and Alessandro were sat on either side of me. Their heads were both bowed as they sat with their hands resting on either side of their bodies. Each was murmuring as if pleading for someone when my sudden movement knocked them out of it. Judas was the first to lunge for me, throwing his arms around me with a muffled sob escaping his throat. Alessandro's head shoots up and he sits back a little more as he stares at me with disbelief, his eyes were red and he looked as if he had been crying as well. He quickly looks away and wipes his eyes before turning to me and smiling, though the smile was broken and empty. Judas's grip tightened on me for a moment as he pulled me towards his lap, rocking me in his arms.

"Oh thank Satanas you are back… you were out for so long… you were so warm and not responding to anyone. I-I swear you were gone from us."

"I'm glad she is back Cardinal but…I think it is best I go; we will meet later si?" He distanced himself from us, shoulders dropped as an aura of sorrow wore on his usually proud form.

"Alessandro, wait please," I called out as he stood to leave.

"You do not want me anymore… I understand the cardinal told me this morning."

"Alessandro please, you don't understand I had to… I was threatened and it felt like my only option. Y-You are Papa you have all the power in the church and all the women you could want, I didn't want to risk you two being split apart."

"Who, who threatened you! I will see that they get thrown to the Ghouls in a heartbeat." Alessandro said, anger crossing his face as he turned around to stare us down.

"I cannot tell you. But… I was told by someone more important that it does not matter. We must keep it quiet though please, I am afraid of what might happen if they were wrong."

127

"Our dark father is not ever wrong."

Huh?

"How-"

He taps near his white eye and nods to me. I touch my face and turn around to Judas who looks at my face, shock spreading across it as he looks back and forth between Alessandro and I. I look about for a mirror before slipping from the bed and out the door. I throw myself into Judas's bathroom and face the mirror, there replacing my right eye was a stark white iris and shadowy sclera that matched that of the Belladonna family and Lucifer himself. I stared at myself in disbelief, my fingers tracing my eye socket as I gazed at the one white eye. After a few moments, Alessandro slinks into the bathroom and joins me at the counter a hesitant hand coming to rest on my back.

"You know the last one to have it bestowed on them was Cassian, and that was as a gift from the one below for coming back to the church, that and picking his prima del madre."

"But what about yours, and Judas's, or your brothers?"

"They were all born with the eye, as were many of the chosen Belladonna before us. Cassian was only given it later in life because he ran from the church as a young boy."

BETWEEN THE POWERS

So you can be born with it or given it… is that how Lucifer chooses the heir?

"So… what does it mean…? What does it do?"

"It means you are a special woman and that we must talk to Caesar. Also… *you* might want this back." In his hand sat a long thin gold chain holding a jewel-covered Satanic Cross at the bottom. "I found it the other day after I went back to the staircase earlier to look for my missing clip on. I don't think Arthur would be too happy if you lost his ruby."

Why didn't the Abbess pick it up…? Or did she leave it intentionally to know if we went back…

Quickly I clutch at my throat expecting to grab the same chain from underneath the ribbon that sat on my neck. It must have fallen and I had not noticed as I was distracted by the two of them. I look up at Alessandro sheepishly and hold out my hands to take the necklace back. He smiles and shakes his head sliding behind me and putting the chain over my head. The necklace slips down my neck and the Satanic cross nestles itself between my breast disappearing beneath the ribbon that held Judas's keys.

#

Quickly Judas and I made our way to the Papal wing to see Caesar, Alessandro had left a few minutes before us to speak with him before we had arrived. As we climbed the staircase the creak of a door swinging open caused me to freeze for a moment and hide my face. A sister made her way down the stairs scoffing as she passed by. As soon as she was down the stairs, I scuttled up the stairs the rest of the way only to run into Arthur. He was standing at the top of the staircase adjusting his jacket, as I ran into him, he let out a disgruntled 'watch it' before realizing who did the bumping.

"Ah, Gale! Fantastic to see you are doing well! I see you are finally enjoying the necklace and oh! I know who you are coming to see." He taps at his white eye and smiles brightly at me catching me off guard as I again touch my face. "I will let you two go I need to get down to the greenhouse before the rest of the daylight is gone."

Arthur shuffles out of the way and down the stairs. The old man had always been more observant than the others whether that was a good thing or not was beyond me. I made my way over to Caesar's door and knocked on the sturdy hardwood, Judas positioned himself just behind me keeping his head down. The door swings open and in front me was a well-dressed older gentleman with a scowl on his face. His black suit jacket was paired with a white dress shirt and a stark white tie that was tucked into a black vest that had glossy pentacle buttons down its length. Tucked into the suit pocket was a pair of black wire-framed sunglasses that he patted down into his pocket as he stepped aside to let us in. The air around me felt tense as if I was not wanted in the space.

I looked around the room at the matte emerald walls that were covered in abstract paintings of women's bodies. Sat over his fireplace was a large silver Satanic Cross with small fleur de lis along its outline and just below that on the mantle was his papal ferula held on a display mount. His bed was almost the same as Alessandro's, large with an ornate headboard and smaller bed posts at the feet. Each corner was adorned with a thick iron loop, one of which had a leather cord hanging down from it. The room was neat; everything had a place and everything was in its place. A service cart littered with expensive bottles and crystal glasses was against the wall near a set of bookshelves littered with older books that bore no names on the spine. Caesar made his way over to the set of lounge chairs and chaise that sat together by the fireplace. We follow behind him as he sits down on the black upholstered chaise, quickly I take a seat and Judas stays behind me as if he were a sentinel.

"So, I see you have met with Lucifer. How lucky, Alessandro texted me you had questions?" The voice that came from the man seemed full of boredom.

"W-Well he told me that I had to come speak to you about um… it."

He lets out a lengthy sigh bringing his black gloved hand to his forehead. "Do you understand who gave you the mark?"

"Well yes but-"

"Are you confused about it?"

"N-no but-"

"Great! Then I have nothing to share, Alessandro likes to direct everything magical my way and it wastes my time. Please leave, I have planned an evening with some very eager young ladies who will be showing up any moment. And Cardinal, make sure that mother of yours moves her up to the Clergy wing, after all, she has met our deity, which is more than I can say for most of you." Giving a wave of his hand, there was a shift of energy as we were compelled out of his chambers.

Asshole...

I stood up and looked at him with mild disbelief, though I did not know what to expect I did not anticipate the arrogance that radiated from his being. I make my way to the door taking another glance around the room before zipping out the door. On instinct, I make my way towards Alessandro's door stopping myself and scurrying down the stairs, Judas and I heading back towards his room. As we drew near his chambers, Lucille appeared in the hallway like a haunting spirit, floating near with her cloud of floral death. She practically was running towards us, and as she drew near her scowl dropped into a look of incredulity and she stopped dead a few feet away.

"Hello, Mother! Fantastic news here, she got to meet the devil himself! Well, she almost died first but she is safe, she made it to hell and back." Judas called out, a pleased grin on his face as he practically skipped to the woman.

"I-I, ahem, I see that. So erm Gale, what did you go to hell for." She said, her scowl wilting as she inspected my face.

"I didn't exactly choose to; I needed an answer and I guess I got it."

"Well, that certainly is something, isn't it? Not many of the sisters get to speak with…the dark lord." She grits her teeth as she feigns a smile, I can't help but let a smile paint itself on my lips seeing her uncomfortable in that moment. She had nothing, I out played her hand.

"Oh! Mother, Caesar mentioned something about moving her up to the Clergy wing now that she has the mark. Is it possible she joins me since we are-" he grabs my shoulder softly and pulls me closer to him in a half hug, "-seeing each other."

"Is that what you want?"

"S-sure I suppose, though if it is all the same to you, I would like to keep my room too in the sister wing in case I need my own... space." I didn't want to always be joined to him, sometimes it was like sleeping next to a furnace.

She lets out a sigh and clasps her hands together making herself look small. "I will have a sibling run some clothes to his room for you then." We stand there awkwardly for a moment before Judas steps off to the side. "I will go make some room then for you Gale, I will be right back!" With that he scuttles off to his room leaving Lucille and I out in the hallway together. As his door clicks shut, she takes a few large steps and gets in my face, her shrinking demeanor exploding into a seething rage in front of me.

"WHAT did Lucifer tell you hm? That you can go about interrupting my plans? That it doesn't matter what you do? If you get in my way no one can protect you. Not even my little Judas, I have been waiting for decades to get this far and you will not get in my way."

"What is your problem with me? I didn't ask for this! I have no control over anything going on here can't you see that!" A hand shoots up from her side as she catches me by the throat and squeezes tightly.

"Don't you talk back to me you harlot; he will be the one to achieve something far greater than Cassian and his bastard sons.

He will-" Judas's door opens and she very quickly retreats a few steps back letting go of my throat. "-Love to have you with him, he seems to have taken quite the liking to you young lady! You are so lucky, well I must be off, things to do places to be."

I leer at the older woman who now stood with her hands folded in front of her, a disingenuous smile across her face but her eyes still filled with seething hate. She turns around and gives a small wave to Judas and shuffles off quickly making sure to bump into me on her way past. I turned and watched as she scuttled off, her black Mary janes clicking on the tile as she left. Why was it only after I had shown interest in Judas that she painted a target on my back? Was there something I was interfering with? Was she afraid I would leak some secret? It's not like I knew much to begin with, Alessandro had to know already he wasn't going back out anymore. I shake my head and make my way to Judas who was poking out of his door with a grin painted across his face.

"Now, you can stay here with no excuse."

"Not like I told anyone where I was going anyway…it is pretty obvious that you have clergy members hanging off of you when you show up with black and white paint everywhere ever so often."

"Normally I am better at keeping everyone who 'visits' clean but the paint smudges very easily some days." His hand shot out to grab my wrist, pulling me inside so that he could shut the door and seclude us.

Taking the chance, I lean in and stand up on my toes to reach for a kiss, but Judas pulls back and leans to the side leaving a soft peck on my cheek.

"Why do you keep doing that?"

"Hm? Doing what?"

"Come on, you have avoided every attempt at a real kiss I have tried to make. You have been doing it for months."

"Oh, that. Well, um, is it to awkward for me to say that I have only purposefully kissed one person and are too nervous sometimes to kiss someone else?" He winced slightly, watching my reaction as I went through a few iterations of shock and confusion.

"What? You can't be serious."

"I don't think the Ghouls fully count but si, only one kiss. Don't get me wrong I want to but... I-I...um well I made a promise to Mother that I wouldn't kiss anyone else after she caught Alessandro and I together in the crypts in the France temple."

I would think the ghouls count? They are people too... Why did everyone only ever see them as creatures?

"Do you really think that applies to me though? Didn't you say yourself we were together…?"

"I did say that didn't I." He smiles sheepishly and laughs rubbing the back of his neck as a rosy blush spreads across his face. "Does that mean you want to kiss me?"

For a man of his age and stature, he sure got fidgety when it came to romance.

I rolled my eyes and took a page out of Alessandro's book, sneaking my hand to Judas's throat though my hesitant movements made Judas laugh more. He in turn grabs my hand from his throat and adjusts it to a better position just below his jaw. He wraps an arm around me and walks us backward to a wall where he helps me apply more pressure. I blush as he shows me how he wants to be grabbed after and after the pressure is how he liked it he slid down the wall so that we were face to face I took the initiative and drew closer. Our lips mere inches from each other, our breath dancing together, I hesitated hovering so close I could feel the heat.

"Of course I want to… I have been wanting to." I murmur, watching his zeal swell.

He panted softly, anticipating the kiss and I could not bring myself to do more than tease in this exact instance. I veered off my path and left a soft kiss on his cheek and giggled as I let go of his throat, taking a few steps away and turning my back. He whimpers at me and slides all the way down the wall letting out a defeated huff.

"It is cruel of you to tease me, that is my job be_la…" He hissed under his breath.

I feel my self-blushing and look back over my shoulder to see him push himself from the floor and charging my direction. He wraps his arms around me tightly and holds me to his chest snaking his hand up my chest. His warm leather glove wrapped around my throat and tilted my head back against his chest. It was his turn to tease but instead of leaving sweet nothings across my cheek or a peck on my forehead he finally leans in, our lips meeting in gentle bliss. My eyes flutter shut as I beg for another kiss, he obliges me our sweet nothing turning into something much more dangerous. His grip on me tightens and I gasp softly for air, a light fuzziness finds its way into my skull though it was not unwelcome. I leaned forward into his grip, his other arm wrapping itself around my waist. I stumble forward slightly; Judas walks us toward his bed letting go of my throat and bending me over the edge.

"May I?" His hands tug softly at my robes and I nod slightly feeling him pull them down to my hips leaving the top half of my body exposed. He runs his leather gloves down my back sliding his hands to the side grabbing hold of my hips and pulling me back against him. I could feel his member was hard beneath his cassock as it dug into my ass. I looked at him as leaned down leaving kisses down my spine, his black lip paint leaving a small trail as he did so. I whimpered softly as I let myself trust his wandering hands. Behind me, I can hear him shed his cassock and undo a row of buttons. He returns against me, pressing his body against mine as he slides his arms under my chest his hands now without the added layer massaging my breast ever so softly. Judas was warm and soft, much gentler with me as it was now the two of us. I bite my lip and wiggle my ass against him to see what he would do.

Letting out a low growl, he squeezed me close to his body his warm breath on my shoulders. His hands slip from my chest and down to my hips pulling my robes off further, the smooth fabric pooling at my feet. Carefully he helps pull me up keeping me close to his body, his hand wrapped around my throat with a thumb on my chin pushing my head to the side. Judas nibbled on my exposed shoulder, taking his time as he kissed his way to the nape of my neck. As he shaped me to his body, I let my arms hang at my side, panting breathlessly as he continued to hold my throat. His scent enveloped me, wrapping me in an intoxicating musk. His hair fell from its perfectly bushed position to tickle at my skin, and with every touch he seemed to grow hungrier for me.

He drops his hands and let go of me for a moment long enough for me to turn around before he pushes me into the bed. I let out a yelp as I fall back onto the pile of blankets, Judas following suit, his arms on either side of my head as he presses himself against my body. As carefully as he could he shifted to one side and used his free hand to pull off the restricting jeans he wore and pushed off his underwear. Our bodies were fully nude as we lay together, I could feel his cock as he slid up against my body, the girthy member pressing into my hip as he came in for another kiss. His lips were as sweet as fresh-picked cherries as he kissed me with more tenderness and want than I had ever felt before. He straddled my leg for a moment grinding his cock against me, a soft breathy gasp escaping his lips in between kisses.

Fuck...

I smile and break away from his lips kissing along his cheek and down his neck. I make my way to his collar bones where I sink my teeth softly into his skin. He lets out a whimpering moan as he takes this opportunity to slide between my legs, reaching down he pulls one of my legs up so he can get a better angle. Instinctually I bring my other leg up as well, he smiles and sits up helping me to better adjust before coming back. I could feel his hand on my thigh as he slid it towards my cunt. Rubbing the slit, he smiles as he dips a finger in, I could feel how slick I was and I look back up at him as a deep blush finds its self across my face.

He teases my clit ever so softly, pausing to rub in a circular motion just barely moving the hood. I close my eyes and bite my lip trying to keep relatively quiet, but Judas simply chuckled quietly and used his other hand to tease my mouth open. He hooks his thumb on my bottom jaw to keep my mouth open and takes time to pay special attention to my clit. His light feathery movements would send tingles up my spine, and as he finally moved the hood, he applied just a little more pressure. With each touch something deep inside me was pulled tighter and tighter, my breath was caught in my throat as I tried hard not to moan.

"Mmm sorella, please don't hold back for me. I want to hear how I make you feel." His voice was rich as he whispered in my ear. "Please bella, I am a man who always gets what he wants..." With that, he slips a finger inside using the side of his thumb to continue playing with my clit.

As I felt him curl his finger inside me, I couldn't help but let out a shaky pant and a weak moan slips out from my agape mouth. With each curl, each stroke I could feel myself being pulled closer and closer to an edge that I had not fully experienced before. The sensations grew and I could feel myself begging to close my legs, to grind against him and push myself over. As I drew in one shaky breath after another Judas moved his hand leaving me aching for more. I gasped and looked up at him, my eyes pleading for him to continue. He smiles at me and gives a soft wink as he fully positions himself between my legs. His strong hands pull my ankles to his shoulders and he comes in closer. I can feel his cock as it brushes against my skin, heat spreading across my skin as I know what comes next.

His free hand firmly grasps his cock as he rubs the tip against my awaiting slit, taking a deep breath in he pushes into me. I groan softly as I feel his girthy member slide into me, my hole stretching just enough to accommodate his cock. Judas's breath was shaky as he exhaled, his body was tensed for a brief moment before he finally carefully thrusts into me. His powerful hips drove into me over and over again, each stroke eliciting sweet moans from his lips. I swallow hard trying to fight moans, his solo of pleasure driving me wild. As he gains a rhythm, he carefully parts my legs letting them fall on either side of his hips so that he may continue to play with my clit. I bite my lip as I whimper at his touch, he seemed skilled in finding all the right ways to pleasure a woman. His hand rested softly on my lower stomach, using his thumb he finds my throbbing clit again rubbing in slow circles. He was going to take his time enjoying my body. I close my eyes and sink back into the bed as much as I possibly could the string in my core being wound tight once more.

My breath was shaky, with every inhale I could feel myself being pulled closer, electricity running through my body. In my mind, I was no longer being fucked by Judas in that moment but instead, I was sinking into a deep pool of pleasure. I could feel the tips of my fingers and toes tingling ever so slightly as a warmth radiated from my cunt. A deep-seated aching throbbing inside me, the feeling so intense that my voice rang out in soft saccharine moans. The thread was being pulled tighter and tighter, the strands coming apart slowly when suddenly it snapped. A powerful wave washed through me, my hands fumbling for the sheets or a blanket to grab as a futile way to hold myself down. It felt like fireworks and ocean waves crashing into the rocky shore, my cunt throbbed tightening itself around Judas's cock.

"Aah-aa…" his voice was hushed, the air catching in his chest as he felt me finish on him. The sudden intensity caused him to fall forward, his hands falling on either side of my head as he gripped the sheets beneath me. Through hazy vision I watched as his mouth fell open; he was panting slightly as he kept going. His movements had started to become more static like he was pushing through to the finish line. In a more tender move, he sinks to his elbows, his lips coming to graze my skin as he kissed and sucked.

"F-fuck…nnn…" his noises hung in the air, each one barely above a whisper. "aa… haa… o-oh Satanas."

He tries to sit himself upright just a bit more, placing his hands on my hips the tips of his fingers digging in as he finally takes one last powerful thrust into me. I watched as the air caught in his chest, his face contorted ever so slightly and his hands dug further into my hips. I gasp as he pulls me hard against him, his cock pulsed as he came inside. He falls forward again his breath ragged as he lay atop me. His arms slid under me as he held us together for a few moments, squeezing tightly as we lay there. For a second a strike of fear ran through me as I remembered the lack of a condom, but it subsided as the thought of being bred by him sent a flutter across my chest. I never wanted children, but maybe... Softly I reach up and brush his hair aside, a smile resting on my face as I gazed at him. A smirk curled at the edges of his lips as he slowly began to regain control of his breathing.

"Oh, Gale...you feel... divine." He slowly pushes himself off me and rolls to the side, his cum oozing from my slit.

"H-how come you are so good at his hm?" I ask with a soft laugh in my voice as I look over at him again.

"I cannot share such a secret with you amore," he sits up and startles as he looks over at the door. "Cazzo! Alessandro, how long have you been there!" Quickly I snap my head to the door and see Alessandro leaning against the hard wood with a knowing smile on his face. His pants were obviously tented and as he stood up straight, he carefully readjusted it before making his way over to us. I sat up and very quickly moved back up against the wall crossing my legs to make room for him to sit. Judas leaned back on his palms as his member very slowly deflated, a sheepish smile on his face seeing the older man come near.

144

"Well, long enough to see you both finish. I see we are sinning without me hm?" he playfully teases coming to sit down, he goes to sit before grabbing a pillow and placing it where he sat down.

"What brings you over here sir?" I ask, a touch worried that he had news for us.

"I was making my rounds and saw a few boxes sitting outside Judas's door. I was going to bring them in but decide just to watch instead." I feel my cheeks growing red and I quickly look away slightly embarrassed we didn't notice him sooner. "It is alright though, it looked fun. Maybe I will get a turn later hm?"

"Am I even allowed up in your room anymore? With Lucille on a rampage I-" I very quickly throw my hands over my mouth as I let slip who had been making my life difficult. Alessandro raises an eyebrow and looks over at Judas, his face going almost as pale as Alessandro's white paint.

Shit.

"Mia Madre...?"

Hello Darkness

"What do you mean by rampage…?" He asked hesitantly.

"You know how I said a sister threatened me…?"

I watched as Judas sat there processing; his face seemed to be one of mild disbelief as he heard me incriminate his beloved mother. Alessandro on the other hand did not look too shocked or surprised. Instead, he crossed his arms over his chest, his white vest puffing out a little as he eyed Judas for a moment.

"She likes interfering with our relationship choices, doesn't she?" his voice was cool, a silent loathing bubbling beneath.

"But she had made a promise to stay out of it after the incident with the Aether and Omega Ghouls."

146

"Since when did she ever stay out of it?! This is, this is absolute bullshit and you know it." Alessandro stands up throwing his hands in the air. "You are 44 years old and still trust every word she feeds you!"

"You don't have to yell alright? I just thought..." Judas takes a deep sigh. "Che cazzo, I don't know what I thought."

"Exactly she got in the way 29 years ago, and she got in the way 25 years ago and she is getting in the way again." I look between the two of them concerned. It wasn't my intention to cause a problem between the two of them, the air in the room felt electric and on edge. My hand wanders down to the Satanic Cross that sat between my breast and I wrap my hand around it nervously.

"I am... I am going to go take a shower really quick." I murmur crawling off the bed. I wrap a blanket around my body and make my way out the door, gently kicking the boxes inside and pulling out a long crimson gown that laid at the top of the pile. Quickly I shut the door behind me as the two of them continue a heated 'conversation' and slip into the bathroom. Setting the gown down on the counter, I look at myself in the mirror. There was black paint smudged lightly across my face neck and chest and little hickies littered my skin. I slid off the Key ribbon and set it atop of the dress before dropping the blanket that was wrapped

around me. I took hold of the Satanic Cross the sharp edges
digging into my hand slightly as I stared at myself in the mirror.

"What did I just cause... why couldn't I just shut up..." I
speak to myself feeling slightly dejected. "I didn't mean to cause a
fight I just... fuck I need some help, don't I?" I gaze into the
mirror staring into my own eyes with a slight frown on my lips.
"Yea... I need help." As the words leave my mouth an eerie black
smoke appears suspended in the air, from the smoke steps a tall
lanky ghoul with a mask I did not quite recognize. It was old,
much older than any of the ghouls here had. It was a rounded mask
that was eerily human but also looked as if it was ripped off a doll.
The silver of the mask was well polished with a small crack
running along the front of it. The ghoul towered above me,
opening its eyes to reveal deep red irises that seem to flicker like a
flame.

"Mona... I am here." His voice was rough and gravelly as
he looked down at me. The anger and calm composure in his eyes
quickly gave way to confusion as he stared down at me. "You are
not her, why do you hold her charm?" the words were cold and
empty, accusatory almost as if I had stolen it. Quickly I scrabble
backwards clutching the pendent wanting to scream but the air
hung frozen in my chest. The black smoke continues to billow
behind this Ghoul, his spear-tipped tail flicking back and forth with
anger. He towered over me and took a step in my direction.

"I-I… it was given as a gift I swear I promise please don't" I drop the pendant as I raise my hands to protect myself fearing that he was going to take a chance to slash at me.

"Gift…?" his voice practically rumbled in his chest his demeanor shifting just slightly from rage to confusion.

"Arthur, the um… the Papa Belladonna the first, he gave it to me. I swear, I swear on my life."

"He had no right… where is Mona…" he growls at me; I could see his fangs flash in the light just a little as he takes a step forward.

"She's… she's dead… she died a few years ago." The ghoul stops dead in his tracks, his tail ceases its flicking and the black smoke dissipates going away completely. He stood there as if someone had paused him. After a moment or so he shifts his gaze to me again the mask that covered his face crumbled and fell to the floor and I got to gaze at his bare face. I had never seen the bare face of a Ghoul before, they always being ordered to wear masks as per Cassian's demand, though I am not sure what I expected. His face was human like though his skin was a light bluish-grey like pencil lead. His hair was neatly wrapped around a small set of horns that curled from the top of his head. The ghoul just stood there, silently for a moment more before opening his mouth to speak revealing a long set of sharpened fangs.

"So, it was true she was dying the last time she called me to her… she sent me away before I could come back." The rage I had previously felt radiating from him melted away into disappointment and dejection. "She's gone…" his tail flicked back and forth again and he wore a frown on his face before taking a deep breath and straightening up before bowing at me.

"You now hold the pendent how may I serve you madam?" his voice was annoyed yet full of morose, he stayed bowed waiting for my words, possibly a command.

"I-I don't know. I um, you are dismissed." I say hesitantly. The ghoul stands up and looks at me again before disappearing into another cloud of black smoke. I stand there absolutely baffled at what has just transpired, quickly I unclasp the necklace and place it on the pile with everything else. Turning back around I grab a towel from the little shelf and hang it on the shower door. It takes me a minute but I finally get the shower going and step inside, the hot water washing over my body. I take my time getting cleaned up hoping that it was enough time for them to settle down. Once done I shut off the water and step out drying off. The bathroom was a bit steamy as I got dressed. The red gown I had pulled from the box was not one that I had recognized before but when I pulled it on it fit perfectly. The soft red cotton clung to my body like a glove along the legs two slits ran almost up to my hips. The chest had a small circular cut-out that displayed my cleavage nicely. The back of the dress was open and dipped down to just above the small of my back. They must want me to start dressing nicer since I have the mark now, I think to myself.

Carefully I put the key ribbon and the Satanic Cross necklace back on, afraid to clutch its pendent as much as I wanted to. I slip from the bathroom and head for Judas's door, but as I near, I can hear them still arguing. Out of sake for peace of mind, I shut the bathroom door and turned to head down the hallway. I make my way down the stone halls and out a small side door that let out into Arthur's garden. The sun was just beginning to set behind the forest at the edge of the ministry grounds so I took a moment to walk around the plots where all his flowers would be planted for this spring and summer. The rose bushes were wrapped in tarps to prevent them from freezing over during the chilling evening. Snow was lightly scattered across the ground covering the pavers, it crunched under my feet as I took a moment to walk about.

Curiosity pulled at my heart and I looked around to make sure no one was around as I ducked into the small white chapel, they used for summoning new ghouls. The space had collected a little dust since its last use but it still was comforting in its own way. To give me some light I looked around for a box of matches and lit up a few of the less melted pillar candles. Their light provides a dim glow to the room, just enough that I can see but hopefully not enough someone can see me from outside. Hesitantly I grasp the pendent again and close my eyes as I face the center of the room.

"I-I need help" my voice shaking just a bit as the words leave my lips. Again, just as before there was a black cloud of smoke that just appeared from the air, and out from it stepped the ghoul, though this time he did not have his mask on. Instead, his hair was down, no longer wrapped along his horns. He was wearing what looked to be a black suit, with alchemy sigils down the side of it. He looked at me with mild concern his tail flicking back and forth as he scanned the room for threats. After a minute he settled and stared at me.

"Why did you call me here..." his voice was gravelly and sharp, displeased with being summoned again.

"I-I wanted to talk to you that's all... do you um... do you have a name?"

"Mona had called me Phantom... I suppose that is my name unless you prefer something else."

"Phantom... that is fitting. Did you... did you really work for Mona...?"

"Yesss…." He hisses out looking a bit pissed off and annoyed at me.

"What was she like?" his eyes soften at my question. He sighed softly and sits down on the ground with his clawed hands in his lap.

"She was kind…and she loved to garden." His voice was less harsh as he spoke of her. "Mona enjoyed having me around while Arthur was busy with work…she may have enjoyed my company too much though." His voice catches a little and he has to pause before continuing. "I should have been with her in her final moments…." I cock my head and look at him my heart heavy for his story. His gaze stayed pointed to the floor as he took a deep breath.

"You said she sent you away, what do you mean?" I pushed, hoping the question didn't step on any toes.

"She had gone into labor two weeks early, and while in the infirmary she called for me to join her for a moment. She had confessed to me that it was twins, one Arthur's and one… mine." His barbed tail flicks wildly back and forth. "The midwives who were assisting in her delivery were under strict instructions to not inform Arthur unless it was his being born first. So that he could be there for his daughter's birth obviously. But my child was the first to be born, he had caused some major bleeding on his way out, so that by the time she was ready for the second one, she was already weak. My offspring was stillborn, not developed enough to survive... but there was hope for the little girl. I was sent to collect Arthur so that he could witness his daughter's birth, but by the time we had returned her heart had gone into distress and both Mona and the little girl were passing. Nothing could be done, as we entered the room, she was fading...I-I left to try and find some better help but before I could she sent me away..."

Hands clenching, I could see the grief choking him as it stopped the air from leaving his lungs.

"We both lost her that day..."

My head shoots up and I see Arthur standing in the doorway of the chapel. The day's dusk barely illuminated his form. Phantom on the other hand was less okay seeing the older gentleman standing there. Arthur's hands were folded as he walked towards us the candle's dim light illuminating the tears that had rolled down his cheeks.

"I knew she had twins... I had known from the beginning that you weren't just her body guard." His voice was a bit strained as he came close enough for the light to illuminate him properly. "Do not blame yourself for being sent away Phantom...it was my fault for being such a prideful young fool. I couldn't accept she had loved us both." Phantom had risen fully and stepped behind me defensively his tail flicking through the air a bit.

"Why did you give me away?" he hissed out.

"She had reminded me of Mona when she was younger, I figured I had gotten my time for closure and to try and move on but you didn't." He smiled weakly at me trying to fight more tears, I couldn't help but come to his side and offer him a hug. "I see you found one of her dresses. I sent some over after I had seen you this morning, it fits you perfectly. A dress made for a Prima del madre."

"Prima del madre...?" I say incredulously.

"You got the mark; you are courting two of the Belladonna men and you can successfully summon a ghoul. You are Prima material though I am unsure which one of my fratellos you belong to. Caesar knows it too, but he won't say anything unless he is completely sure. The union of a prima to her chosen sire is a very rigorous ceremony. Mona never got to do the full ceremony; she was never given the blessing just as Lucille wasn't."

"You must be mistaken, I mean. I am just some girl that ran away to this church to flee from dangerous men...I didn't ask to be wrapped up in all of this this isn't my choosing."

155

"We don't get to pick our paths in life sorella. Only accept it as it comes to us."

I stand there, tears still pooling in my eyes from learning what truly happened to Arthur's wife. They spill over my cheeks and I crumple to the floor, my knees hitting the old wood hard. Phantom crouches uneasily as he attempts to rub my back and Arthur takes a few steps back.

"It isn't a bad thing sister. I um... I can tell you need to process my apologies for intruding." He walks back away to the open doors standing with his back turned patiently waiting for us. His silhouette against the dusk sky was small, not that of a powerful satanic ex-pope but just a man. I stayed on the ground as tears rolled down my face, not sure of how to process everything shared with me. I was prepared to hear Phantom's story, that was it but to learn they suspected me of being a Prima. That was not something I was prepared for. The Ghoul stayed crouched next to me softly rubbing my back in an attempt to console me, his tail stopped flying back and forth coming to curl around my knees. He did not have to be kind to me at this moment, but the ghoul had made the choice that I was better off with him there.

#

Arthur had left the summoning chapel after a little while of waiting. The sun had set, the sky was dark and the candles in the chapel barely provided any light to me. I carefully blew out the candles, their smoke dancing off into the air, and made my way out of the chapel. Phantom guided me back into the ministry, his hands were hot as he pulled me along by my wrist. Once inside he bows his head to me flicking his tail impatiently.

"You are dismissed." My voice wavered a little as I felt like he needed to stay a bit longer, but as I spoke, he stood up and disappeared again. It felt odd summoning and dismissing a creature like that. Like I had more power than anyone should have. Alone again, fully alone I lean back against the cold stone wall and sink to the ground. Prima del madre? Seriously? I never wanted to be anything more than a sister. To take care of my jobs and have time to myself where I didn't have to fear someone using me.

Now I am entangled with currently the two most powerful men in the Satanic ministry. Ever since Papa came home things have been getting strange, before I never had much interaction with the clergy. Sure, Lucille was there to make sure we all were doing our jobs and attending the sermons. Arthur was frequently working with sisters out in the garden, and Caesar had sisters going in and out of his room quite frequently. None of them though interacted with me quite like they have been these last few months. In less than a year my life had been turned on its head and I was scared.

157

BETWEEN THE POWERS

I sat in the corridor quietly thinking about the changes that kept happening. Each time I had been a little more settled or content with the change something else would happen. Was I being prepared for something? I run my fingers through my hair and sigh looking up at the sconces that lined the walls. What if I was being prepared for something? The devil clearly has a plan set in stone, so what is my path? I fumbled through my thoughts a while longer until someone calling out my name gained my attention.

"Gale? Where the hell are you?"

I turned my head to see Alessandro appear at the end of the hallway; he looked around almost frantically until he saw me sitting against the wall by the garden door. He froze staring at me, like he had seen a ghost before shaking his head and lightly jogging over to me. His dress shoes created an echo as his feet fell on the stone tiles.

"Where did you go? Where did...?" the words trail off for a moment as he looked me over. "Why did you disappear?"

"You two were arguing and I needed a moment to myself," I say as I carefully rise from the floor dusting off the red gown I was in. Alessandro seemed to be looking through me as I stood before him. "What?"

"Nothing, it's nothing. Come on it is late yeah?" He reaches for my hand and I pull back a little.

"You look like you have seen a ghost what is wrong?"

He looks up into my eyes and feigns a smile, "Nothing please stellina, let us go, yes?"

Reluctantly I let him grab my hand, though as he grabbed my hand he seemed to be trembling ever so slightly. Something was bothering him but I wasn't sure if I was going to get it out of him easily. He seemed to drag me with him, his pace was fast as we walked, almost ran back to Judas's room. Alessandro opened the door and Judas looked towards us with a small scowl that faded as he saw me in the doorway. My eyes immediately dart around the room as something had felt off, on the floor was the letter addressed to Judas that spoke of Alessandro's dethroning. That's it, that's what was bothering him. He finally found out why he was brought back early from his tour. It wasn't just to have him there for the rituals, they were replacing him. I look to Judas my eyebrows furrowed.

"Yea, he knows now…" His voice seemed a bit bitter as he turned his gaze to the floor again. "All three of us are caught up now."

"You knew? Since when?!" Alessandro hissed as he looked down at me.

"I had seen the letter the other day while I was poking through his stuff… and then he explained it to me." Alessandro

159

scowled at us both and promptly left the room. I felt like running after him would have been a mistake and so I sat in the door way watching as he walked off down the corridor.

"He's going to need some time; I just hope moth-... Lucille doesn't come and yell at me." He reaches a hand out to me, "Come, sit with me."

I sigh a little as I take one more glance down the corridor, Alessandro was already gone. I stepped inside and shut the door looking down at the boxes that sat just aside the door frame that held all the old dresses that Arthur sent for me. My heart felt heavy as I realize fully why I was given the items. They belonged to the last prima del madre, first of mothers, and by some way of Lucifer, they fit me. It was as if through small gestures Arthur was testing me, gauging if I really was what he thought I was. My eyes flit back up to Judas whose gaze was back to the floor, his graying blonde hair falling softly as he sat there.

"He is pissed at me... it is not like I wanted to take over. I was content being just the little head Cardinal." He sighed and ran his hands through his hair. "We knew this was always a possibility, especially after they had reprimanded Caesar and made him step down."

I take a few steps towards him and sit down on the edge of his bed, "I hope he will be okay..."

"Oh he will be… he has always been resilient his whole life. I have never seen anything truly get in his way." He chuckled lightly as he sat up and brushed his hair back, "he could be stuck in the bottom of the ocean and still find a way to get out of it."

"Well, let's hope this doesn't get in his way…"

Every Heart breaks Sometimes

It had been a few weeks since Alessandro had been around us, we saw him of course in passing and at the ever-so-rare sermon he would give. He didn't stop to speak with us and our attempts of speaking with him were ignored. Judas had attempted to send messages through ghouls or by slipping notes under his door, but he never spoke back to us. I was starting to give up hope on getting him to come back to us. I couldn't blame him though; his lifelong lover and the woman he was interested in knew that he was no longer in power. We had known something major and life-changing, and we didn't share it with him. I would be fairly upset as well if people I loved were hiding things from me. But I would also want to try and work it out, or at least attempt to in the interest of us. Judas seemed to be unbothered by how long Alessandro stayed away from us.

"How come... how come you aren't more frantically trying to speak with him about this?" I ask softly as I sit down with him in the main lunch hall. It was a quiet Sunday afternoon and many of the sisters and ghouls were still in bed. Many trying to sleep off the hangovers they still had from Saturday.

"He does this when he gets upset, it is a process with him my dear." Judas's voice was calm and quiet yet his eyes betrayed him. He looked nervous or at the very least upset as well.

"So what? He does this every time he gets into an argument?"

"No, only when he feels betrayed by those he cares for. He won't even let moth-... Lucille speak with him. Only the occasional sister and his ghouls." I groan slightly and roll my eyes.

"I understand what it feels like to be betrayed by ones you love, but... you are supposed to talk to them about it."

"He will come around I promise, if you feel like you must though you know where he is going to be." Judas leans over and places an arm around my shoulder. "I will not stop you if you feel like you have to go speak to him, but he might not speak to you."

Sister Salacious
BETWEEN THE POWERS

I sit there silently as I think about what he has said. I
didn't want to push Alessandro's boundaries but at the same time,
there was a feeling in my heart that my time with him would be cut
short. Judas and I sit and eat our lunch together, the occasional
sister or ghoul appearing to grab a bite before going back to
wherever they came from. I wanted to say more, to protest and
drag Judas with me but he had already settled in to wait for him.
As he finishes and leaves to go do the rest of his tasks for the day, I
stay sitting there in the lunch hall.

The lunch hall was large and empty, the rows and rows of
empty tables and chairs making it seem abandoned. Even the
window to the kitchen seemed abandoned as those in charge of
cooking were further in the back. It felt lonely in here as I went
over my thoughts, truly lonely. Judas was settled on waiting for
Alessandro, and I don't know what Alessandro has been doing. But
the warning that the devil gave felt like a warning. I was going to
lose one of them in April and I wasn't sure who. My thoughts
continued to race, one of them was going to die and I didn't know
who. My hand slides up my chest and I grasp the Satanic Cross
tightly. Its sharp edges bring a comforting pain to my hand as I
continue to overthink. My own mind was so focused on the dark
thoughts that it conjured up that I almost didn't notice the hand that
was hot to the touch on my shoulder.

BETWEEN THE POWERS

Phantom had appeared behind me, his hand on my shoulder as he looked down at me. My gaze shot up to meet his he had a small frown on his face; his burning gaze filled with worry.

"I'm sorry... I didn't mean to summon you... you can go if you need."

"No, you need someone...I know that you are scared of what Lucifer has planned for your future."

"How did you- "

"I can hear your thoughts and words when you take ahold of that pendant, and I mean, every thought and word." He crouched next to me his hand coming to rest on my thigh instead. "I promise, whatever your future holds you will still have one of your lovers."

I shake my head a little and scoff, "I don't want just the one though, I want both..." I never fully thought about it before. When I could freely go between their rooms it felt like a little game, like there was no real reason I was doing it aside from it made me feel good. But now after Lucille threatened me, the dark father warning me and Alessandro not being around out of anger I feel, empty. Like a part of me is no longer there. Judas made me happy; he fulfilled my every desire but he was also a very busy and devoted man. Having both one so devoted and one so, aloof had made the days more interesting. It felt as if I needed both, my soul felt incomplete even though when I had arrived, I didn't want or need either of them. I sat there with Phantom lost in thought, was it lust that had brought me to them? Could it have been their contrasting behaviors in how they showed me affection? Was I only enjoying their...

"Um, please don't think about that please, or at least let go of the pendent if you must" Phantom spoke sheepishly.

"Oh, I am so sorry," I blush as I quickly let go of the pendant and look away for a moment. "I don't know what I should do, I mean... I think I love them but...'

"Do you trust yourself enough to say you love both of them? Or do they thrill you?"

"They excite me sure but, I can't help but feel like I need them..."

"Do you think you can talk to Alessandro and tell him that?"

"Judas, says to leave him alone..."

"He also said that if you feel like you must then go, his relationship dynamic is not the same as yours. So come on." Phantom stands up and offers me a hand. "Let's go talk to him."

#

BETWEEN THE POWERS

    I stand in front of Alessandro's door, my hand shaking just a little as I hesitate to knock. What if he was pissed at me for not bringing up what I found? I looked over at Phantom who was still looking around making sure no one else saw him, he briefly looked down at me though. There was a softness to his eyes, that is before he smiled at me and knocked heavily on the door. He smirks at me and slips away just far enough that Alessandro won't see him when he opens the door. I look back towards the door my heart pounding in my chest as I waited for Alessandro to answer. The silence was deafening as I waited, there was nothing though. Not a clink of a bottle or a groan of discontent.

    It was silent behind the door. I knock again, practically banging on the door. Nothing. My gaze shoots to Phantom who was watching with mild concern. As I looked up at him though his concern shifted to worry and he shoves open the door. It wasn't locked, Alessandro seldom locked it, but he still wanted people to knock out courtesy. I slip past Phantom my eyes scanning the room for any sign of him, his bed was a mess with an open bottle lying on its side among the blankets. The kitchenette lights were off and there was a trail of blankets and clothes leading between the bathroom and his bed. Quickly I walked towards the bathroom, the door was open and the light was on but there was no sound, no singing or running water. I braced for the worse as I walked in the doorway.

Alessandro was passed out in his bathtub, his arms over the side and his head resting against the wall of the tub. I step closer unsure if I should panic further or not, my heart hammering away in my chest. As I grew closer to him and my shadow crossed his face his eyes shot open and he startled backward, well as backward as one could startle in a bathtub full of lukewarm bath water. He sucks in the air quickly, his eyes wide as he stares at me his hands gripping the sides of the tub.

"Vaffenculo, what the fuck are you doing here?!"

"I wanted to talk to you…"

"And we don't knock suddenly?"

"You don't need to be bristly Alessandro, and I did knock. Quite a few times actually." I cross my arms a little as my anxiety starts to shift towards annoyance. He sits up more in his tub and takes a deep breath before pulling the plug and standing up. The water ran down his body making him seemingly glimmer in the bathroom light for a moment. He looked down at me his eyebrows raised and a small scowl on his face.

"Okay, well I am obviously awake now, what do you want."

"You are still being bristly…"

"And I am going to be, you scared the shit of me while I was enjoying a soak and a nap. So come on, what are you here for?" The bitterness was still thick in his voice that usually wore the warmth of a summer day, but it felt deserved.

"I wanted to talk, about well... your dethroning I guess."

"How much did you know? Like did you actually know?"

"I only knew what I read in the letter; I had read it the previous night though I suppose Judas has known for a while."

"I will talk to him when I am ready to talk to him," he crossed his arms over his chest as he still stood there in the tub his body starting to dry in the open air.

"I know, he told me all about the thing you two do when pissed at each other. But I am not here for him, I am here for me. I miss you, and I think this is a little unfair to be pissed at me for just barely knowing before you."

"No one was going to tell me though officially huh? Not until he had his shit together to just move in to replace me."

"You can't honestly believe that that is what he ever wanted." I started in, defending the cardinal who wasn't even here to cover his own ass.

"That is not the problem, it is that no one can tell me when this shit is out. I would have loved to have known why I was

169

fully dragged off stage. Why did no one tell my ghouls, they had to chase after me. I mean fuck I don't know, I am a favorite am I not? So why wait months to tell me that I am no longer of value to the ministry."

"You are... at least to us you are."

"I was going to lead this ministry into the future, to finally get us to the top, to the peak and now I am stuck here like a dog in a cage because that bitch thought I was to shit at my job. I would love to see her try to do what I did. What any of us did! It isn't easy writing music and performing in front of thousands, I had them wrapped around my finger and now she wants to just hand it off?" he throws his hands in the air as his voice raises a little in pitch. "I gave them my everything and she gets to decide my future? She shouldn't be making decisions about my life. Any of our lives! And for Judas to not tell me makes it that much worse, he knew. He fucking knew I wasn't going to be able to go say goodbye... that I wouldn't get to wish the fans well and to introduce them to the next in line... the others have..." he deflated slightly his arms coming to cross his chest again before he steps out of the tub and grabs a towel. "I won't get to tell them why I got removed from stage... why they won't see their beloved Alessandro anymore..."

He wraps the towel around his hips and walks past me, practically through me as he heads back to his room. I followed close behind trying to think of how I could possibly comfort him. Alessandro walks over and sits on the edge of his bed his arms resting on his knees as he sits there.

"I don't get to tell them goodbye…"

"Is that what this is over…? Not being able to send your fans off to the next one like your brothers had?" Cocking my head, I hoped his body language would give away the answer. "Not being able to end it on your terms?"

"It is more than that, I loved performing and having the adoring crowd screaming for me. It felt like I was needed… wanted by so many and then suddenly it was taken away."

"I'm sorry… did you talk to Cassian about this?"

"He is under her thumb; the choices have already been made even if I did want to protest this and get the decision reversed I can't without potentially fucking with Judas's future." I walk closer to him coming to rest my hand against his back softly. "I…I don't know anymore."

"I know I am only one little fan in the ocean but I still need you… do you think that could be enough…?" He looks up at me, tears obviously in his eyes that have yet to spill over. He swallows hard and wraps his arms around me as he buries his face in my stomach. His body shakes ever so slightly as his tears wet my robe. I carefully put my hands on his head and neck and hold him against me as he cries.

He had enjoyed the thrill of being on stage and loved by many, it makes sense to be upset if no one told you that you were officially done. I held him tightly as he squeezed me, I was afraid to let go that if I were to let go, he would stop. I let my fingers softly run through his hair, the black strands soft to the touch. There was the occasional grey hair in the mix as though time was slowly catching up to him. He didn't act like he was an old man; he was still lively and full of spark. And yet as I stand here holding him, he didn't feel like a spry young man he felt, defeated, older, and lost. My heart ached for the pain he had felt, he didn't deserve to have his spirit and passion crushed like this. Yet there was nothing more I could do at this moment aside from holding him here and letting his walls crumble.

I looked over along the wall at Phantom who lingered in the shadows unsure of how he still hadn't been noticed. He had a slight grimace on his face and had his tail wrapped around his legs loosely. I gestured at him that he could go but instead he sat down on the floor next to the wall. Alessandro must have felt me moving as he pulled back softly and wiped his eyes, his gaze rising to meet mine. I couldn't help but pout slightly as I looked at him, he was hurting and I felt useless in my abilities to help him. Softly I pulled his head against me again so that I could continue to hold him there with me. He wrapped an arm around my hips and pulled me against him again his eyes closed as we sat there together, just existing for as long as he needed. Alessandro pulls in a long shaky breath and finally sits up keeping his arm around my hip. He opens his eyes and looks dead ahead, his face creasing into a frown as he sees Phantom sitting there.

"Ghoul, where is your mask and why are you in here, I didn't ask for you." Phantom doesn't answer he just stares back flicking the tip of his tail ever so slightly. "Hey, can you even hear me? Get back to the ghoul wing and go get your damned mask, I didn't have them all made so you can go about without it."

"His mask broke…" I murmured, looking back over my shoulder before returning my attention to Papa.

"WHAT, Jesus Christ ghoul what the hell have you been doing to…." Alessandro looks up at me and I smile with a goofy toothy grin. "What do you mean it broke? Like you were there?"

"Well, it isn't exactly like he had a new mask; it was ancient practically."

"Excuse me? These were brought in just last year how could it have broken already?" He stands up and starts to make his way towards the ghoul a little. "What is your name? I don't think I recognize you." Alessandro squints at him, but Phantom continues to sit there flicking his tail as if he was waiting for someone else to introduce him. "Come on, I don't need insolence if you are going to invade my space what is your name?"

I sigh and shake my head as I look at Phantom, "His name is Phantom, and he really doesn't have a mask. Come on get over here." I beckoned Phantom over; he rolled his eyes and pushed himself off the floor walking over to stand next to me placing a hand on my shoulder as he did. Alessandro watched the ghoul with mild disbelief until he saw the hand go to my shoulder. His face drops as he looks between me and the ghoul, his eyes darting between the little golden Satanic Cross on my chest and the maskless ghoul who gripped my shoulder.

"No... there's... you are kidding right," I shook my head a little as I grabbed the pendant and dismissed Phantom. "Are you going to continue keeping secrets!?"

"I only found this out the other day when you and Judas were arguing. I never knew Arthur had given me a ghoul with the necklace."

"He didn't, he gave you a test... and somehow you passed without even knowing why. Do you know what this means!"

"That there is a possibility that I am the next prima? Yeah... Arthur also told me about that."

"Well, we need to share the news! I mean it is great, isn't it?"

"Alessandro, I don't want to do that just yet. I feel like I need more time with you before we decide that I am what you think I am. Your life just got turned upside down and Judas is trying so hard to live up to the expectations being placed on him. This would only add more drama, wouldn't it?"

"Yes but- "

"No but's please…" I walked closer to him and grabbed his hands. "Please, I want things to settle before we go and make more of a fuss huh?"

"I… fine. I will respect your wishes my dearest but this is amazing news! Does… does Judas know?"

"No not yet, I wasn't sure how to bring it up to him. He has been busy with trying to write songs that Lucille will approve of and I really don't need to interrupt that. Lucille already hates me enough; I don't need to get in the way of this too."

"Oh my dear…" He let go of my hands and wrapped his arms around my shoulders pulling me close to his body, his skin was cool to the touch as he pulled me in. "I thank you for sharing with me first then. This has made my day a little bit better…"

175

Alessandro softly rested his chin on top of my head and held me there with him for another moment.

"Hey, what do you say we head out? Just you and me to go celebrate huh?"

"Won't someone want to know where we are?"

"They won't notice that I am gone for now, come I need to get out of the ministry for a little." He lets go of me and seemingly flies to his closet poking around for an outfit that is inconspicuous but still fits his personality. He pulls out a few black items not letting me see them as he then slips back into the bathroom to get dressed. I roll my eyes a little and go sit on his plush bed while he gets dressed.

Thirty minutes had passed and Alessandro finally opened the bathroom door and stepped out with a smile on his face. He was wearing a pair of black suit pants with a partially unbuttoned black pearl snap with a black vest that had red embroidery work to pull it together. His hair was fluffed and combed inwards giving him a faux hawk. Around his neck was a small silver necklace with a pentagram dangling off the bottom of it and a thin black leather collar. He looked good, there was no doubt about that but where were we going to go where he didn't stand out.

"How do I look huh?"

176

"Like you are emo…" I laugh softly and shake my head. "And perhaps like you are trying too hard to be 'hip'."

"Hey now, that is not fair. I haven't had many reasons to dress up however I wanted to the last few years." He looks happy as he sticks his hands in his pockets and poses a few times at me before walking over to me. Alessandro grabs my hand and pulls me up onto my feet. "You aren't embarrassed by me, right?" he said teasingly as he leaned in to steal a kiss. His lips were soft as they met mine for a brief moment before he pulled back and bit his lip.

"No… though this is never a look I would have imagined on you."

"Good, means that I can still surprise you." He steals one more kiss before going to his nightstand and pulling out a car key with a small Satanic Cross key chain. Alessandro slips it into his pocket and beckons me to come with him as he goes to the door. I stand up and follow behind him.

"Wait, I'm not dressed for this."

"Baby girl you are wearing a skin-tight black dress with a high collar. You look stunning, let's go I promise you will fit in."

Alessandro practically dragged me through the halls of the ministry and down a set of stairs that I had never noticed before. As we flew down the stairs, I recognized that we were in a

177

parking garage and I looked at him mildly confused. He shot me a 'just you wait' look and pulled me towards the front of the garage. Alessandro beelined to a sleek black 60's model Impala with a small silver Satanic Cross hood ornament. The car looked like it was in pristine condition, its chrome accents were well-polished and the white walls looked unused. He unlocks the car and quickly heads to the passenger side to open it up. I walk around admiring the car for a moment before ducking into its crimson-red interior. The seats were a soft well-maintained leather that felt smooth to the touch. Alessandro shut the door and skipped across to the other side jumping in, as he jammed the key into the ignition and turned it over the powerful V8 roared to life. Its purr echoed through the garage as he put it in drive and slowly took us out of the hidden garage and out into the night.

Let Down and Let Go

Alessandro took us out on the open road, the dark moonless sky shrouding us in a cloud of black that was only lifted as far as the headlights could reach. The purr of the engine was soon drowned out as he slipped a personal CD into the radio and turned it up. As a familiar song echoes through the car I look towards Alessandro. He looked like he was having the time of his life, his lips dancing as he sang along to the melody. I couldn't help the sinking feeling that enveloped my heart as I knew his time could be coming to an end soon. The irony of the song tugged at my heartstrings as we flew down the highway towards the shining lights of the city. I watched with silent agony as I knew so many things, I was afraid to share with him, and yet he was happy blissfully unaware of the next twist in his story. The music continued to ring through the car as more classic hits were belted out, but my mind was too busy mulling over itself to truly listen to them. My eyes shifted back to the open road as we flew past other cars as if they were standing still.

We eventually made it into the city, heading towards the downtown, a cheeky smile plastered on his face as we pulled up outside of what looked to be an old and mostly abandoned factory building. I look over mildly perplexed at why we would be here. The street was lined with cars and from the building I could hear a heavy bass groaning through the walls. Nonetheless, Alessandro was excited as he practically jumped out of the car and came to open my door. I take a deep breath and swing my legs out of the car, carefully standing up as my skin is licked by a brisk breeze that comes blowing through. Alessandro grabbed my hand pulling me towards him as he shuts the door and locks the car. I look up at the old decaying red brick building, the windows still intact but years of use and weather damage made the building decrepit. My eyes flickered about the area taking in the lack of people outside, the dimly lit street, and the two men who stood at the end of an alleyway.

The two burly men had yet to look in our direction but as Alessandro pulled me towards them their scowls had shifted into wide, mischievous grins. The two of them step back and to the side, their hulking shoulder bowing as Alessandro walks near.

"Tonight's going to be a riot, good to see you, Mr. Belladonna."

Alessandro winked at me as he pulled me to a door that was lit only with a single ominous bulb. "You trust me, right?"

"Well yeah... but what is this place?"

"Oh, you will see..."

He stands up straightening his shoulders and opens the door bowing his head for me to enter. The door opens and from it radiates the familiar haunting sounds of dark 80's goth music, it was practically screaming at us to shut the door again. He gestures for me to enter so I step around the door walking into a scene fresh out of an old cult film. The room was lit with an eerie red glow, a thick mist covering the floor that billowed and rolled as people moved through it. The walls were draped with cobwebs and tattered, torn tapestries, across the ceiling were exposed industrial beams with lights and speakers bolted on securely. In the center of this, goth club, was a large circular bar that also encompassed the DJ. An older-looking gentleman sat at the controls, his hair was spiked and teased in different directions, the dark strands catching the red glow of the room giving the effect it was on fire. Everyone looked like they were dressed in some ensemble of punk or goth, and as a few of them turned to greet the newcomers their faces lit up as they watched Alessandro enter behind me.

Groups of people hollered at him, thrilled to see he had returned and even a few came up to greet him with various handshakes, high fives, and even a hug. The music was blaring around us, its aggregate melodies pulling at my body to dance but I

instead kept in behind Alessandro as he made his way to the bar.
We weave through the crowd; the blitz of musky colognes and dark
floral perfumes swept my mind into a small frenzy. I was
overwhelmed by the smells and sounds but it felt like a scene from
a movie, like I was the outsider being brought into the flashing
lights of a club I had no reason to be in.

Alessandro lead us to the bar, pulling me along until we
finally got up against it. He could sense my apprehension and
leaned in wrapping his arms around me. "It's just for a little, I want
to celebrate with my little Prima del madre."

I take a deep breath and wrap my arms around his
willowy form, "alright fine, I guess I could use a drink."

"That's the spirit!" He leaves a kiss on my supple cheek
before pulling away to order a drink. I watch as the bartender sulks
around the counter, her eyeliner looked as if she had been crying
but it looked almost intentional. She looked me up and down
before turning to Alessandro with a sickly-sweet smile, leaning
against the counter she opened her mouth to speak.

"What can I get for you sugar?"

"Hey Brenda, I see they made you cry-laugh again, was it
a regular or a newbie this time?" Alessandro smiles at the woman
as she leans against the counter. She was practically pushing her
breasts out to him as she folded her arms under her chest. I watch
as Alessandro's eyes flicker down to her exposed cleavage before

he glances back up at her face with a sly smile. "You know I will take one of your cranberry Cosmo's though can you do a heavy pour? I am out celebrating tonight."

"Oh yeah?" She leans back resting her hands on her hips, "And what pray tell are you celebrating hm?"

"Well let's just say there is a very special woman in my life now...." I reaches over and grabs my hand as I watch the two of them interact. I could feel the loathing that radiated off the bartender, her gaze flickered over to me with mild disdain in her deep hazel pools.

"Well, hey! That's great, I will bring you two a bottle of our house red." I watched as she strutted away from us, her eyes shooting daggers one last time over her shoulders before leaving. I looked over to Alessandro whose eyes seemed to be glued to her hips as she disappeared around to the other side of the bar. His mismatched gaze returns to me as he sidesteps, our hips meeting with a bump. A warm hand finds its way around my hips as he pulls me close looking out across the sea of alternative people dancing and having a great time.

"I am so glad you told me first... it means the world to me."

"Well... Arthur still knew before you." Alessandro looks down at me and frowns for a moment before shaking his head.

"Doesn't matter, I knew before Judas and that makes me feel a bit special."

I roll my eyes as I slip my arm around his waistline, the two of us standing there together reveling in our moment. That is until I heard someone clear their throat behind us. I turn around and the bartender hands me the bottle and glasses with a scowl. One that instantly softened as Alessandro turned back around and picked up his cocktail. His head was on a swivel as he locked for an open path, grabbing my wrist and pulling me along to a little corner booth that had been open. He squeezed us through the undulating crowds of people, dragging me through like a fish on a line. The crowds were thick, people chatting and dancing with each other not noticing the two of us as we snake around their bodies. The lights were dancing to the music and the fog was kicked up into an eerie mist. Alessandro broke through the wall of people pulling me through with him, but something touched me. I let out a small yelp as I startle forward into Alessandro, someone or something has grabbed my ass. My heart races out of my chest as I fear that the assailant will continue, the unwanted touch making my mind race back to those days at the church. A wine glass fell from my hand shattering on the ground in front of me, the sound was enough to startle Alessandro.

I look up at Alessandro who turns around to look at me, his eyebrows furrowed slightly as he looks down at the broken glass. He took a step back prepared to help pick up the shards before something caught his eye. Behind me was a guy who looked wholly out of place amongst the sea of black, he looked more like someone plus one that they dragged off a college campus. The man had a smirk on his face as he eyed me up more before meeting Alessandro's mismatched gaze. Alessandro looks back down into my face seeing the disturbance and fear in my eyes as I wanted to flee in this moment. My body was trembling ever so slightly as I looked for a way away from everyone. Alessandro places a hand on my shoulder and pulls me around behind him so that he could stand face-to-face with the perve.

The offender stood over Alessandro with a good 4-6 inches on him, he was fit and in better shape than my lean, willowy lover. That didn't stop Alessandro though. He quickly downed the cocktail he had, setting down the glass and taking in a deep breath when in a burst of rage that I had never seen before Alessandro pulled back and swung on the taller man catching him square in the jaw, knocking him sideways. A gasp rippled through the crowd of people that were directly around us. Alessandro rubbed his hand, flexing his fingers while leering at the man who had groped me. The man stumbles sideways a little, a look of anger sweeping across his face for a moment as he stares down Alessandro.

"Do not, fucking touch a woman like that. Especially not mine." He hissed through his teeth before turning back to me, his body was tensed as if he was waiting for the man to retaliate but it

185

never came. Alessandro placed a hand on my lower back and ushered me to the corner booth we were heading towards. I set down the bottle and remaining glass that I had in my hands, trying hard to not knock it over as my hands were still trembling. I turned again to face Alessandro my eyes flickering to the crowd ever so often as I watched for anything else to happen.

Alessandro kept his eyes on me; he looked as if he wanted to pull me in to comfort me but hesitated. I wrap my arms around his torso and bury my face in his chest as my body continues to tremble. His chest trembled a little with each breath he pulled in, and in that moment the rest of the world went silent as I listened to his breathing and his heart that pounded in his chest. Alessandro wrapped an arm around me, turning his head to watch the groper with his little group of buddies.

"Fucking pussy!"

I could feel as Alessandro wanted to pull away again to go after the man but I kept my arms tightly around him.

"Says the man who would rather grab at someone instead of being proper. Get the fuck out of here."

"You want to say that to my face old man?" the man sneered, though I could even hear his friends trying to pull him away from the situation.

"Unlike you, I have a very beautiful woman who needs me in this moment." Alessandro looks down at me as I stay clung to his body running a hand through my hair before looking back at the asshole. "But if you are feeling froggy then jump, it has been a good while since I fought." Alessandro was tensed, his body pulling away from mine as he was ready to take on the younger shithead.

"Fuck you old man..." The man struggled to come up with anything else to say as his buddies started to drag him away from us.

Alessandro shook his head as he wrapped his arms around me again holding me for a moment as he spoke to a few concerned bystanders. The music of the club continued to buzz on in the background, the world kept spinning even if in my head my world was coming apart at that instant. The safety of Alessandro around me though kept me grounded, I didn't want to let him go. Sucking in a deep breath, his cologne swirled around me like a cloud of leather, old whiskey barrels, and orchids, it was a comforting scent, to say the least. After what felt like an eternity I pulled back and looked around my surroundings, I wasn't in a church, I wasn't going to be taken against my will. I was safe, or at least as safe as one could be in a club with one of her lovers.

"I am sorry princess; I didn't know that that stronzo was going to grab you like that." He leans down and leaves a kiss on my forehead as he helps me sit down in the booth. "Forgive me diavolina, I wanted this to be a fun little thing for us since it has been a stressful few weeks."

"It's… it isn't your fault people are just gross."

"I know but, you don't deserve to be treated like that by anyone. No one does but especially not you." He reaches across the table and grabs my hands.

"Thank you…"

"Of course, I try to not make a habit of violence first but I..." He takes a deep breath and looks back over at the crowd of people dancing. "In that moment I could only feel anger, you looked so afraid…"

"I know, I… let's not talk about this, come on we have some wine and a little space to ourselves."

Alessandro shakes his head for a moment before putting on a smile for me. He grabs the wine bottle on the table and pours wine into the glass. The deep crimson liquid splashed into the bowl of the glass. I stare at the wine for a moment and look back over to the shattered glass on the floor, watching as someone comes to sweep it up. The shards seem to sparkle as they were swept away with the dust, leaving the floor empty as if the incident didn't even happen. My eyes scan the sea of people looking for the man who had touched me, though in that moment I could not see him. I turned my head back to Alessandro, his eyes searched mine trying to find what I was thinking.

"Maybe we should have a drink and head back to the Ministry eh? I don't think bringing you to a club was maybe the best idea on my part."

"I'm sorry, I wanted to enjoy tonight…"

"No, it is not your fault my dear, here you want to try first?" he slides the wine glass across the table to me. I stare down at the crimson liquid before carefully picking up the glass by the stem. The wine had a strong herbal aroma, though right behind the scent of aged herbs came what smelled like smokey oak. I crinkled my nose hoping that the flavor was not as strong as the smell was. Bringing to glass to my lips I let the wine splash across my tongue, it was pungent and harsh. I swallow it quickly not letting it linger much longer in my mouth; I set the glass down and shake my head a little.

"I can't it's not one I can drink," I say softly as I push the glass back to him. He nods his head slightly and picks up the glass taking a sip, he seems to be unbothered by the harsh flavor.

"Do you need me to go get you another drink then my dear?"

"No… I think I will just hold off for now."

BETWEEN THE POWERS

Alessandro takes another sip of the wine; his eyes still search mine as he thinks of something else to say. We sit together listening to the various sounds of dark vapor waves and goth metal as it swirls about the club. The mist lingered on the floor as it grew thick again. As my mind continued to spiral, I let my eyes wander. This club felt like a scene out of a new-age horror movie, eerie and full of attractive people though it felt as if danger was around every corner.

After a while longer Alessandro finished the bottle by himself, his face was a little flushed and he had a smile on that grew every time his eyes returned to me. I knew he was far too drunk to drive us home, and I didn't feel safe enough to drive his car myself but there was no other option. I slip from the booth and help get him up, a waitress wanders over and allows me to pay the small bill before we slipped from the club. He leaned against me, not heavily as he could still walk fine himself but enough that I could feel his weight on my shoulders. We step out of the door back out into the alleyway, the cool air sending a chill down my spine as I lead him back to his car. Our footsteps fell heavily on the messy concrete, Alessandro giggling like a little schoolgirl as he leaned against me. I rolled my eyes and sighed as I slipped my hand into his pants pocket to pull out his keys, my hand brushing against something else for a moment as I did so.

"Mm… Come on Gale we can play back at the ministry..."

"Oh hush, I just needed your keys. I am not going to let you drive like this."

"Mm… smart woman, I like that about you…"

We rounded the corner my eyes focused on the very tipsy Alessandro in my arms when I heard a scoff. I turned my head to see the same asshole from earlier leaning back against the broken façade of the club, his arms crossed over his chest as he wore an angry sneer. Alessandro raised his head and eyed the man; his white and blue eyes filled with disdain. I shook my head and pulled at Alessandro, my hand gripping the waistband of his pants to pull him easier in the direction of his car.

"Aw, did the old man get too drunk? Now he has to have his babysitter drive him home?"

I closed my eyes and pulled on Alessandro whose whole body seemed to tense at those words. "He isn't worth it Alessandro… come on let's get home," I murmur as I pull his willowy body towards his glossy black car.

"Come on old man, rematch. Step away from the bitch and fight me." The man stood up off the wall and pulled off his jacket in a move to try and intimidate us. I felt my hair bristle on

191

the back of my neck as Alessandro pulled away from me, his movements a little unsure as he swayed ever so slightly.

"Excuse you?" Alessandro said, his voice suddenly cold and empty as his body grew rigid. "One does not… call a woman a bitch unless she asks you to." He took a step forward and I knew what was coming next. I wasn't going to let Alessandro get his shit rocked though for trying to defend me. A tinge of panic washed over me as I grabbed for Alessandro again not knowing how to prevent this or stop him. But as I reached, I felt my Satanic Cross shift from its place between my breasts. I had a way to stop this; I slipped my hand down the neckline of my gown and pulled out the Satanic Cross clutching it tightly as I looked up at the two ready to square off. He said he could hear my thoughts, right?

Well hear me now, get out here damn it, I think hoping that that was enough to pull him out. Behind me a black cloud appeared and Phantom stepped forward, I could hear his low rumbling growl as he placed a hand on my shoulder.

"Stop them please…" I whisper in a hurry nodding my head as the asshole tensed his body to strike. Phantom's furious gaze flickered towards the two men, his lean muscular form quickly stepping between them. Alessandro stepped back in shock, looking back at me with a 'you can't do this' look in his eyes. The other man gasped seemingly in fear at the sudden ghoul in front of him, it wasn't common for the ghouls to be seen outside of the ministry unless on tour with Papa. Though most people assumed that they were just a bunch of people in masks dancing around on stage. Phantom's hand darted out and grabbed the man by the collar of his shirt, his tail flicking wildly behind him as he pulled the man in close. The stranger put his hands up in a pacifying move as if to say he had meant no harm. Phantom was not going to be gentle with him though. He forcefully pushed the man backward letting go of his collar as he did so causing him to tumble to the floor.

"What the… What the fuck is this …" The man croaked out as Phantom towered over him.

"This is what happens when you mess with a woman of the satanic ministry." I hissed through my teeth. My own rage and anger surprised me as I scolded the man. Phantom took another step to him, his shoe stamping dangerously close to the man's groin.

"Look I-I am just joking around… there's no, there's no reason to do this." He scrabbled backwards for a moment trying to get away but each movement to flee from Phantom only resulted in the ghoul growing closer.

"Apologize…" Phantom said, a low threatening rumble emanating from his chest as he spoke. "Now…"

"What? No, I didn't fucking do anything man." He scrabbled backward more as Phantom's hand darted down to grab him again. "Alright alright fuck man I'm sorry, I'm sorry just leave me alone." Phantom straightened up and leered down at the man before turning back to me cocking his head as if he was asking if that was a job well done. I gave him a small nod and he stepped back away from the man coming to stand in front of Alessandro instead. Alessandro frowns as the ghoul takes a seemingly protective stance in front of him from the other man. He climbs to his feet and stares at us, horrified as the ghoul makes another threatening lunge at him making sure that he didn't connect. His feet carry him away as he dashes fast down the street, I couldn't help but feel a little guilty but then again, he was being a prick.

"Bella... you can't summon the ghoul in public like this! I am going to get into so much trouble." Alessandro whined at me, his face a little flushed as Phantom wrapped his arm around his hip.

"Well, I can't have you fighting like an idiot either, especially while drunk."

"Not drunk, just tipsy..."

"Not safe to drive. Look I will get us home, Phantom can you help get him into the car?" I ask softly looking up into the ghoul's eyes. He shrugged and guided Alessandro to the passenger side door, I quickly walked around and unlocked the doors sliding into the driver's seat. Phantom hooks his hand in Alessandro's waistband and carefully shoves him into the car using his grip to guide him down to a sitting position. Alessandro whimpered slightly as the ghoul's hot skin brushed against him, his eyes darting to his waistband and back up to Phantom.

"Little handsy there eh?" Alessandro teased as he arched an eyebrow. Phantom frowned and let go quickly, his eyes darting to me.

"Yes, you can go, thank you… seriously thank you."

He nods to me and takes one more seething glance at Alessandro before disappearing into the smoke. I turn over the engine, a chill running down my spine as I listen to her purr. Alessandro looks over at me, his face a bit red as he wears a devious smile.

"Mm… You know how to take care of me eh? How about I take care of you when we get back…" He purrs at me, his hand coming to rest on my thigh. He slid his hand up my leg squeezing a little as he brushed my inner hip. I inhale sharply and look over at him before brushing his hand away.

"Alessandro, please. Let's get you home first and then maybe."

BETWEEN THE POWERS

"Ah fine… that ghoul of yours seems a bit… handy."

"Ew Alessandro," I say looking over at him my jaw drops a little as I pull out and take us home.

"What? He is a cutie for a fire ghoul, have you not thought about it?"

"No, of course not." I hadn't exactly been thinking about doing anyone aside from the 'tipsy' man in the seat next to me and the cardinal back home who was likely very worried.

"You are missing out; the ghouls each have their specialties. I prefer our Omega ghoul; he can manhandle me any time."

"Oh my god." I laugh in disbelief as we carry on down the road together.

"What can I say? I know I am a whore, eh? I am a pretty boy after all." The two of us laugh for a moment, the stressful tension that had kept arising slowly dissipating. As we flew down the road my eyes drifted back to him ever so slightly, he kept his eyes on me, a goofy smile on his face every time our eyes met. I shook my head a little after the fifth or sixth time our eyes met and turned on the radio to fill the empty hum in the vehicle. The eerie ringing of bells fills the space around us as his classic rock CD begins to play.

#

Once we had returned to the ministry, I made sure to park carefully and summon Phantom to help me drag Alessandro back to his chambers. Alessandro had of course tried to flirt with Phantom but was met with the coldest gaze I have ever seen a fire ghoul give another person. I helped Alessandro strip out of his outfit and hunted down a washcloth to clean up his face. Though he would not hold still for me, he was too preoccupied with the position I was sitting in. I had straddled his lap so I could hold him still, this had him excited and antsy as I removed the makeup from his face. His fingertips dug into my hips as he held me down on him whining that I was more focused on taking care of him first. With him being wine drunk, he became needy, his hands pawing at me as he begged for my attention. I finished wiping off his face, though there were still little bits he would not let me get. I started to stand up from his lap so I could go put the washcloth away when he wrapped his arms around my midsection tightly and would not let me go.

"No, no baby…No, non stai andando da nessuna parte bella. Resta con me."

"Alessandro, I have to go put this away come on. Let go, baby…"

"Heh, you called me baby…" He smirked a little and nuzzled his face between my breasts fighting against the fabric that covered them. "Resta con me, tu dai tanto tempo al cardinale. Che dire di me hm? Tuo papà?"

"Papa, come on now I am just going to go put the washcloth down."

"Si, si… just putting it down but then you will find other reasons to stay from my arms. Please bella…"

"Where do you want the wet washcloth then hm? Just let go I promise I will return."

He wines at me reluctantly and lets go, his lip jutting out a little as he pouts. I slip from his lap and walk to the bathroom to set down the washcloth, stopping to admire myself in the mirror again a little. Having them practically head over heels for me all the time seemed to be doing wonders for my ego. I ran my fingertips across my jawline and smiled at myself, my white and hazel eyes sparkling in the mirror. I lingered there for a while longer, maybe a bit longer than I had intended when I heard someone whimpering again.

"Mia Bella… Please I have been good Papa, no?"

I roll my eyes and laugh softly sauntering over to Alessandro, who at this point had undone every button possible on his body and was waiting for me to come near to help him pull it off. An excited smile crosses his face as he watches me walk back toward him, a playful wiggle of his hips makes me laugh slightly.

"Gale… Do I possibly get my turn alone with you?"

"Mmm, what do you mean?" I ask innocently as I reached out and started to pull his jacket and shirt slowly from his body. My hands were gentle as I tugged the fabric from his shoulders.

"You know what I mean… I saw what you had let the Cardinal do." He pouted at me again, "When do I get a turn bella? I know how to make you feel good."

"Alessandro, keep begging and it might be longer." I scold him playfully. In all honesty, I didn't know. Getting intimate with Judas by ourselves was not something I was anticipating and the Christmas incident seemed like it more focused on Judas being with me again. Part of me wanted Alessandro, I wanted to be able to just drop my dress and let him go but yet I held myself back from it every time it arose. Maybe I feared it, I couldn't tell though. I reached for his waistband to slip him from his pants when his hands grabbed my wrist.

"Want to keep the pants on?"

"No I…" He pouts and lets go. "I guess you can remove them, I just wish it was for other purposes."

199

"Does it really bother you that bad that I let Judas go first?"

"Maybe…Non voglio altro che mostrarti un buon momento. Ma tu resisti, perché?"

"Papa, you know I cannot understand you fully when you go Italian."

"Bah, you need to learn. But why do you resist me, my love?"

"I don't know, it just never has felt like the right time…"

"Do I come off too strong? Am I too much bella?"

I rolled my eyes and shook my head as I carefully slipped his pants from his hips. "No, I just, I really don't know and I haven't convinced myself I should."

"Aye, please baby…"

"When I am ready, I am ready," I say firmly. As I pull his pants the rest of the way off and set them with the rest of his clothes he burrows into his pile of blankets.

"Well, if you do not wish to sleep with me, can you at least stay the night for me? Just this once…"

"Sure, I can, though I don't have any change of clothes with me." His face lights up as I say this. "Who said you needed them; we always sleep naked in Papa's room." He chuckled scrunching up in the blankets more.

"You promise to behave?"

"On my life, hands stay where you put them." His hands move out from under the blankets he was covered in and keep them where I can see them. I smiled content with the gesture and unzipped my dress carefully letting it fall. I had taken to not wearing a bra anymore, and this night was no different. As the fabric fell into a heap on the ground, his face goes bright red. I walked towards him ready to slip in next to him when he whined at me again. "Bella, the underwear, no?"

"You have yours on, it will be fine." He frowns at me and slips his hands beneath the covers for a second. They return a minute later with his black underwear as he chucks them across the room to his laundry basket. "No, I do not."

"You cheeky little shit…" I laugh and take a deep breath slipping my panties from my hips, kicking them aside so that they may be with my dress in a heap. "Better? No getting handsy."

"I promise, but maybe being against Papa will make you change that, no?"

I slip into his large plush bed with him, crawling across the satin sheets and letting myself flop down next to him. In an instant he opened the blankets and wrapped his arms around me, dragging me closer to him. He pulled my back to his chest, curling his body around mine before quickly burying his face in my neck.

"Hey, hey. No funny business."

"I only cuddle Gale; you are so warm though and smell like honey. I will only cuddle…and maybe smell."

"Weirdo…"

"Your weirdo… I am a strange little man I know. But I…" His words stop for a moment as he seems to be picking what he says next with some consideration. "But I love you, and I hope you love me too."

I close my eyes hoping that maybe that was just the wine talking, but I knew that it wasn't. It wasn't a word that was used lightly by him, when he really loved something, he had a hard time saying it. He pulls me in tighter to his body the intimate heat from him warming my heart. He took in a deep breath, his face nuzzled neatly against the back of my neck. The pads of his fingertips dig into my stomach ever so slightly as if he is clinging to me like this would be the last time he will ever see me.

"I love you too Alessandro… you know this…"

"I know… I know, I just feel second fiddle sometimes to Judas."

That hurt just a bit. I mean I had been giving more of my time to Judas, but only because he knew more of my past and well, now I live with him. My heart throbbed as I thought about how he must think I think of him. I did love Alessandro, he was a handsome, charismatic man who made me feel like I could be free and wild. Yet I restrain myself around him every single time.

"I'm sorry…"

"No it is okay; I am just jealous. But I am a big boy I can handle a little jealousy." His voice sounded tired, like someone flipped a switch and he started to power down. He yawned and pressed himself harder to me, I could feel every part of his body against me as he nuzzled closer.

"Thank you for staying the night with me…" He murmured leaving a soft kiss on the back of my neck. "Goodnight stellina…"

"Good night, Papa…"

Alessandro was very quick to fall asleep, though he usually was. His body went limp slowly as he drifted off, the tenseness in how he was holding me faded. Though he would twitch a little in his sleep and latch on to me again as if I was a teddy bear someone was trying to take away. I lay there awake for a while longer, my eyes focused on the window next to his bed. I couldn't stop thinking about why I kept rejecting his every advance and move unless Judas was present. Did I trust Judas more or was it that I was still afraid like I was during the Halloween ritual? Either way, it was unfair to him. It's not like I didn't want to, hell at this very moment with his cock pressed against my ass I wanted him. But something made me hesitate and I could not figure out what. It was like someone was making me wait till the perfect moment. I closed my eyes and let my mind kick the idea around until I eventually fell asleep curled up in Alessandro's arms in his massive bed.

One Step Forward, Two Steps Back

I woke up to a rather pleasant but odd situation while wrapped in Alessandro's arms. I woke to him whimpering softly in his sleep, his body softly grinding against me. His arms were low around my waist, wrapped around so tight that his fingertips dug into my hips. His member was solid as it was rutted against my back ever so slightly, his voice groaning ever so slightly as he did so. I tried to move to see if he was actually awake, but every little wiggle I made to look at him made his grip tighten. I giggled under my breath, my cheeks going red as he seemed to be engrossed in this dream. It was kind a cute to have him rutting against me like this, but I should probably wake him up. Waiting for another moment before gently starting to wriggle to turn around. I got to my back and his motions stopped briefly as his arms pulled on me tight. I gasped as he tightened more, my hands pulling at his arms to get enough space to turn around completely. Resting my hands on either side of his face, I rubbed my thumbs against his cheeks.

"Alessandro… wake up silly come on…" I would whisper before leaning in to leave a kiss on his forehead. "Come on baby… wake up for me." I cooed.

I move my hand to his shoulder and lightly shook him, just enough that he grumbled at me, his eyes slowly blinking open. He opened one eye fully and looked at me though he didn't process the situation consciously until I shook him again. Both eyes fly open and he very quickly lets go of my body, his face going bright red.

"Ah, shit! I am sorry my sweet…"

"Let me guess? Good dream?"

"Very…" He mumbled slightly as he snatched a bunching of the blankets to cover his hardened member. He was blushing and looking away from me like he was caught doing something he shouldn't have been.

"I didn't mind… I thought it was kinda cute." I laughed softly my eyes softening as I looked at his nervous face. "Oh come on Papa… don't want to at least finish that little scenario."

"Bella as much as I would love to, I don't think I can…not with you in the room anyway."

"Oh? Well…" I took a deep breath and bit my lip for a moment. "What if I wanted to join in and help?"

That certainly caught his attention. His head jerked up and a cautious smile drifted across his lips.

"Oh really? In… In what way hm?"

"Well to be honest it was kinda hot having you rutting against me like you were. Using me like a toy without being in me…" He had done the same thing when we were beneath the stairs, but while it was unintentional it felt more intimate.

"Would you… let me continue perhaps?"

I giggle and nodded rolling back to my other side and wiggling my ass at him to tease him. "Come here Papa… come grind against Sister."

Alessandro quickly scooted forward again, throwing his arms around my hips again. He cautious slipped one hand to my chest, hovering for a moment to check my reaction before grabbing and kneading at the fatty tissue. His other hand pulled me closer using my hips to keep me forced back against him how he wanted it. His body was warm against mine, his breath danced on my skin as he rested his head against the back of my neck. I could feel his cock against my ass as he pressed himself hard against my body, a smirk coming to my lips. There was something intimately erotic about being rutted against by your lover as he held you close. His hips rocked against me in a soft rhythmic pattern; his breath was shaky as he used my supple tissue to please him. Alessandro whimpered softly as he buried his face into the back of my neck.

"Aa~ah..." he panted, his hands still controlling my body as he held me back in the position that best served him at that moment. Alessandro's lips met my skin, leaving a soft trail of kisses along the nape of my neck. His hand that was toying with my breasts slipped down my body to wrap around my hip, his other hand slipped to my ass grabbing at the tissue. I whimpered as I felt him squeeze and knead at me, the sensation of his fingertips digging into my skin made me want more. I rolled my hips back against him, eliciting a gasp from Alessandro as his grinding faltered for a moment. He breathed out heavily against my skin before squeezing at my ass again.

"Mnn... keep grabbing on me like that and I might just have to fuck you."

He gasped to feign shock, then while letting out a soft chuckle "maybe I should keep grabbing then, no? Make my dirty girl needy for her Papa..."

"Ah ha... maybe you should then." I hummed as he continued to knead at my ass. His cock still grinding slowly against my rump and his hand cupping my ass seemed to ignite a little flame in my core and I couldn't help but feel like I should be more involved. A needy whimper escapes my lips as I roll my hips back against him again.

"Is someone being a needy girl for me? Does she want more from her Papa?" He murmured as his lips continued to graze my skin. His breath shook in his chest as pushed hard against me, a weak moan slipping from his lips. "Does she need Papa to fuck her?" He growled low in my ear. His words send chills down my spine, my hips twitch against him as if my body was begging for his touch.

"Mnnf~ Please Alessandro... I want you..." I whined softly; the words even surprising me as they fell from my mouth. With little hesitation his hand slips from my ass and down between my thighs. His fingertips dug into my skin as he guided my legs apart, he shifted his position and I could feel his member as it throbbed against my perineum.

"Are you sure princess...?" He hummed quietly as he grasped his member rubbing the tip along my awaiting slit.

"Please..."

"Heh... good girl." He purred as he pushed forward, easily slipping into my wet cunt. Unlike Judas whose girth stretched me out nicely, Alessandro's length hit my cervix. I gasped as he hilted me, the pressure from him inside making me moan quietly. It felt full and I liked it. Behind me, I could hear Alessandro's breathing hitch in his chest, his hips twitching before he caught control of himself. He laughs soft and low as he holds onto my hips, steadying his breathing for a moment before cautiously rocking his hips. Every move was gentle, at first. Slowly as he gained his control over his own body he would move with powerful deeper thrusts, he never moved quickly with it as he seemed to enjoy my whines and moans that slipped from my lips with every push. The tips of his fingers dig into my hips as he uses his grip to keep me still, though it felt like he was sliding me along the length of his cock as if I were a sex toy to him. I tilted my head to the side just enough to listen to his breath as it trembled in his chest, punctuated by a wanton grunt as he pushed all the way inside again. A low growl left his throat as he suddenly pushed the palm of his hand into the back of my hip, forcing me onto my front. As he rolled me, he found himself on top, his thighs straddling my legs as he kept himself firmly inside of me. Alessandro pushed himself up with his hands on my lower back, with this new position he could grind himself deeper into me.

"Brava ragazza. È bello averti finalmente avvolto intorno al mio cazzo…" He groaned as he continued to pump deep inside me. I could feel him pushing against something inside me, and with every stroke, it tightened the spring in my core. A moan slips from me as I bury my face in the plush bedding beneath me. "Tch… head up bella, I want to hear how much you like it." He said as he wrapped my hair in his hand and pulled back. I picked my head up as he pulled controlling me by my hair, his knuckles resting below my shoulder blades as he kept my head pulled back and my back arched. I stabilize myself by crossing my elbows underneath me, closing my eyes as he fucks me roughly.

"Mmn~ careful Alessandro please…" I whined as he continued to hold onto me, but he seemed to be lost in his own pleasure to hear my words. His hand let go of my hair for a moment, instead slipping to my throat and pulling me back more. He leaned down pressing his chest against my back as he tilted my head to the side. I felt his breath against my skin for only a moment before his teeth met my shoulder. I cry out softly as he sinks his teeth in further, a searing sting radiating from the spot as he sucks on the skin. His movements were becoming stiff and I could tell from his labored breathing he was going to spill over soon. But that didn't stop him from moving to my neck and biting down there as well. My skin throbbed and I could feel my heartbeat in my cunt as he continued to fuck me roughly.

There was nothing gentle about what he was doing to me in this moment, he was marking me as his and having his way with me. Though the pain of his bites gave a dull aching undertone, my mind focused on the ever-growing buzz I felt in my core. Alessandro was lost in his own enjoyment of my body, his teeth sinking harder into my skin leaving a perfect imprint in my flesh.

211

BETWEEN THE POWERS

The searing pain shoots through me again and I cry out in an achy whimper that was soon overwhelmed by the coil finally coming undone. My mouth falls open as I feel my body fighting me, my fingertips clutching at the sheets as my cunt pulsed around him. Like pouring dye into water, the pleasure exploded through me before slowly seeping through my entire body. That seemed to be enough for Alessandro as he let go of my throat dropping my shaking body to the bed. His hands returned to my hips as he dug his fingertips in, slamming me all the way down on his member as he spilled himself inside of me. An almost guttural groan leaves him as his hips twitch against me, spasming as he fills me.

He wavers for a moment before withdrawing himself and falling to my side, a satisfied smirk across his lips as he remained closed. "Mm... Mia bella, small question..."

I turned my head to him, my cheeks a bit pink as my breath is a little tensed. "Hm?"

"Birth control?"

"No..." I hide my face in the bed for a moment.

"Aha... well I suppose we might end up with an heir from me yet." He chuckled as he pushed himself up with his elbows. His eyes open as he looks over my body, lingering on the three purple and yellow bitemarks he had left on my skin.

"Would you want that? I mean… considering what some of you say I am, that is my job isn't it?"

"I suppose that is true. I wouldn't mind having one of my own… But the choice is yours, if you want one… None of us can force you to do anything." He hummed softly as he admired my body a while longer. It wouldn't be a terrible thing I suppose if something took, especially since I knew I would be losing him in about two months. I stared up at the lithe man as he gazed at me lovingly.

"Well, maybe something will take…"

"You think?"

"We can only hope yeah?" I laughed at the idea that before always felt like a nightmare and buried my head against the bed again, listening to the gentle creak as Alessandro slipped out of bed to go cleanup for the day. I raised my head to watch him slip to the bathroom. He hesitates for a moment and looks at me again.

"I think you would make a beautiful mother sweetheart…" and with that he stepped in and shut the door.

I sit up on the bed, a chill running through me as his seed dripped from me. I hope he didn't mind the wet spot. I carefully rolled from the bed, running my hand through my hair I sauntered to the bathroom. The shower was running so I slipped inside so I could grab a wash cloth and quickly wipe myself down. I would take a shower later when I got back over to Judas's room.

#

It had been about 9 weeks now since the club incident and my intense morning with Alessandro. I had been bouncing freely between the two since Lucille wasn't able to do shit yet, though she had continued to threaten me and lecture me in the hallways as I passed between my two lovers. I had convinced Judas I preferred it when he finished on me rather than in me to give Alessandro the chance to breed me first, and as far as I could tell it was working. I had started staying in my room more often when the symptoms started to flare up, I didn't want them to know just yet. Not until I was sure anyway. Alessandro finally broke his silence with Judas and had gone to talk to him, which lead to a rather awkward situation when I walked in on Judas being pinned, ass in the air while Alessandro fucked him. However, they have started to grow more comfortable with me seeing them intimate with each other. Come April I finally decided it was time to test and tell them.

I took a pregnancy test this morning well three, waiting anxiously for the results to appear. I clutched my Satanic Cross necklace; I knew Phantom could hear my nervous thoughts but he kept himself away for the moment. Though the metal was hot to the touch so I knew he was listening to me. Pacing back and forth,

Judas lightly knocking on the door as I waited. I kept it locked and told him to stay out for a bit.

"Gale? Is everything alright in there?" He asked softly trying the knob a few times. "Is something wrong?"

"No nothing… I just need a minute longer please." I whined trying to get him to fuck off. It had been about 15 minutes and I waited to see the second line appear on the final test; the others had been positive but they could have been false. Hesitantly I grabbed the stick and closed my eyes as I turned it over. I peered carefully at it and all air left my lungs as I saw two blue lines, clear as day.

"Holy fuck! Phantom, come here!" I shouted, summoning my ghoul to celebrate with him. Judas could hear me and knocked again a bit more insistent.

"Cara mia? What is going on in there?" Judas murmured through the door, hoping that I would open it for him.

Phantom appeared in his usual smoke cloud; his typical salty demeanor was replaced with an excited aura as he hugs me tightly. His low voice rumbled "Congratulations, hopefully it stays yeah?" I could feel tears running down my cheeks, I never wanted kids and yet so badly did I want this one to make it to full term. He set me down and steps behind me as I walk to the door and open it for Judas, hiding the test behind my back.

"Gale, what is going on?"

"I need you to close the door," I said with a smile, practically squirming out of my skin as I waited with eager anticipation. Judas shuts the door, an anxious look across his face as he watches me standing there in front of the ghoul. I watched as his green and white eyes flickered across my body and then around the bathroom, suspicious of whatever it was I was hiding. "Judas, I need you to promise me something."

"Si, what is it?" he hummed, stepping forward. His warm hands come to rest on my hips as he looked at me with caring patience. I carefully pulled the test from behind my back, biting my lip in anticipation as it took him a moment to figure out what he was looking at.

"Don't get jealous yeah?" I giggled softly as he takes the test, his face lighting up as a gentle pink tint comes to his cheeks. He quickly slips his free arm around my hips and pulls me against him, a burst of almost victorious laughter leaving his chest as he squeezes me into him. His warm musky scent wraps me in a comforting blanket as he leaves kisses across my face. For a minute he seems nothing but joyous until he pauses to think.

"But? I have not been...?" He looks into my eyes the joy falling just a little, though a smile still beamed brightly at me. "Is not mine, is it?"

216

"No, it's Alessandro's most certainly," I said softly as he handed me back the test.

"Well, we should go tell him, no?" His voice broke just a little as he kept on the smile for me, obviously disappointed but happy for us anyway.

"We will soon, I promise." I kissed his cheek softly. "I promise I will carry yours too… I wish I could tell you why I picked his first, but I am sure you will learn soon…"

"I do not like such ominous words, but if you promise mine is next then fine." He laughs with unease pulling me tightly to him again. "Looks like the line will get its heirs after all hm?" Judas's voice was gentle as he teased me, nuzzling his nose into my hair as we stood there for a moment. Phantom rested his searing hand on my shoulder for a moment, nodding to me as I looked back at him and nodded back. He disappeared in his cloud again leaving Judas and I to our moment together. After a little longer of him holding me close, he steps back with a grin.

"Come, let's go tell Papa yes?" he purred tugging my free hand to lead me out of his bathroom.

We walked briskly through the stone halls, weaving around anyone who was left standing in our way. I kept the test tucked against my wrist so no one saw it as Judas was practically dragging me to Alessandro's chambers. My heart stops for a moment as I watch Lucille pass us on the stairway to Alessandro's room, her eyes flickering to my hand before back to me. As we fly past her, she stops staring at my hand, her calm face slowly shifting to an almost mortified gawk. She saw she had to have seen. Judas doesn't acknowledge his mother though as we race by to focus on the mission at hand. As we get to Alessandro's room Judas burst through the door with an eager smile on his lips.

"Alessandro amore mio! We have... our beautiful bella has news for you!" Alessandro quickly looked up at us, his face seemed laden with sullen thoughts. He raised an eyebrow looking at me as his face shifted away from the almost morose moment he was having before we came in.

"Well?" he said tentatively.

I shut the door behind us carefully striding over to him while Judas stayed by the door, his arms crossed over his powerful chest. I hide both hands behind my back and came to stand in front of him. He looked up at me almost confused for a moment, his gaze shifting to Judas and then back to me. Pulling the test from behind my back I hand it to him face down, he takes it with a small smirk. Turning it over he sees the blue lines and almost explodes forward wrapping me tightly in his arms before looking to Judas again who shook his head. Alessandro hugged me tighter, pulling my chin up to look at him as he took my lips in a passionate but almost frantic kiss.

218

"Oh! What wonderful news from my beautiful Gale!" He exclaimed continuing to hold me close. I could hear Judas chuckling in the corner before a slightly bitter sigh left his lungs. Alessandro buried his face against my neck as he squeezed me tightly. "Bella, is it mine?" He asked, the words rushing from his lips, pulling back as he rested both hands on my cheeks.

"She wouldn't let me, so it has to be yours fratello." Judas spoke up before I could answer, all I could do was nod in agreement.

"Yes, I wanted yours first…" I murmured before Alessandro cut me off with another strong kiss.

"This is fantastic news! My day has turned around for me after all!" He says sitting back down on the edge of his bed, pulling me into his lap as he does so. I notice a familiar envelope sitting on his bed, the wax seal broken but it obviously being the same Satanic Cross and 666 of Cassian's stamp. I reached for the letter curious about what the old man had to say, Alessandro quickly snatched it from me and held it away from me so I wouldn't read it.

"Hey! What is that Alessandro?" I say trying to grab at it again. He only shook his head and kept it away from me, as if me reading what it said would make it all the truer. Judas looked to Alessandro, the pleasant smile on his face shifting to a worried frown as he watched him keep the letter from me. He walks towards us and catches Alessandro's wrist pulling the paper from his hand.

"No... no, no they can't!" he groaned as he read the letter, his voice almost distraught as he read the letter over and over again. Panic grew in my chest, my stomach churned anxiously as I tried to catch a glimpse of the letter in Judas's hands. Alessandro collapsed backward into his bed, covering his face for a moment. The air of the room shifted, no longer were we celebrating the possibility of a new Belladonna, something more sinister this way came. I whined at Judas to show me the letter finally just hopping off Alessandro's lap and grabbing the letter from him. Judas looked down at me, his eyes filled with rage for a moment before he broke. I looked at the letter in my hand, and a chill ran straight through me.

[Alessandro Belladonna]

You will be sent to the Italy chapter until the 27th of this month, you will leave tomorrow with no protest. We need you to check over the completed new chapel that has been erected outside of the Vatican. There will be no ghoul guards sent with you as you shouldn't need them.

Sister Salacious
BETWEEN THE POWERS

This is your last official duty as Papa, and you will not fail.

Abbess Lucille

"What! They are sending you off?" I say quickly turning my head to look at Alessandro who looks less than pleased as he stays sprawled out on his bed.

"They are sending me to a hostile area with few ghouls, expecting to check over the new chapel that was set up with much protest." He groaned sitting back up to look at us.

"What? Only a few ghouls? That is ridiculous, we always send a full pack of ghouls with every Papa that goes over there." Judas murmured looking at the letter in my hand with suspicion and anger.

"I know, I do not think they wish this trip be safe for me though…"

My heart beat rapidly in my chest, is that what he had meant by the end of April? Not the true end but nearing the end? I looked panicked between the two, I wasn't ready to lose one already. Tears prickled in the corner of my eyes as I tried to think of anything to say. Judas wrapped his arm around me and pulled me against his chest, my tears quickly spilling over as I felt fear through me. I could hear Alessandro sit up, placing a warm hand on my lower back.

"I will be back I promise, no need for tears…" He cooed gently. "Come Sister, I promise all is okay I will make sure to return just for you and Judas, okay?"

Yeah… sure.

Part II: Water

Left Behind

Just like the letter had stated, Alessandro was flown out to Italy today. A pit seemed to open in my stomach as I watched him get on that plane and disappear into the sky. Judas watched with me; the air catching in his throat as he watched equally concerned as I was. His red cassock billowed in the wind as we stood on the airfield watching Alessandro disappear into the clouds. His hand on my hip tightened its grip for a moment before we turned to return to the ministry. The car ride back was silent as the two of us were lost in our own thoughts. I had leaned my head against his shoulder though; my eyes focused on Lucille who had an all-knowing smug look across her face. She sat there watching us momentarily, Judas not once acknowledging her.

BETWEEN THE POWERS

When we finally got back to the ministry, Judas slipped out of the vehicle first and waited patiently for me holding the door open. Lucille made it her mission to get out first, her bony hand pushing me back against my seat as she neared the door. The cloud of flowers that covered her choked me as she leaned into my ear.

"I hope you are ready for one hell of a funeral little girl…" she hissed as she climbed out of the car. My heart stopped in my chest. The fuck did that mean? Was she really going to?

I looked at her as she stood up and patted Judas's chest before making her way back into the ministry. Judas winced a little as she touched me, his eyes shifting to me as he waited for me to step out. I carefully step from the car and fix my dress looking up at Judas, trying my damnedest to hide the worry in my eyes. He grabbed my hand nervously; his usually sure grip was loose like he knew something that he wouldn't share with me.

We walked back inside and made our way back to his room, though he wouldn't let me in like he normally did. He stopped in his door frame and turned to me giving me a nervous kiss before shutting the door in my face. I heard the click of his lock and went to grab the key I had for his room off my chest, but the key was gone. He had to have taken it off me without me noticing. I knocked for a moment hoping that it was a mistake but he went silent and shut me out. My heart sunk further in my chest

225

as I was terrified of what the hell was going on. Was he upset that I picked Alessandro's first? Or did he know something I didn't?

I huffed as he wouldn't let me in, turning on my heels I quickly scurried off to Alessandro's room. But when I had climbed those stairs and got to his door it too was locked. I didn't have his key as he had normally kept the room unlocked for me to come and go as I pleased. So, if it was locked that meant someone did not want me in there. I growled and left to go sit in my room. Something wasn't right and I could not pinpoint what it was. I sat down in my cold empty room, anxious thoughts chewing at my mind.

Staying like that for the rest of the night, eventually going to bed with my Satanic Cross clutched tightly in my hand, the weight of fear and anxiety sat heavy in my chest.

#

The next morning instead of the brassy ring of the waking bells we were greeted with the dull aching drone of mourning bells. Those only rang when important members of the clergy had passed. I sat upright quickly as I heard the dreaded tone, feeling my heart race in my chest as I went to throw myself from bed. Quickly as I turn to put my feet on the cold stone, I feel an arm tighten around my hips. It was hot and strong as it pulled on me. A long slender black tail reaches out and wraps around my ankles. I turn around to see at some point in the night Phantom had been summoned, and now he was not letting me go.

"You know what those bells probably mean…" he grumbled as he looked up at me from his curled-up position in my bed. "Don't leave… stay with me… I can comfort you."

"No… he… he said till the end of April… she…" My heart broke in my chest as Phantom softly pulled me back to him. He was never this tender but, in this moment, he could feel everything I was feeling and hear my thoughts as they spiraled out of control. Tears spilled down my cheeks as he pulled me close to him, his scorching skin was comforting as he let me cry against him like this. His massive hand stroked my dirty blonde hair as he hummed a soft song to me. His chest rumbled as he hummed, and as much as I enjoyed the calming melody, he hummed my heart slowly shattered in my chest. Those mourning bells had to be for Alessandro, I knew Lucille had a plan for him but it wasn't supposed to be this soon…

I did not bother leaving my room to find Judas only occasionally leaving to use the bathroom, dread hung over me like a thunderstorm. Heavy and suffocating as I clung to Phantom for comfort. He knew what it was like to lose someone you loved so dearly. My chest was aching from my sobbing, Phantom's grip on me was tight as he knew I couldn't be alone in this very moment. Around late afternoon a knock appeared at my door, I ignored it though. Whoever it was could fuck off because I do not think I could take any interactions right now. The knocking was persistent for a while until finally, Judas pushed open my door. I lifted my head for a moment and caught a glimpse of him in his full black cassock, his paints clean but the obvious run marks from him crying glistened in the dim lighting of my room. Quickly buried my face in Phantom's chest hoping he would get the message that I didn't want to talk to him now. Phantom carefully pulled his mask off to look at Judas, he gently shook his head and my cardinal approached my body.

He hovered behind me, unsure of how much closer he should get to me. Carefully though against Phantom's silent warnings he sat down on the edge of my bed and placed a hand on my back. I reflexively arch away from him as I tightened my grip on Phantom's shirt.

"Bella… Please talk to me…" he pushed out, sounding half his size.

"Go away… please…"

"I know you heard the bells… they can't find him so they are assuming the worst."

"Judas, please I… I can't just, just go please.. " I say my voice seeming shattered and empty as I keep tucked up against Phantom's tall body.

"Lucille put me in charge… She refuses to make my Papa yet stating that Cassian isn't ready for it…" Every word was hollow as he continued, and I could hear the wringing of hands in his voice. "I'm not ready for it…"

"Judas, I said leave… please…" He paused for a moment before continuing with his words.

"I didn't want this… I did not think she would go this far to get what she wanted…"

"Leave!" I shouted as I turned to face him, tears staining my face. "Just… go I can't not with everything going on…" I murmured burying my head back into Phantom's chest. Judas retracts his hand and sighs knowing that I was not going to let him continue. He stands up slowly and shuffles back to my door. I could feel his eyes on me as he longed to make me feel better.

"I love you…" He let the phrase linger in the air for moment, his hand resting on the door as he gripped it softly. "They are making me record and release my first song next Friday…" and with that he slipped from my room.

Phantom rubbed my back slightly before sitting up slowly, his sharp features softened as he looked down into my eyes.   "I am sorry, you are too young to have your heart shattered like this…" he murmured as his irises flickered with a subdued flame, his long white hair framed his face like a waterfall.

229

"He… He can't be gone, can he?"

"I could always go to hell and look for you… but that means I have to leave you for a day or two." The offer felt unreal, but he could traverse the other side and find information that I couldn't.

"I have to know… please…"

He stood up carefully and looked down at me, his tail swaying gently as he slowly let go of my ankles. "Why don't I give you something before I go? Just so you aren't so alone.. " he rumbled softly. In his hands, black smoke swirled before leaving one of Alessandro's jackets in his hand. He carefully hunted down the sample of Alessandro's cologne and spritzed the jacket. Once he was satisfied with how strong the scent was, he held it to his chest for a moment before handing me the warm familiar fabric.

"I will be right back, okay?" He turned and stepped into his black cloud disappearing leaving me alone and cold in my room clinging to the jacket. It felt as if Alessandro had just taken it off and given it to me. I curled up in a tight ball on my bed as more tears spilled down my cheeks, holding the jacket against my chest, cradling it as if it were the last thing I had of him. It very well could be the last thing of his that I was allowed to have. The world melted away from me as I continued to mourn the death of one of my lovers. I tossed and turned restlessly hoping this was some hellish nightmare.

#

Judas, walking back to his room and shutting the door behind him, fell back against the wood as he sank to the floor. His hands ran to his head as he crumpled again, anguished tears leaving his eyes. The usually strong and gentle man collapsed in on himself as he became a young man again being cursed at for even existing. It felt as if it was his fault that Alessandro was gone like this. They had been together for his entire life, practically inseparable even with all the changes their lives had taken. His heart was crushed, his lifetime lover was dead and his other lover was devastated, angry even. Thoughts raced through his head as he ran his hands through his blonde hair, his fingers curling as he held on tightly. Judas hung his head as the tears continued to run, his makeup running with it leaving black water trails down his cheeks. The safety of his room turned cold and empty as he craved to be held by one of his lovers.

Lamenting in his room, unable to move away from the door, gentle sobs left his chest as the situation sinks further in. It was his fault, no... his mother's fault that Alessandro was taken away from us. She wanted him to be in control so badly that she offed one of the few people he cared immensely for. The pain of losing Alessandro clouded his brain, his lover, the one man who he

231

trusted and craved intimately was dead somewhere overseas and there was little chance that he would ever see him again to say goodbye. And that was the worst part, knowing he would never have that chance to tell him goodbye. To see that goofy smile as Alessandro would look back at him during sermons. He no longer will get to listen to Alessandro's voice as he would guide him through rituals and ceremonies. No longer will he watch Alessandro flounce around and flirt with everyone on stage. To hear his laughter at a stupid joke, or be scolded playfully for doing something wrong. I no longer smell him on my clothes as I go back and forth between them, no longer sneaking off to explore each other like naughty teens over and over again. That was all gone, Alessandro was gone…

The pain ate at him inside, pushing him to do things he knew he should not do. He pulled his body off the floor and shuffled to his bed, sinking to his knees, and reaching under his bed. Pulling out a bottle he looked at the amber liquid his eyes watching it as it splashed around inside the bottle. A voice screamed in the back of his head to put it back and ignore it, but he needed something to mask the pain and so Judas found himself at the bottom of a bottle trying to process the loss of Alessandro.

#

The next few days blurred into weeks as I milled about, no sign of Phantom any attempt to summon him was met with a cold Satanic Cross and no ghoul. I was too hurt to try and hunt down Judas. His first song came out on the 13th, and as much as I wanted to listen to it I could not; the idea of Alessandro just being gone like that, no longer serenading us with his voice sent pain through my chest. I tried to avoid leaving my room as much as possible, I didn't want to be a part of any of the mourning festivities they had set up. That and I was avoiding Judas as much as possible; I couldn't look at him. It wasn't his fault that Alessandro died and yet, his mother had him practically steal the throne out from under our beloved Papa.

Shuffling from the room; Alessandro's jacket hung across my shoulders as I made my way outside to sit in Arthur's garden. I needed to get out of my room since it had started to grow stuffy. My feet carried me down the familiar halls to the doors, then out to Arthur's garden when I shuffled slowly to the far side of the garden and sat down on the pavers, hiding amongst the belladonna and lily of the valley that grew. I had my knees pulled to my chest as I listened to the world around me hoping it would help drown out the thoughts in my head. Not even the birds would sing for me though, the wind barely rustled the leaves in the trees. Everything around me fell silent, and I was left to my thoughts sitting in the garden wishing more than anything that Alessandro would just come skipping from the doors looking for me. I sat there hollowed and empty listening for anything that would ease my sorrows. He was supposed to be back today, maybe if I just closed my eyes, he

233

would come walking out for me. Burying my face in my knees, my hands lightly clutching to his jacket as I closed my eyes and waited. He couldn't be gone... I needed him.

#

Judas was lost in a haze of liquor as he mourned his lover. Lucille was less than pleased that he sunk into the bottle just as quickly as Alessandro used to, but she felt that taking that from him too would only enrage him. She needed him pacified if she was going to continue running the ministry from behind the scenes again. He would often find himself sipping on some harsh burning liquor at night to keep the thoughts from bothering him. Judas tried to for weeks to continue to do his job and balance the few things Alessandro had done before on his shoulders while nursing a new bad habit. Poor choices were made as he slipped further into the bottle, new scars appeared on his body and he no longer could look at himself in the mirror.

Standing at his window in his room, his green and white gaze sweeping the grounds as he lifted the bottle to his lips again. The booze burned his tongue as it flooded his mouth and slipped down his throat. His face was painted with a semi-permanent frown as he watched over the garden. His eyes flickered up to the empty window of Alessandro's room, his gaze lingering as he wanted nothing more than to see Alessandro step to the window. But as he stared his heart sunk into the pit of grief that pooled in his stomach, quickly he looked away and took another sip. His eyes linger over the garden, his breath stopping in his lungs as he catches a glimpse of Alessandro's jacket. He only saw the jacket disappear amongst the belladonna and lily of the valley, but that gave him enough hope in his broken heart to go search for him. He set the bottle down on his nightstand and carefully fixed his black cassock before emerging from his room and walking to the door that led out to the garden. His head was on a swivel as the warm air hit his skin. Eyes frantically scanned for any sign of his Alessandro as he made his way towards the belladonna patch.

Judas's heart raced as he weaved through the flowers, the liquor in his system making it difficult to stay fully vertical as he was practically running to the belladonna. His footsteps pounded on the pavers, disregarding how dizzy he was feeling as he flew towards the spot where he saw the jacket.

Rounding the last bush, he saw the jacket and was filled with hope before the world came crashing back through him. It was just me sitting there curled up in Alessandro's jacket.

"Gale…" he murmured quietly looking down at me. I was curled up tightly, Alessandro's jacket clinging to my shoulders, my eyes closed tightly as if I were waiting for something.

"Gale please…"

BETWEEN THE POWERS

"Gale...look at me..." he pleaded, begging that I just acknowledge his existence.

#

I kept my eyes closed as the warm spring air lingered, the sunlight warming my skin as I clung to the jacket on my shoulders. It felt peaceful as I let myself just pause here in the garden. For the first time in these last few weeks, I didn't feel the tears spilling down my cheeks as Alessandro's scent wafted itself to my nose. I heard someone's footsteps approaching, assuming it was a ghoul who's just playing around. I zoned out and focused on the warmth on my body and the scent of Alessandro. For the smallest moments, I swear I could hear him calling my name.

There it was again, someone calling my name. I buried my face against my knees for a moment listening as it is called again. Then a hand touched my shoulder, quickly slipping to the side of my neck. It was warm, and shaking as it gripped me softly. I raise my head to see Judas in front of me on his knees, before I even had a chance to speak, he fell forward wrapping me tightly with his arms. He stunk of alcohol and was sobbing gently against my neck as he apologized over and over again. I say there stunned as he clung to me as if I was the last person on this planet, his words were broken as they spilled from his lips.

"Judas…?" I murmured trying to get him to sit up. I paw at him lightly to get off me but he wasn't budging as he kept his face buried in my shoulder. No doubt crying harder as he could smell Alessandro on me again as his scent intermingled with my own. "Judas… please…"

"I shouldn't have let him go… I shouldn't have left you alone. God, I am sorry, I am so so sorry. I need you please… please don't make me go." He cried softly, his words muddled, keeping a tighter grip on me. At this point I feel us falling backward, my body pinned to the ground by him as he sobs into my neck.

"Ho bisogno di te, per favore non posso essere di nuovo solo…"

"You don't have to go…" I sighed softly as I listened to him. It felt as if this was his first chance to fully process this since Alessandro's death. I stared at the blue sky, tears prickling in my eyes as he continued to mourn against my skin. His pellegrina ruffled as the wind picked up softly, the leaves in the trees rustling and birds finally singing as the world unpaused itself.

"I missed you… so god damn much. I should have come to you…" he murmured; his words muffled in my skin as he held me tightly. Nothing was going to pry his muscular grip from my body. Judas's scent enveloped me again, tangling with Alessandro's and the alcohol on his breath as the wind swirled around us. My chest clenched as the tears rolled down my cheeks again.

"I'm sorry for pushing you away…"

"No… no you had every right to push me away… it was my fault I told Lucille I did not want to go to Italy… I didn't think she would send our Alessandro." He admitted. "That should have been me in that plane… I should be the one dead…"

"Stop that… you didn't know…"

"But it's true… I would give my soul, my life for him to walk among us again…"

"Please… don't say that…" I couldn't begin to imagine trading one life for another, needing both of them felt like a curse only I was meant to endure. But I couldn't imagine how he felt, losing his lover of decades…

"He deserves to be here with you… not me."

"God damn it… please I love you. I love both of you…don't… don't go…"

"I won't… I need you…" his voice was hollow as he continued to hold me, his shoulders shook with each exhale as he tried to slow his sobs.

"I never want to leave your side… please…" he murmured leaving a gentle kiss on my neck.

"I won't make you…" Promising almost silently as I laid there beneath him watching the clouds carefully scroll past us, it felt like a lie, but a much needed one. The tears stain my cheeks again as everything melted around me, but finally after weeks of hiding, I felt like I finally needed someone.

He slowly pushes himself from me, his gaze on my form as he looks down, tears still slipping down his cheeks. Judas wipes them away with the back of his sleeve, the fabric slipping slightly as he does so revealing the bruising and scratching from anxiously inflicting pain.

"Oh Judas… no…" I say pushing myself up off the ground grabbing his wrist and pulling his arm to me. Quickly I pull the sleeve up higher and feel my heart break all over again. "Baby no…"

"I know… I shouldn't have…" he murmured staring at the red marks across his skin. He turned his head away from me as if he was ashamed for hurting like he was. The pain of losing someone so close to him was too much to bear inside and so, he dashed his pain across his body and drowned it in liquor.

"I shouldn't have pushed you away…" I murmured softly as I left a small kiss on the marks. "Come on… we should go get

239

cleaned up…" He nodded in agreement and carefully pulled us up off the ground. Alessandro's jacket fell from my shoulders, picking it up and draping it across Judas's shoulders, I felt guilt for hoarding its comfort. He looked at me as if he was going to let the tears spill down his cheeks again. Together we shuffled inside and headed towards his private bathroom.

The door clicks behind us and he hangs the jacket up on the door hook, burying his face into it for a moment to be swaddled in his scent one more time. My heart breaks a little as I watch him rub the fabric between his fingers, his eyes locked on the Satanic Cross patch that had adorned the breast of the jacket. I turn around and move to the shower carefully getting the water running while Judas is distracted. The water was hot as it came pouring from the faucet, after adjusting it for a moment before settling with the temp and pulling the stopper. I turned and looked into the mirror for a moment, the bags had settled under my eyes and I looked momentarily dead inside. His self-love notes were gone, not even one left anywhere around the mirror. The sticky residue from them residing there clouded the edges of the mirror. A bottle sat knocked over on the counter accompanied by a small pocket knife that was left open. I cringed slightly as I stared at the blade, understanding why it was there. I closed my eyes and picked it up, closing it quickly before slipping it into one of the drawers. I turn to Judas watching him as he continues to rub the fabric gently between his fingertips, like a child holding a comfort blanket.

"Come on sweetheart… let's get you out of that cassock…" I hummed as I walked closer to him. My hands reach out carefully pulling him away from the jacket, his eyes flickering to stare at me instead. He looked broken inside… lost even. I tenderly undid each button of his cassock, slipping it from his shoulders and letting it drop to the floor before slipping my hands along his skin, pushing his shirt up his torso. What before was an intimate ravenous act was now caring and gentle as if he had needed me to do this for me. My chest clenched a little as I spot more marks and bruises across his skin. He was hurting… and I was too afraid to be near him to help. I closed my eyes for a moment as I finished pulling the shirt from him. Taking a step forward I rest my head against his bare chest for a moment, my ear pressed to him as I listened to his heartbeat. At least he was still here with me… My hands slipped towards his waistline to pull off his pants when his hands stop me.

"I can do that… don't worry about it…"

"Alright then," I murmur softly as I step back and carefully slip off my dress, letting the soft fabric crumple on the ground. I felt Judas's eyes briefly flit across my body before he turned away. A sigh slipped from my lips and I stepped into the black tiled shower, the warm water pouring over me. I closed my eyes and sat there under the spray as I let the thoughts cloud my mind. She had to have planned this; did Lucifer lie to me? I felt

241

Judas step in behind me, his arms sliding around my hips as he pulled me tightly to his bare body. The water cascaded down our bodies as he buried his face in my shoulder, his nose pressed against my skin, his warm breath dancing across my neck. We stood there under the flow for a good while, listening to the sound of the water hitting our bodies and flowing down the drain. I never wanted to part from him in this moment… he was all I had left.

Heart to Heart

"I'm sorry Arthur… I can't imagine how hard this is on you." I finally say as we sit across from each other in his chambers. The air around us was suffocating, weighed down with the grief that still consumed The Ministry. The tea in my cup was starting to grow cold and I was reluctant to sip from it. It felt wrong to even drink in his presence, that I had lost that little perk of our relationship when that plane crashed. Losing someone who was practically family was a special kind of grief, one that rots out your core as you continue with your own existence.

I sigh as I look off to the side where Caesar stood, his hardened gaze pointed out a window. Caesar was one of the few men I wouldn't expect to grieve openly, especially not over someone he saw as lesser. Perhaps he would bury himself in the crystal decanters of liquor he kept, or in the bodies of women who

243

threw themselves at him. But here he was ignoring the conversation yet lingering in the space as if to still mourn with family. Arthur raised the ornately patterned cup to his lips, hesitating to take a sip. His mismatched gaze was pained, closing his eyes he took a mouthful of the bitter brew and nodded for a moment.

"Oh, I am no stranger to grief… it has been my bedmate for years." The older man says finally, breaking the silence. "He was not young… but he certainly had more ahead of him." Caesar scoffed in the background, shifting his position so that he could lean against the windowsill.

"What was it like? Meeting him for the first time?" I asked, attempting to drink the cool tea. Arthur thought in silence as he looked back through decades of memory, leaning back in his chair a bit more before setting the little cup off to the side.

"Alessandro was… a wild one. Cassian had picked him up in Rome during one of his yearly visits. At that point I was already in the process of becoming the next Papa, so I did not get to meet him until he landed in the city." A smile tugs at the corner of his mouth. "12 years old and fueled with fire… Cassian was almost certain that he would get arrested. I knew he just needed patience, and so we gave him patience."

"You gave him patience brother. I gave him work and put his nose to the grindstone. Alessandro needed guidance or he would have failed in his duties... He still failed in his duties." I could hear the bitterness that rose in his tone. Looking over his shoulder he swallowed back words of anger, disappointment. "I failed him, had he been more prepared he would not have been revoked from his papacy. He would not have been put at risk."

"It was not your fault fratello, we knew that Alessandro was not destined for a long run... he partied too much. The nightlife ran in his blood." He retorted, a fondness on his tongue for the energy that was once held in Alessandro's life. Caesar did not enjoy the pushback, his face contorting into a resentful scowl as he stormed from the room. Arthur shook his head. "I knew he would do that, blame himself. Caesar really did try to straighten him out, he had gotten extra time to prepare for his role and wanted to ensure that Alessandro did too."

"I'm sorry again I..." My own grief still felt like it was underserved in this space. Perhaps I should skulk off to Judas and find solace in his warmth, leaving the older Belladonna to carry their own sorrow. "I have nothing I could say at this moment that feels appropriate. I only knew him for a few months... Nothing substantial."

"Love can do that, make someone more important than we previously could ever imagine." His gaze shifted to the painting

245

on his wall, lingering. "You have every right to mourn." Not like he does. I have the rights of a new girlfriend, a hook-up. He could tell from the way my face seemed to drop that I was not comfortable in accepting this 'right' to grieve. As if any one person could control your right to mourn.

"I cannot tell you how to grieve Sister Wenstrom… But perhaps you would benefit from finding busy work, I know gardening has been my crutch for decades now."

"Thank you, Arthur." I pause as the words catch in my throat. "I think I should go…" Finishing my drink I stood up and gave a bow to the man who was 50 years my senior, letting the sorrow drag me from the accepting space. Maybe I should have stayed, be there for him as I have been for Judas. Though it felt as if I was intruding. Before when we met to talk, his grief over Mona and his life felt as if it were meant to be shared. Even after the incident with Phantom, I was welcomed in his room. But today those green walls felt judgmental, accusatory, as they screamed in their silent font that I was undeserving of my pain. Maybe I was just feeling guilty; after all, I knew he was going to die, but the plane going down felt too soon. Lucifer even said that it was too soon when he came to the sounds of my pitiful prayers and begging. Even the devil can be wrong sometimes, that or he lied.

Lost in my own mind, I wrapped my arms around myself as I continued to shuffle down the stairs and through the halls. My mindless sauntering had begun to drag me towards Judas's office, the new office. With Alessandro out of the way, Lucille wasted no time in moving Judas to where he needed to be. His office was gutted not even a week after the announcement, only his bedroom remained relatively untouched.

It wasn't long till I found myself at his door, waiting quietly, anxiously for him to open it. Hoping that perhaps his mind could feel the presence of his shaken grieving girlfriend. But, in a rather unkind twist of fate, I began to smell flowers. Not just any kind either, the same pungent and distasteful odor that his mother wore. Turning my head, I spotted her as she stalked closer, rapidly closing the gap. My mind screamed for me to open the door, to grab the gilded handle and push, but I froze.

"You better not be coming to bother him again. He finally has agreed to put that stupid bottle down, and has work to do." She snapped, shaking her finger at me as if I were some insolent child going to bug their father. "I swear, that is the next move. Getting rid of you, you and your distractions so that I may set him up with someone of my choosing."

"What is your problem with me?" I finally snap, trying not to choke on her perfume as it crammed itself down my throat.

"My problem is that you have been nothing but a bad choice for my son, you and Alessandro. He deserves better; I could marry him off to a much more suitable woman right now if it wasn't for his indecent desire to be with you." Her hand shot out as I reached for the handle, grabbing my wrist with an iron grip. "Mark my words, little girl. Once I am finished sorting through the congregation, your head is next."

That was a threat clear as day, another genuine threat from the mouth of that vile woman. One that I wished I could slap out of her maw.

"I don't know what you may think I have done to your son. But getting rid of me will do nothing for you." I snapped, trying to rip my hand away from her. "You will only cause him more pain." Lucille let go, straightening up as we heard the click of shoes coming past the hall. Even when she simmered with rage she knew she had to keep up her illusions. That if others caught on to her, she would lose the control she had. The control she only gained because she was sleeping with Cassian, who by all means was still in charge and had final say. The footsteps retreated as quickly as they came, leaving the two of us in a standoff. If she began berating, I could open the door and expose her to Judas. But she knew better.

I watched as she ran her hand over her hair, straightening cut the grey fly-aways.

"Your time will come. And when it does, I will find a better fit for my replacement, abbess, or abbot. Someone who shares my outlook on control." Her lips were pursed together so tight, one could have assumed she was talking from her asshole. Pushing past me, she opened the door and stepped inside making sure to slam it in my face. No matter how much I hated her, I still had to admire the protectiveness she had over her son. There was no doubt though that she was a helicopter parent when he was growing up. Fine. With the door shut in my face, I pressed my back to the wall and slid down. The hard stone scratching against my exposed skin brought a grounding sting to the forefront of my mind.

Replacement felt like an odd word for her to use, in the same way that a mother fosters an Oedipus complex with their child. I wasn't replacing her in his life; I was filling a different role. One of pleasure and love and emotional stability, not motherly care and guidance. Unless she meant I was her replacement in The Ministry, which also felt wrong. At this point, I was becoming the Prima del Madre, the Satanic pope's baby mama. Not the abbess, or whatever her job was outside of making people's lives miserable. My gaze flickered up from my knees to the door that sat across the hall. The little round window that was embedded in its polished wood was void of light, the glass reflecting this pitiful scene.

Sister Salacious
BETWEEN THE POWERS

A woman on the ground, dressed as if she was to attend a ball, her makeup streaky and filled with blemishes from crying. Around her eyes were puffy and red, and it was clear from the state of her hair that she was struggling to keep up with her own emotional struggle. Even the soft autumn glow of her skin was beginning to fade, leaving behind the pallor of sick. That woman was me, only a few months ago did I feel like I was running on top of the world. And now look at me. Hanging my head, I waited for the wretch to leave so that I could talk to Judas. Minutes dragged by as sitting on the cold hard stone began to cause my legs to go numb, she was running out her time.

The door creaked open finally, cold air rushing out of the office in a tidal wave as her flowers began to make their exit. How something so beautiful can become a bad omen was beyond me, but she did it.

"You know Judas, your father was running much of the ministry by himself at your age. He even found 2 of your older 'brothers' by the time he hit 40." She said, her voice airy and light as she talked to Judas. "I could see you being one of the greats, your name could go down in history! Judas Belladonna, the one who took over the world!" His face grimaced as she finished that sentence, pushing her out of his office.

"Yes… thank you, mother. But now is not the time to be discussing that we have other matters that need to be dealt with… Like the investigation as to why the plane went down."

"That was weeks ago, 2 months is certainly long enough to leave the investigation alone. If the ghouls didn't find anything then, they won't find anything now." Her gaze dropped to where I was sitting. "Mm, you have a stray Judas. I would suggest dealing with her."

He looked over to where I sat, immediately divorcing himself from his mother to come help me up. His hands were warm as they found their way to my back, lifting me up onto my feet.

"You may go now Mother; I am sure Cassian would much rather have your presence for the afternoon don't you think?" Judas said though I could feel her gaze digging into my skin. Maybe I need to start recording what she says around me; Judas already has a dislike of her but won't get rid of her because she is his mom. "Sweetheart, mia bella, what's wrong?"

I waited till she began to walk off, watching to ensure she was out of earshot before letting the tears come back. "I miss him." My voice broke as Judas placed my hands in his. "God, months before I wanted nothing to do with him, and now I miss him…"

251

Judas laughed slightly as he kissed the top of my head, pulling me into the office where he could close the door behind us. He knew how I felt, a thousand times over and then some.

"I know, I miss him too." Leading me to his desk he pulled out a folder from behind his computer. "I had to keep this from mo- Lucille. But…" he opened the folder and pulled out a series of photos. Most had looked like random snapshots of debris and damage from a fire, but one caught my eye. One of the ghouls was standing next to debris, and from his hand dangled Alessandro's lavender robes. But they looked fresh like they were just pulled from the dry cleaners and brought to the scene. Picking it up, I tried to look for anything else out of place. At this point we didn't even have a body to mourn over, his coffin was filled with a dummy that had his face cast so the congregation had a figure to mourn. But the longer I looked the more I saw that didn't make sense. His belongings that he had packed for this trip were scattered like someone had been searching through them. Nothing had any damage to it aside from parts of a plane that were scattered and a few scorch marks on the ground.

"I'm sorry, are these from *his* wreck site?" I asked quietly, trying to make sure that that was what I was seeing. It felt too staged, but how would I know what a staged wreck would look like?

"They are. I had sent Willow, Branch, and Mist to go investigate. I figured earth and water ghouls would be our best bet in case anything was buried." He picked up the other pictures and shook his head. "It makes no sense that the plane would go down, we have technicians who maintain the private planes. Ale had ghouls with him on his flight crew, even a Quintessence. By all means one of them should have been able to recover him…" His voice wavered as he set the images down and leaned against his desk. "He should have been able to come home… even if it was only as a body."

"I know…" My voice was flat, empty as I moved to sit in one of the little red chairs that sat in front of his desk. "I don't think there is much we can do at this moment. Even if we did find him, it would be too late." He scoffed and shook his head.

"It's always too late here." Putting the folder away, he seemed reluctant to drop it but moved on with the conversation. "Lucille is demanding I get music ready for the rest of my album. 45 and I can't even make my own choices without her hanging over me. Do you know how embarrassing that is… 'Judas, the Mama's boy'." His voice was bitter. Ever since Alessandro had disappeared, he seemed to continue to grow bitter. Not like I could blame him, I had found myself growing increasingly anxious and that perhaps it was a mistake being a part of that ritual on

Halloween. How could happiness and pleasure be a mistake though?

"I'm sorry Judas, I seem to be saying that a lot to everyone. Your older brothers, you, the siblings who come to ask me what's going on…" My hand went to the necklace and squeezed. "To Phantom…" As it grew warm, I quickly let go and closed my eyes.

"We can't bring him back, I can't change the past, I can't even get my own mother off my ass." He stood up and began to pace, digging into the chest of his cassock to produce a pack of cigarettes. Pulling one free, he rested it between his lips and produced a lighter. Sucking in, the tip starts to glow a cherry red, smoke weakly dancing from its tip. "Do you know that she keeps coming in here, suggesting that I… get rid of anyone who stands in my way? As if murder is acceptable in 20XX."

Do I tell him about her threats?

No…

"It's not like this is the 1800s and executing people is normal," I say trying to lighten the mood. He raised his hand as if to signal me to stop talking. Taking a drag of his cigarette, he blew the smoke at the ceiling and shook his head.

"She wants me to use power and control I don't have yet. By all means, I am still 'just' a cardinal." A bitter laugh. "Cassian won't even change my title yet, I apparently haven't 'earned that right'. Even though, no one else is here to take the papacy and I have been 'promoted'. He is still holding that stupid grudge..."

"So what are you going to do? Just bite your tongue?"

"I don't know... Whatever I do though, I can't risk adding bodies to my name. I have to be careful or else we will fail before reaching our zenith..." The cherry of his smoke reflected in his black sclera, a spark being lit in the background. "I refuse to be snuffed out and silenced like mio bello was, or abandoned as our predecessors were."

#

Leaving Judas's office after a lengthy conversation, I felt lighter and yet burdened with more information. Alessandro's crash felt staged, no corpses, no blood. There was hardly any debris from the plane itself, and the damage looked intentional. That and there was really no sign of him even being on the plane aside from his personal effects. Even with the ghouls who scraped the grounds for anything that remained, not even a whisper of his physical form was there. Part of me longed to go back to worrying about whether or not I had a choice in who I fucked. Debating the crisis of predestination over free will, not whatever twisted game

255

this has become. Lucille seems to be gunning for me but in subtle ways. Threats, comments, and half-assed attempts at upsetting and manipulating her son just enough that he would be too busy to focus on she was doing. It wasn't working, but in some ways, it felt as if it was.

With Alessandro gone, Judas had become short with me. Not all the time. In snippets, small glimpses of anger break through his usually quiet demeanor. His wrath would break through and he would become cold, focused solely on his goal within the Ministry. The anger felt forced compared to the grief that coated his soul like bitter ash after a raging fire that had been put out by rain. Lucille was wearing on him. When he wasn't locked in, he was searching. Nothing I did could distract him long enough to help me break him free of this obsession. I needed to talk to someone who wasn't going to judge me or rat back to one of the upper clergy.

With my head ducked, I made a beeline for my room in the sisters' wing. Watching the tile disappear under my feet, I try to avoid running into anyone. Weaving past the other shoes and hemlines that appeared in my field of vision, I finally appear at my room. Shoving open the door, I dash inside, looking around at the familiar one-window bedroom. It was visually cold, bare stone walls and the absolute minimum amount of furniture that someone would have here. My bed was still rumpled from the last time I slept under its covers, and everything had a stale scent of deodorant and cologne. If anything it reminded me of being back home in my parent's room when they decided I needed a lecture.

Grasping the cross around my neck, I squeezed tightly as I uttered a few words to summon Phantom again. Since Alessandro's death, my ghoul had been reluctant to leave my side unless I asked him to go. Judas had been uncomfortable with the creature practically hanging off me, worried that the Ghoul was trying to wedge in as the new third. I didn't blame him considering his track history. While Phantom was attractive and certainly sweet enough, I didn't see him as anything further than a friend. As I finished my little call out, a cloud of black smoke again appeared from nowhere, the ghoul stepping forth as he wrung his tail.

"Is something wrong Gale?" He asked, red gaze searching my own for any context of his visit. I shook my head, though we both knew that was a lie.

"It's nothing major but something about his… passing feels wrong. Judas showed me pictures today from the wreck sight and it looked staged." Sitting down on the edge of my bed, I ran my hand through my hair, plucking out the spider lace veil I wore. "I could be wrong but, no body, barely any damage to his stuff… it feels manufactured."

"How many plane crashes have you seen before?" He asked, leaning back against my small oak desk. "And I mean really seen, not just those that had been devastating enough to appear all over the news."

"Well, none aside from the few that appear on TV but those were always larger crashes. A 747 doesn't exactly just make a small hole." Rubbing the veil between my fingers I stare at the floor. "Have you noticed Lucille has been increasingly hostile towards me? I mean whenever you are listening er... are around."

He shrugged as he leaned his head back in thought, his tongue pressed against his upper lip.

"She was always a bit harsh when I was around Mona... Like my general presence upset her. But I wouldn't say I have seen her be directly hostile, though I would be lying if I said I was listening all the time."

"I feel like she might have something to do with the plane going down. I mean..." Dropping the veil in my lap, my gaze again rose to meet his as he dropped his head. "She had made direct threats against his life before, or at least they sounded like threats on his life. And both of them have had issues with her being strict in the past."

"She probably did, let's be honest here she doesn't exactly sound like the accepting type. She likely knew about Alessandro and Judas and thought it would be best to put an end to it. You have to admit their relationship is a little weird to those who don't know the history of the 'family'."

"Well, they aren't family, I know they all throw around brother a lot but I know guys from high school who grew up together and would call each other brother. It is just like two boy best friends who grew up with an interest in each other's bodies, nothing more than that." That caused Phantom to laugh, crossing his arms over his chest he shook his head.

"That doesn't make it any better for strangers who only hear 'brother' and see a bunch of people who share the same last name, but still. If she didn't like it, since she has the power to, she could have removed him easily. Whether that be murder or kidnapping would all be up to what she was feeling."

"See, when you put it like that it makes it sound like she would have just decided to on a whim. Lucille doesn't feel like a person to just *do* things. She plans and executes it." This was frustrating, not knowing what that woman was up to while the cards were scattered across the table. It seemed I was playing go fish while she played chess, a whole different game miles ahead of me.

"And you know this because? What are you suddenly an expert in all things shifty mom-related?" I leered at him and rolled my eyes. He has become more comfortable with me, and with that, he has started giving me more lip.

"No, but she is a woman in power. A flick of her hand and she could have her son and Cassian running around like chickens with their heads cut off to do what she asked. Granted, looks like Judas has been digging in his heels…"

"You could have that power too. I mean, you are Judas's girlfriend technically. If you get him to marry you, you could in theory take over for Lucille."

"Marry him…? I don't know, lately he has been becoming distant. Verging on pompous without Ale here, I know he is hurting too but…." My hand moves to my stomach and I frown slightly. Alessandro wouldn't want me to just run though, would he? This child is of the bloodline; he would be the heir. "I mean, I want to think I still love him… but pain changes people. Is he even the same Cardinal I met on that ritual night?"

"Well, I wouldn't recommend running just yet. You said it yourself, pain can do things to people, and it probably doesn't help if mommy dearest is lingering over his shoulder all the time." The ghoul paused and stood up, pushing his mask off so that he could look me in the eye. "Hear me out. What if I follow Lucille for a little while? See if anything shakes loose. If she really is set on getting rid of you as well, then it would help to have evidence to further break Judas from her."

"This feels like plotting." I protested, though as I did so Phantom squatted down in front of me. The seams of his new black skinny jeans cracked slightly as if they hadn't been worn in all that well.

"It's not plotting if it's for your protection, it is my job. Trust me here yeah?"

Reluctantly I nodded in agreement. Phantom stood up and ruffled my hair, soon then making his way out of my room. It felt wrong but he was right, I needed proof. I needed evidence she staged the wreck, that she was coming after me, and that she was manipulating Judas even though I knew it in my soul. Laying back in my bed, I stare up at the ceiling. Anxiety swirled in my chest like a stormy sea, bucking back and forth as it dragged other emotions into its turmoil. I didn't want to fear her, but with every interaction something inside me screamed to fight back. That she was a danger to me and to everyone within these walls.

Time to Dance

"Wake up my dear. I can't let you sleep through this meeting…" Purred a distantly familiar voice. It had been months at this point since I last heard from Lucifer. Our first and only full meeting before today was when he gave me that foreboding warning. *'She cannot do anything until the end of April of this year, go to your loves it will not affect their fates. Take this bit of knowledge with you though. Three great men will fall when the fourth rises, Death will come scythe in hand and no one can stop the reaper.'*

Just as he had said, she had done something at the end of April. Now it was almost the end of July, the sweltering summer days dragging on as the world had plans to change for fall. But only one great man had fallen…

"I said wake up." The world around me grew hotter, enough so that I threw myself into a sitting position. My eyes open to scan the empty space, waiting for it to once again burst into flames as it had prior. Pushing myself up, I groan in pain, searching for Lucifer.

"I'm up... You lied to me. Only one has died." Crossing my arms, I began to walk in the direction I first saw Lucifer. "Alessandro is dead, and that's it. And now I have Lucille up my ass worse than before."

"Tch, you have little faith for someone who is supposed to become the Prima del Madre. He isn't dead, just gone. Others will die before the fall, do not think that The Ministry is safe now." He hissed, descending from the darkened sky to meet me on the mirrored plane of fire. "You have doubts of your relationship with Judas, no?"

"Well yes. He hasn't exactly stayed sweet and kind like I had first fallen for. I find it hard to believe that he will continue to have my best interest in heart with Alessandro gone."

"And are you still naïve and afraid like you were when he had first met you?"

"Well no." That wasn't a fair comparison to make; I was being exposed to new things, he had someone die. "But-"

263

"People change. You can either change with him or let yourself stagnate." He staggered closer to me, staff in hand. "Judas is a scared man, he knows that it is very likely his mother killed Alessandro, and that if he doesn't perform, they will kill him next. He is just a dog chasing his tail."

Cocking his head, the enigmatic demon brought his staff to my chin. With a gentle push, he forced me to look up into his black and white gaze, a smile creeping over his face. "I can see why they both enjoy you. You have quite the mind… Gale my dear, you should be able to figure this out."

"Figure what out?"

"What do you need to do in order to survive Lucille, it should be obvious at this point." He withdrew the staff and stalked towards the billowing hellfire that lined the space around us. With a hand of swirling humanity, he brushed through the flames as if moving through water. "Adapt to survive, or suffer under the weight of your role. Lucille wasn't always a venomous wretch, ask Cassian even."

That was the one person of the upper clergy I had avoided talking to, the patriarch. Cassian was still by all means in power even though he kept himself from view. We collectively knew he called the shots when it came to major decisions with the ministry. The other Belladonna's simply were there to show face and gather

264

new members, they played the part while Cassian picked the direction.

"I can't cause harm to her, I feel like that would break any connection Judas and I have." I could hear him growl, frustrated with me before taking a deep breath and walking back over.

"You aren't causing harm. You are finding a way to outwit her, to beat her at her own game. If she wants to threaten you, make threats back. I did not give you my blessing just for you to cower away from a challenge. Fight. Back." With that, he placed a taloned hand on my chin and lifted my face. A simple kiss was placed on my lips before the hellfire faded away and I was left back in my cramped one-window room.

I knew I wasn't a fighter; I barely was a runner. I fawned. People pleasing to get through the hard points so that I could weasel away in the end. I didn't have the proverbial claws to defend myself, though in theory if I could get over my fear I could. Laying there, my gaze traces over the stones of my ceiling. Following hidden curves and patterns that snaked across as I let my mind try to conjure up a plan. Phantom was going to follow her and collect information that we could use against her. I could finally meet Cassian, but almost no one traveled through the catacombs to go visit him. They were winding tunnels filled with the skulls of our dead and his 'lair' for lack of a better term lay at the end of it. Once he had found the 3 older Belladonna men, he retired to the cavern to work from the shadows and be left alone. Arthur was well old enough to take care of the throne and the others in line. And Lucille had stuck around to raise Judas so it wasn't like he had to be visible.

Sitting back up, I pause for a moment and wipe off my lips. They were warmer than usual like Lucifer's kiss in the dream state lingered on my lips in the real world. A tingle arose in my chest before I stood up and made my way from the room. I couldn't be developing feelings for another, not roughly 4 months pregnant with my dead partner's child. Then again, I don't think it would count since he was approximately the equivalent of a ghost right now. Unable to affect me in the physical world aside from whatever bleeds through the cracks.

Now, I was unsure of how to find my way to Cassian's lair, seeing how I had never had a reason to go find it before. I didn't want to just go wandering through the catacombs unaccompanied; that felt like a death sentence if I were to get lost or caught by someone on Lucille's payroll. She had ghouls at her disposal that would have no issue dispatching me. I could bet on one ghoul being able to do what I ask, but he was busy. Perhaps I could snag one of the band ghouls who worked for Alessandro before he had been pulled from the stage. They would have the motivation to help me if they knew I was looking into his death, but there was a good chance that any one of them would also snitch. Perhaps I should ask Caesar for help; he has a reputation for getting into trouble and doing what he can to intentionally piss off Lucille. I just had to hope that I wasn't on his shit list.

I set my heading and make my way up to Caesar's room; the first time I was up there, I had heard a woman in the middle of having her face ridden into the mattress. The only time I had bothered to come to talk to him was when he was getting ready for a 'session'. While it was important to address my eye, he seemed displeased to be bothered since we already knew what it meant. After spending so much time around the monastery and hearing stories of his prowess, I would be lying if I said I wasn't jealous. If sex hadn't made me so nervous when I first joined, being wrapped around his fingers might have been a fun way to spend my summers past.

Through the halls, I weaved around the many brothers and sisters who were making their way to lunch. Some overlooked me, walking past as their stomach did the driving. Others glared down at me, their eyes digging into my skin. Even with one dead, I was regarded as the local whore. Frankly, the amount of slut shaming that came from people who were supposed to be open-minded was astounding. But everyone has their own beliefs.

It didn't take me long to find myself in front of his door once more, hesitating to knock. I could feel the judgmental stare that I would get if I didn't ask him in the 'correct' manner. Taking a deep breath, I straightened out the blue gown that was stretched across my frame. Attempting to smooth out any wrinkles that remained from falling asleep in it before raising my hand to knock on the door. But before my knuckles even made contact, the door was ripped open, Caesar standing above me with an eyebrow arched.

"Yes?" he growled, obviously unamused by my presence.

"Sir, my apologies for bothering you but I was hoping I could ask you for some help."

"Help with what exactly?" His tone was bitter and low, like at any moment he would slam the door in my face and tell me off.

"I need an escort... a Ghoul preferably that will not snitch back to Lucille..." Caesar arched an eyebrow and stepped out of the door frame, ushering me inside with a flick of his head. Stepping inside quickly, I ducked my head as he shut the door behind me, holding my breath as I waited for him to speak again. He sighed, his oxfords clicking on the hardwood as he walked towards the chairs awaiting by the obsidian fireplace.

"So you need help sneaking around, and I am assuming it is *from* that crazy bitch that Judas calls a mother. If you are here asking for an escort Phantom must be busy." He says, almost dismissively. I followed his path and sat down across from him;

my head still ducked as I wanted to avoid his gaze. "What's in it for me?"

I didn't think about what he would want in return for this favor. Honestly, I had been operating under the assumption that because it would piss off Lucille he would just go for it. A single ghoul being lent to the mother of one's future 'nephew' seemed like nothing, but he wanted something. My gaze rose to meet his, my hands coming to rest in my lap as I stared blankly into that mismatched gaze. All of them had it. That look in their eye like they could take over the world if they wanted to; they had power, and they knew they did. But he wore his ambition behind a thin sheet of glass; with one small crack in his containment a supervillain could be born.

Swallowing back my fear, I clenched my jaw for a moment as I tried to scrape together anything worthwhile.

"I don't believe I have much to give you…" He smirked.

"You people are all the same, coming to me because you assume I have an answer for you. And yet you do nothing for me. What is with that hm?" He leaned forward, his arms on his knees as he leered at me. "I could pull a ghoul fresh from hell for you, right this moment even, that would be loyal to you and only you. But I need something in return. Something of value to me."

This was the man known for being the most promiscuous; in short, he was a man whore. When he wasn't busy running security with an iron fist, he usually had someone strung up in his room. Shabari rope was his medium, and he was practically Picasso. He wouldn't want my body, would he…?

"I am not giving you myself. Judas and Alessandro have reserved that right…" *Fuck I wouldn't mind it though…* "Whatever you need or want from me to do this, it cannot involve me in any form of intimacy."

"Who said I needed your body? You are already filled with the offspring that came from my brother's seed. I don't feel like being tunnel buddies with him." His nose crinkled as he sat back and adjusted his lapel ever so slightly. "Other women, sure. If they needed a task, I would take sex as payment if it was something they wanted to offer. Pleasure is a trade I rather enjoy dealing in when people want to do it. No, I need something much more important."

He paused for a moment. "If I am to summon a personal demon for you, I need part of your soul. I would use mine, but." He shrugged and ran his hand over his bald head. "I don't have enough of it left to just use on favors like this. All tapped dry. And, of course, payment… but that can be discussed later down the line. I want to be able to call in a personal favor at any point."

"You're joking, right? Just… a favor?" I asked hesitantly, trying to decide if I needed to laugh or not. However, I felt relieved that he wasn't asking anything of me at the moment. "No one believes in souls like that, and if they did exist, it's not like you can just scrape some off… can you?"

"There is a lot more that you don't know about. See, while Judas and Alessandro play house and rockstar, prancing about the ministry, the rest of us have work to do. Arthur has gotten too old to help me, too weak. While his connection to the devil is still strong, he doesn't have the power and the command he used to." Caesar watched me before continuing. "Look. You want a job done, a ghoul escort of your own? I need part of your soul. Just enough to summon something. You should be familiar with a ghoul on a leash. You have Mona's, you have part of her soul even hanging around your neck like a little prize." My hand moved to the necklace that always sat on my chest, a gift given to me by Arthur.

"Part of… part of her soul?" I ask incredulously, not quite sure that I believe it yet.

"He failed to mention that, didn't he? That necklace is tied to a ghoul, your ghoul, Mona's ghoul. The only way we can do that is by taking part of someone's soul and trading it with the ghoul in question. Then, we take part of their soul and mesh it with whatever is left after the trade to imbue it in an object. Usually, it's

271

something small that can easily go overlooked, like a necklace. Sometimes, it is the gem itself that is the cursed object; other times, it's the whole item. Whatever is more capable of holding onto the soul's energy." I blinked at him, almost dumbfounded, as I rubbed the necklace between my fingertips. This wasn't just a gift from Arthur to say that he accepted me into the family. Rather, insurance that part of Mona would keep living on through me and Phantom.

"Hmph, I think you get it now." Standing up, he outstretched his hand to me. "So, do we have a deal? You need a ghoul. I won't ask questions about why, but I need that slice of your being. Then you can piss off Lucille all you want."

"And what if I don't want that? What if I just want to borrow one of your ghouls?" I ask, weighing my options.

"Then I won't be able to promise that they will stay loyal. They have been on this earth for years; selling out one measly sister would mean nothing to them as they are not bound by any contract outside of the band."

"Fuck…"

"Yeah, fuck. Now, do we have a deal or what? I have other things I need to do with my time." His gaze seemed to go right through me as I rose slowly and took his hand. A grin spread across his face as his grip tightened. His black and white eye began to glow an ominous green tint that began to smoke from his socket, the flesh on that half of his face going translucent to reveal his skull beneath.

"This might hurt a bit." Caesars voice had split in half as it left his lips, baring his teeth as he squeezed tightly.

"What?!" Before I could pull my hand away, electricity ripped through my body. Every nerve was on fire as I could feel something being pulled away from me. The energy felt as if it was being sapped from my body, and just as soon as it had started, it had ended. Ceasar pulled away his hand and nodded, looking at his palm as if he could see what he had taken, his face returning to normal.

"Good. Be back here tomorrow night and I will have a ghoul for you. Until then, I would recommend staying out of trouble... Wouldn't want this to be for nothing, eh?"

My world felt like it had been cast in jello, everything wobbling and swaying in front of me. Or was it me who was swaying...? My legs shook under my body before giving out like pasta under a boot heel, the world going black on me as I hit something hard.

A Light in the Dark

"Ah fuck… ow…. Ow," I whimper as I manage to push myself up into a sitting position, my head spinning as I start to come to. The last thing I could remember was shaking Caesar's hand and then electricity ripping through my body as he stripped away a part of my soul. My hand went to my chest as I searched for the necklace, clutching it tightly. This was still Mona's necklace, a part of her soul and Phantom's resided here. Now I would be getting my own…

Finally, I began to scope out my surroundings. I could tell from the plushness of the bed alone that I was not in my room, but it was too dark to tell whose room I was in.

I began scooting in the direction of an edge, sliding across what felt like a bare mattress until I managed to find the drop-off. Hopping off, I shuffle around the dark, arms outstretched as I felt for anything that might give me light. It took a moment as I bumbled my way into an end table and a chair before finally finding the curtains to rip open. As the fading sunlight flooded the room, I recognized it immediately. Alessandro's room...

I had been avoiding this room as much as I could for weeks now; it felt wrong without him here and they had kept it locked for the most part. Even now, the room felt lifeless as it flooded with dusk. The royal blue walls seemed to have lost their shimmer, the random bottles on the floor were missing, and his bed was stripped of the ample pillows and blankets he had. The air had grown stale; any remnants of his cologne were gone. It was almost sterile now, like it had become a guest room, cast off to the side to be filled with the next wandering stranger.

Walking back towards the center of the room, my gaze returned to his bed. The massive 4-post bed with bodies of naked women caved into the posts, where much of this adventure had started. My heart sank as I tried to imagine him sitting there in the middle, a book in his hand, as he would watch me mend a tear in his jacket. He wasn't here anymore. I would never get to watch him fight off sleep again just to chat me up or deal with his lewd jokes as he would go about applying his face paint. I would go so far as to say he was robbed of a long life; dying at 52 felt too young when his older brothers were in their late 50s and 60s. Hell, if Cassian was truly still alive, he should be in his 90s. So why were his wings clipped so soon? What made him worthy of death? I could ask that question for years and probably never get an actual answer.

The sorrow that began to rebuild itself slowly turned to rage. It wasn't fair. Judas was likely right that all of this was staged; Lucille had been making half-assed threats for weeks. It would be below her to not carry through with at least one. I needed to find a way to exact revenge, to show her that she can't continue screwing with us. I needed to separate her from Judas before she poisoned his mind beyond repair.

Quickly, I made my way from Alessandro's room to Caesars. Not bothering to knock, I shoved the door open surprised that it was unlocked.

"Give me my ghoul. I'm not playing games anymo-..." Maybe I should have knocked. Caesar looked back over his shoulder as the woman he was with let loose a scream. She was unable to cover up her body as her hands and ankles were strapped onto a black and red St. Andrews cross. He sighed as he turned to face me, using his body to cover the naked lady. However, I am not sure that was a much better choice as he only had on his slacks, and in his hand was a cat o'ninetails.

"So knocking is suddenly a lost skill, hm? I know stripping parts of one's soul does not affect manners, maybe passing out made you forget them." He chided, the disappointment thick in his tone.

"I-I… usually knock. I'm sorry." Swallowing back my embarrassment, I straighten up and nod towards him. "I need my ghoul now. I have things to do, and I am not waiting for you to finish playing hide the pickle with…" Leering at the woman for a moment, I recognized the face. "With Sister Madeline. Please." I could tell that I had pissed him off as he slid the impact toy off his wrist and chucked it onto the bed. Stalking over to his little nightstand, he dug around momentarily before pulling out a little velvet bag. Closing the gap between us, I held out my hand for him to deposit the little trinket.

I had never had the pleasure and misfortune of being this close to him, not even at the ritual as he had his hands on my chest. Standing toe to toe, his bare-chested form towering over me, I was wrapped in the alluring pull of his noir cologne. My breath halted in my lungs as I stared up at him, hoping the blush on my cheeks went ignored as I waited for my item.

"Take it. Get out." He growled as he thrust it into my grip and grabbed the door. "Knock next fucking time." I began to walk out of the room, stopping just outside the door as a question came to my mind.

Sister Salacious
BETWEEN THE POWERS

"Wait, how do I-" the door slams shut in my face. I
deserved that for barging into his space like I had; I wouldn't have
been surprised if he had withheld the item from me, either. Could
have punished me how he saw fit… *what is wrong with me? Jesus.*

Staring at the little parcel in my hands, I went down the
stairs and back towards my room. I knew it was my safest place to
go if I wanted to stay hidden from Lucille while I summoned the
new ghoul for the first time. The halls were oddly empty though,
my footsteps echoing as I scurried through. People were missing or
busy. Either way, it made me uneasy; normally, a few stranglers
were lingering along the stone walls as people waited for dinner to
be served.

Slipping into my room, I pinned myself against the door
for a moment as I tried to make sure no one was going to just
appear and catch me. My fingertips moved to open the little bag,
pulling delicately at the maw until I caught a glimpse of silver. It
had looked like a ring with a thin band, and set in its claws was a
deep blue stone cut like a heart. It certainly was an impressive little
ring for being something so simple, something that held part of my
soul and that of a ghoul. Testing it across my various fingers, it
slipped effortlessly onto my ring finger, the metal cold to the
touch. With Phantom, I just needed to say his name or say I needed
him, even simply thinking I needed help summoned him to my
side. Hell, sometimes I could even use a little chant I made up, and

he would appear all the same. But Caesar was too busy to explain how this one worked, was I to assume it was the same concept?

Clenching my fist, I closed my eyes as I tried to imagine what their name might be or even what type of ghoul I would be summoning. The ring grew colder, even with my hand clenched like my new fiend knew I was trying to think of how to summon them. The world around me was cool as well, numbing my senses until a hand appeared on my shoulder, and claws began to dig into my supple skin. Opening my eyes, I looked up into the face of my new 'friend,' though I was expecting to see a mask like the one I had with Phantom. Instead, staring back at me with silvery eyes was a ghoul of pure black. His hair was like freshly spun silk, wispy and a cottony white as it hung down to his shoulders. I winced away from his hand as his claws dug in further, a whimper slipping my throat. But that small objection was enough for the creature to quickly retract his hand.

He had stepped back from me, a cloak shrouding his form for the most part. The ghoul was impressively tall, and yet he was thin. His face was gaunt, cheekbones sharp as the rest of his features seemed to be more dead.

"Um… Hello." I say hesitantly, unsure if he can understand me. "I'm Gale, I had Caesar summon you to… help me with a few things."

"*And what is it that I am to help you with…?*" Hissed with a voice that was filled with multitudes as it rose from the depths of hell.

"Well, I need to make my way through the Catacombs to find someone. And then I will likely need a hand with setting up a trap for another…"

"*So we are to cause problems? I am not surprised… I was summoned and given to what? A child?*" The being was dismissive, unsurprisingly so as it looked me up and down with distain.

"Hold on, I am not a fucking child, first and foremost. And I resent that you would think so." I retorted, feeling the fire return to my chest. "Second of all, you are here to help me. I don't care if you are the most lackluster and useless person to help or if you carry my plans out like a good little soldier. Until I have my answers and my plans are executed, you are mine." The ghoul looked taken aback for a moment; his silvery eyes focused on me as he opened his mouth to protest. But deciding against it, he closed his mouth again.

"Good. So you understand me then." Taking a deep breath, I smoothed out my gown and tried to compose myself so that I came off as strong. "First things first. I need you to walk with me through the catacombs. There is someone down there who might have information about my partner's death or about what the hell the Abbess's plans are. I do not know what to expect, so do not ask me." The ghoul nodded as he looked to the floor, his boney, clawed hands picking at the outdated Victorian suit that lay across his scrawny body beneath the cloak.

"What's your name?" I ask with a disgruntled sigh, figuring that in my efforts to be tough, I may have come off as an asshole.

"*River,*" It managed to push out. I couldn't help but laugh slightly, not at the name itself but more at the fact that it was probably one of the most stereotypical names you could possibly give a ghoul of the water persuasion. Well I assume he was a water ghoul with that name.

"Well, it is nice to meet you, River. I'm sorry for being harsh but... I have a mission, and you have become integral to it. I hope you understand."

River shrugged at me, disinterested still in what I had to say. Out of all the ghouls that Caesar could have summoned for me, he picked one that did not give a fuck. Maybe Phantom was the same way though, when Mona first called him to her, gruff and aloof as he wanted nothing to do with people. I would just have to deal with it until we were done, and if I was lucky, River would cooperate.

"Right…" Pinching the bridge of my nose, I straightened up and brushed off any perceived dirt. "Catacombs first. Then… with whatever I get there, we can make a better plan. You are not to share what we are doing with anyone, right? I can try to make it worth your while, but I need you to understand that this must be kept from everyone… you are here to help me, to serve me. All others are to be assumed as hostile."

"Why the secrecy?" The ghoul murmured as he adjusted the cloak that had threatened to slip from his shoulders. "It would be safer to do this alone if you needed silence."

"I think…" A sigh leaves me as I scratch at the back of my head, anxiously picking at the stands of hair under my fingertips. "I think that the Abbess here has been trying to find a way to get rid of me. And I am almost certain she got rid of Alessandro."

"Mkay… and Alessandro is?"

"One of my partners. The other one is her son, and she has been weirdly overprotective of a grown-ass man." The laugh that slipped my lips was bitter, uncomfortable, and nervous. "She doesn't favor me, and as soon as she discovered I was involved with both of them I ended up with a target on my back."

"Heh, so a mama's boy and his over protective mother. Got it." The ghoul nodded; his silver gaze flickered to the door.

"So… catacombs? I have never been in them, at least not the ones here…"

"Well, I know that there should be an entrance in the mausoleum on the grounds. When I worked in the library, before my reassignment, I saw a few old documents about how this place was built. The mausoleum is out by the forest edge, and within it supposedly is a door to where we need to go…"

"Alright then, let's go," River said, assuming this was just that easy as he began walking towards the door. For someone who came off as abrasive, he seemed to fold rather quickly with some pushback. That might be a problem later…

"No, hold on. No one can see that I have you. Lucille treats me like I am oblivious and her son like he is incompetent. She keeps making threats against me, and if she figures out I have help, more help, I am worried those threats are going to become reality." My hand clenched as I focused on the ring. "I don't need you right now… I will summon you again when I get out there."

River stared at me as his form began to sink into the ground, the hardwood rippling like water. His silver gaze was locked onto mine, eyebrows furrowed as he went under. It felt almost wrong sending him away after summoning. Most of the ghouls didn't seem to care that they were pushed around; they were summoned lackies. Phantom didn't care all that much as that had been his life for years… did River?

While my morals battled in the back of my mind, I slipped from my room and through the stone halls. It was hard being a stealthy woman while pregnant, but no one questioned me as I pushed through one of the side doors and followed the well-worn path in the grass. It wound aimlessly up to the doors of the mausoleum, as a concrete path wandered in the other direction towards the public parking lot. The vast marble structure before me towered into the sky; its stained-glass windows were colorful breaks in the white stone. The door was pushed open, propped with a large polished stone that had flecks of silver. The little voice in the back of my head fretted that this was a bad idea, we had never met Cassian before. He always sounded scary, creepy; after all, who would go hunting for young men who had received Lucifer's blessing?

Perhaps I should have asked Judas more about the man he called father. But it was too late now; I sucked in a breath and walked into the marble halls. Wandering until I found a door that led to a staircase. It was cracked open as if someone had already been through here, or maybe Cassian just wanted fresh air in the crypt.

Clenching my fist, I focused on the ring once more, though this time I had the ghoul's name in mind. River rose from the ground like a specter from the sea; his face still twisted in a confused scowl. As his feet hit solid ground, the willowy figure hunched over and snaked nearer.

"What?" I whispered at him; my eyebrows furrowed with concern. If he couldn't work with me, I might be screwed.

"You just… sent me away, like I am nothing? What the hell?" He hissed quietly. "Is that what this will be? I am your fucking errand ghoul? 'Come River, leave River, fetch me something to eat River.'"

My feeling was right; he wasn't going to be as okay with it as others would be. But this was a terrible moment to have this discussion.

"Now is not the time for this argument, we have to get moving…" He was right though, perhaps I shouldn't have just sent him off like that. "Look, I'm sorry but we can… discuss this more when we get out of here."

River huffed, shaking his head in disbelief as he pushed the door open further and began slinking down the stairs. It had taken us a good 20 minutes to find the way, wandering through the bone-lined halls. The air was thick and stagnant, decay lingering in every breath. Our only light source was a collection of flickering torches and a few well-placed portable lights. It felt as if we had attempted to walk back to the dark ages, but our time still had its claws in the world around us. The catacombs could have stretched for ages, but it wasn't long till we spotted another doorway. A large ghoul stood next to it, his mask old and doll-like and his uniform nothing more than slacks and a button-up.

I wanted to get closer, but something told me that he might be a problem if I did. River narrowed his eyes at the ghoul, his tail lashing back and forth.

"Why aren't we going in there…?" he says in a hushed tone, hiding in the shadows with me.

"Because… I don't think Cassian is alone."

"Who would be-" The door opens and I grab River's cold hand, yanking him around the corner with me into the dark. My eyes slammed shut as I held my breath, every nerve on fire as I recognized the voice at the end of the hall. It was the abbess. Of course, it was. She leached into everything that I tried to do now, she was everywhere.

"Thank you, Cassian, I should be back for him before the end of the week. Just setting some final things into motion and then we can have total control again." The voice of a snake would be far more pleasant. "Just think, our little J will be on top of the world and you will have everything you ever wanted again."

286

"Judas is too weak; a little tragedy will toughen him up enough to lead us properly... I knew I shouldn't have hunted them all down at once. It made them all too dependent on each other." Croaked an older voice, the words rancid as they slithered down the corridor. The putrid scent of overused floral perfume began to draw closer, my grip tightening on my ghoul's hand.

"What about the girl? Judas is too attached to her, and she has the eye... by all means, she is now a part of this. I don't need competition for my position."

"What is she going to do? She is fat and meek. If we get Judas in line, he will pull her in. Just make sure that Phantom Ghoul is out of the way. If she thinks she has any sort of power, this will be harder than it needs to be."

"Phantom won't be a problem; I have a plan to deal with him. He will be rendered practically useless to her once I catch him."

What were they going to do to Phantom? Fuck as soon as I leave here I have to find him again.

"Good. Now go on... I will tend to my disappointment. You have a ministry to run." Their voices were practically on top of us, Lucille walking down the same hall we just come from. My heart sank low in my chest, everything trembling as I attempted to regain my composure. In the walls of the Ministry, I knew Judas was always nearby. But here, she could bury me if she caught sight of me poking around. Waiting till we were sure they had both gone, I stuck my head back out to the main hall. The ghoul guard had moved, and a light shone from under the door. Looking over my shoulder to River, I motioned for us to move forward.

My hand trailed over the skulls that were pressed into the walls, fingertips gliding over the bones as I moved with caution. River huffed behind me and walked past to the door, giving me a look of 'you can't be serious.' Stopping in my tracks, I frowned at him. I thought I had made it clear that this was supposed to be a quiet task and that I couldn't risk being caught. But he didn't seem to care. With a sigh, I followed his lead and crouched down, pressing my ear against the door. Cassian should be by himself or talking with his guard… I hope.

Holding my breath, I sat as still as I could, listening for anything that would clue me into my next move. It was silent, for the most part, anyway, aside from the occasional cough that had made it through the old wooden door. Pressing myself against the grain harder, I closed my eyes as if it was going to help me hear better. It felt like ages dragged past before I heard a different sound. It was a groaning like someone was in pain or uncomfortable. It would carry out for a minute before Cassian's voice would come rumbling out.

"Shut up. You did this to yourself..." The groaning ceased, coughing taking over the silence again before going quiet. He wasn't alone, and whoever he was with wasn't holding up well. The groaning returned, followed shortly by the slamming of a hand against wood.

"I said shut the hell up." The rancid old man shouted, his voice rattling the wood against my head.

"And why should I...? No one can hear but you, strontium..." *That voice...* "Just give me water please, that is all I ask."

"No, I am trying to read. And I cannot read with your constant bitching."

"Maybe... and hear me out. I wouldn't be bitching if someone hadn't used me as a kickball last night." The voice retorted; its familiarity was uncomfortable, pulling my heart as if there were a hook in it connected to the person who was speaking. It was smooth and yet wrought with pain and loathing; there was even a twinge of rage in its tone.

"You always think that you are so important. You had chip on your shoulder; I could have left you in Rome in that gutter you drank yourself into. But no, I picked you up despite my best interest. Look at how you have repaid me. By being a fucking embarrassment. Do you know how many rumors we have had to squash? We put on the illusion that this is a bloodline, that this is a family of power and strength. And you are out here, galivanting with the cardinal flaunting your promiscuity. Flirting with patrons… fucking ghouls. A slave to your lust. You are a disgrace."

"I am a mistake. You fucking knew this when you gave me the whole 'destined for greater things' speech. Not my fault you decided to drag me out here to fucking California." A bitter laugh barely made it through the door as I felt a knot in my throat.

"I…" Cassian's voice stopped. "I thought I was saving you from a worse fate. No child should have been cast out of his home with a bottle in hand just for being strange."

"Maybe I deserved it. My mother knew I was a fuck up when I came out with an eye as black as sin. Try as she might, but nuns can't exactly beat that out of you."

"Alessandro, you could have been so much more if you hadn't been reckless. Lucille caught on fast as to what you and Judas were up to; we are lucky she didn't take this to the council." *No,* he couldn't be alive. He had gone down in a plane crash in April, how can he be here…

"And what are they going to do, huh? Slap me on the wrist? Disown me from the family? Yeah, that will be a good look for you. The anti-pope doesn't even have absolute power over his church; we would be torn apart." He began to laugh, wheezing

290

through the pain. "It's easier to make someone go missing, huh? And what? You are going to keep me down here like your little pet?"

"Not at all… We have a plan. Some people need to be taught a few lessons around here…"

"Judas is a good man… leave him alone."

"Oh… My boy, you are sorely disillusioned… Judas isn't the only one who needs to be thrust back in line. Think a little harder."

"Leave her out of this too! She's done nothing but what we have asked of her-" He shouted, though his voice was quickly cut off by a yelp as it sounded like someone planted their foot in his stomach. The coughing returned, and my hands turned to fists as I froze. River looked down at my body as I stay locked in place, his boney claws grabbing my shoulders as he dragged me from the door as only one thought remained.

I have to get him out of there…

Round and Round

"Judas, I need you to believe me here, alright? I know what I heard." I protested as he rolled his eyes and continued to play his game. "I was down there, alright? I fucking heard his voice!"

"Gale, I can't just go and confront Cassian. You likely heard someone else…" He murmured, voice cold.

"You are acting like a fucking scolded child; what the hell Judas? What happened to the Cardinal? Hm? The man who gave a fuck, who cared when I was upset?" I watch as his hands tighten on the controller.

"You don't think I am trying? Do you know how exhausting it is to go day in and day out being reminded that someone you love is dead? All the while going crazy because you feel it… you feel like he is out there." He paused the game and

292

chucked the controller onto his little nightstand. "I have my mother up my ass about the band; I have clergy members asking what I am going to do about my lack of an heir, found or birthed. My own ghouls seem to have no interest in talking to me, and now the woman I love; the woman carrying my dead partner's child is going out of her way to tell me that he is still alive. I am trying to find peace for a moment."

"What about the papers you showed me? The photographs? You were certain just a few days, a few weeks ago that Alessandro was taken and the crash staged."

"Yeah, and minds change... I have better things to do now than go chasing after a delusion. I want to believe he is alive but he should have been back by now." He rubbed at his face in frustration, a disgruntled sigh leaving his throat as he held out his hand to me. Of course, Lucille already got to him...

"Come here..." Walking closer, I let him grab my hand to pull me into his arms. His head came to rest on my swollen stomach, my hand moving to his messy blonde strands as I smoothed out the strays.

"What am I supposed to do then? I heard his voice, he is alive and being tortured down there..."

BETWEEN THE POWERS

"Just shhh…" He hushed me, sending us into the quiet. The only sound coming from his console as the fans buzzed and the game's pause screen played a casual tune.

It frustrated me that we couldn't agree on what to do. When I had accepted that Alessandro was gone, Judas insisted that he was still out there. And now as I am convinced that Alessandro is being held prisoner right beneath our feet, Judas just wants to relax and try to figure out his new job. This back and forth was starting to grind my gears; it was almost as bad as when my mother insisted that we move in with my grandmother before changing her mind the next week and forgiving my father for his affair.

Judas left a kiss on my stomach and chuckled. "Your mother is driving me crazy…" He said with a soft voice to the life growing inside me.

"Tch Judas." I swatted the back of his head lightly, moving out of his arms to sit next to him. "I need to know what I am supposed to be doing… You don't believe me about the catacombs. You have given up on finding him, and I have no job waiting for me in the library. Lucille refuses to assign me anything. I feel like I am going nuts."

"You are supposed to be relaxing… I know it is hard with everything, but one of us needs to relax." He looked to me, his mismatched gaze empty before he pulled on the mask. "Why don't you stay here tonight? I could rub your back, cuddle you, pamper you like a Prima del Madre should be pampered."

"I would rather go back to my room for the evening. I have a few things I have been needing to do that I have been putting off..." My response frustrated Judas, his brows furrowing at me. "Just for tonight, I can come by tomorrow."

"Fine. Go tend to your little issues, my love. I will be here." He murmured as he grabbed my hand and left a half-hearted kiss in my palm. "One of these days, I will get to worship your tender flesh again..."

I rolled my eyes at his passing comment, leaving the room with little hesitation. He had been becoming a pain as stress built in his life. I know I was his, we were even supposed to set up the ceremony for next year when he got settled into his position fully. But the promise of forever came with the heavy burden of being attached to someone who no longer was the man you fell in love with. I needed Judas in my life; my heart still longed for him. But the Judas in that room was not the one I fell for... I need to talk to Phantom.

While the walk back to my room was a short one, it felt like eons passed before I could summon Phantom to me. River had been crashing in my room, anxiously holed up as he waited for me to come back. The water ghoul had detested being sent away and

295

brought back all the time. Yet when he and Phantom interacted it was like placing two strange cats together in a small box. You never knew what sort of reaction they would have.

"River. Be nice." I warned as I grabbed my pendant to summon Phantom. Like clockwork, I called for him and he appeared in his cloud of smoke.

"So. What did you find out?" I asked, crossing my arms as the cloud disappeared.

"She has something planned, I don't know what but she and Cassian have been having a lot of meetings. And… I don't know. Whenever she sees me, she makes odd comments about who 'we ghouls really belong to'. She has warded her office too; I haven't been able to get in and poke around." The fire ghoul's ruby gaze raked over the willowy River who sat in my bed. "Bitch has been covering her tracks…"

"So, we have nothing." I groan as I rubbed at my forehead for a moment.

"Well, not nothing… We know she and Cassian have been busy and we heard Alessandro in the catacombs." River pipped in from behind me. "We just have to figure out how to get him out."

Phantom gave the ghoul a snide grin, rolling his eyes before returning to me with a raised brow.

"So what? This is becoming a rescue mission?"

"No. Maybe... I haven't decided yet. I want to get him out of there, if it really is him but it also sounded like perhaps Lucille had another plan for him. Maybe she is bringing him back once Judas gets settled in, like a really fucked up forced retirement." I hated that idea just as much but it meant he would be alive still.

"Hah. Good one. I wouldn't count on it but you are the boss." Phantom bowed his head to me before leaning back against the door. "How much do you trust Lucille to make the ethical choice here?"

Damnit... he was probably right.

Alessandro wasn't going to be returned, not with how Lucille does her bidding. I had ghouls though. I had two who I trusted, one more than the other at the moment but enough to go get him. I walked over to my desk and rested against its cool surface. My eyes traced over the wood grain as I tried to think of a plan.

I couldn't just send them in half-cocked; Cassian would be watching. As far as I knew, he never even left his chamber unless he had to. I could talk to Judas about fitting them with proper uniforms, and send them in under the guise of a delivery or a summoning. One could stay behind and look for Alessandro, if he was still alive, and get him out of there. My fingertips tapped on the desk as I closed my eyes. This wasn't who I was. I wasn't some all-powerful, sneaky badass. I was just someone who wanted to keep their head down and move through life unseen. But no, I got involved with the Antipope and his boy toy.

Shit...

"Alright so..." Pushing off the desk I turned around. "I can't go down there myself and be any real use. I know you two don't owe me anything but if I can get you the uniforms can you go down there and get him out?"

"What?" Phantom said, disbelief in his tone. River couldn't help but laugh, practically cackling as he coughed up a lung. "You think we can just walk in there and come out alive?"

"If he is still alive down there, if it is him, then he should be rescued. If he isn't alive or it isn't him then well... I guess I can feel better about the situation and putting it to rest."

"So let me get this straight. You want us to go down there and pull out your 'dead' boyfriend. And then what? Are you going to hide him here? Take him back to Judas and hope he doesn't decide to rub it in his mother's face. Do you know how stupid this sounds?" Phantom huffed, his tail lashing behind him as he grew animated. "Not even Mona was this ballsy, she worked in the light and was kind to get what she wanted."

"Mona's partners were either attached to this fucking necklace or were the only available pope at the time. She didn't have to go save one." I retorted as I stepped up to the hulking ghoul. "Now either I get my help or find others who will do it."

Rivers laughing stopped and I could hear the bed creak as he stood up, clearing his throat.

"Right, so you want to run a rescue mission... Tell us the plan." Phantom glared at River as the ghoul came around to stand next to him. "I mean, I won't say it is a good idea. But what do I know? I have barely been on top for a week."

"Thank you..."

#

Ghouls were set, uniforms were fitted, and it was show time. After I had gone back over the plan with Phantom and River, I sent them on their way. Realistically, I had low hopes that they would return before this evening. So that meant I had to keep people busy. Lucille was already on one today as she was distracted with the new flow of siblings who had entered the Ministry. Cassian would be harder to redirect, but if they were as smart as I hoped they were, they would be able to get him out of his nest long enough to check it out. Judas was mine to deal with… and that would be easy. He wanted my attention and my affection, and I could almost guarantee that he would want a feminine touch.

Throwing on a flattering emerald floor-length Bardot gown, I made my way to Judas's office, where he sat with his nose in paperwork. I could let him work, but where's the fun in that? My knuckles rapt on the door as I pushed it open, a smile creeping across my face as I entered.

"Baby, do you have time for me?" I purred, the sound of my saccharine voice enough to pull his attention from the papers. He grinned at the sight of me, leaning back in his chair as he looked over the edge of his desk.

"Mm, I see you have come around Sorella. How are you doing today?" He mused, tapping on the arms of his chair. There was a hunger in his gaze that I hadn't seen in a while, one that was near predatorial even. The last person to draw such a reaction from the Cardinal was Alessandro, and when I saw it, Judas was shoved against a wall, his length devoured by a man of higher power.

"Well, you have been working so hard and I feel better today…" Shutting the door behind me I sauntered closer. "And so, I figured perhaps you would like a little entertainment." Clicking the lock, I made my way around his desk so that I could sit on the edge.

"I mean, if you still find me as attractive with how… well." I looked down at my body, the swollen belly being the most noticeable change in my form.

"Oh, mia bella… of course, you are still beautiful. Your body is a work of art crafted by Lucifer himself. You could never not be stunning." He said softly, his hands slipping under my gown to rub at my thighs. "I could rule the world with you at my side…"

I chuckled lightly, watching as he left innocent kisses along my belly, moving up toward my breast. My mind went quiet as I focused on his touch again. The warmth of his leather gloves as they pawed at my thighs, the weight of his head as it rested against my chest. I sighed as I relaxed into his touch, allowing my legs to be pushed apart. My hand moved to the back of his head to tangle in his blonde hair.

Judas seemed enraptured by my flesh, pushing the hem of my skirt up my legs until he got to his prize. His mismatched gaze flickered up to meet mine, his tongue running across his lips as his pleading gaze asked for permission. Sex always turned him submissive. He had power in his day-to-day, so the bedroom was one of the few places he gave it up. I hesitated to nod. As much as I wanted to feel him and keep him there with me, part of me had

301

grown to loathe his childish behaviors over the last few months. But I needed to make sure he was still focused on me. Nodding, I rest back on my palm to allow for easier access. His hands surged forward, tugging off the soft cotton underwear that had hidden my slit from him. The panties were discarded, dropped to the floor, and quickly forgotten about as he pushed my legs further apart.

I hissed slightly as my hips griped at me, my current state preventing my usual range of motion. Judas took notice, slipping his arms under my thighs. He pulled my body closer, leaving his black crescent kisses up my skin. Everything tingled as I rocked my head back. I was here to be his distraction, yet he was still the master of my mind. His tongue traced over my flesh, innocent circles that danced closer to my cunt. A shudder ripples through me as he drags his tongue through my slit, savoring my juices. From his lips slips a pleased groan.

"Mm… Cara mia…" He murmured between laps. Focused solely on the gentle folds between my thighs. As much as I wanted to shut out the pleasure, his skilled tongue would not let me distance myself. Every lap was a thrilling sensation: waves of electricity shimmered through my body. To my surprise, his fingers ran up through my slick, taking the opportunity to push in. His ring and middle curled up into me in a 'come hither' motion that begged my body to sing for him. Lazy moans wandered from my throat as I let myself lean back onto his desk, papers crunching beneath me as they gave away to my weight. The tingle that danced over my skin was intoxicating, every move of his jaw pulling strings on my body as I twitched for him.

"Again amore... I need to hear you again..." He panted, eating my cunt with a persistent hunger. As if my slow oncoming orgasm would feed his body and soul.

Fuck I was almost there. It had been so long since I had allowed him this tender act of worship, I almost forgot what it was like to feel as if I were the center of his universe. His eagerness knew no limits, his eyes fluttered shut as he buried his nose firmly against my mound. I was soaking and couldn't tell if it was from my body or from him, but he didn't mind.

My hands clenched at the fabric of my dress, his tongue focusing solely on the swollen bud of nerves. Judas would lap and lick, sucking at my clit as he felt my thighs tightened around his head. I fell helplessly to the orgasm that came ripping through my body, my cherry throbbed with each drag of tongue. Electricity raced through my core as I arched from the desk, my hands gripping the smooth hardwood.

"That's it... there you go, princess..." He purred, his voice followed by a meticulous click as he began the unbuttoning of his cassock.

BETWEEN THE POWERS

As I felt my heart flutter and my body begged to regain composure, there was an abrupt knock on the door. Judas's head shot up, hands fumbling to fix the cassock. Bringing the back of his hand to his mouth, he wiped the remnants of his black lipstick and me clean from his face as he stared at the door. Again, knocking, this time harder and with a greater urgency. It was as if someone was trying to break it down.

"Hold on hold on!" He shouted as he helped me sit up. His hands deftly pull the hem of my dress back down my legs while I frantically try to make myself look presentable. The banging turned into the knob being tested, and as my feet hit the ground the door flew open. Lucille waltzed in, her hands folded in front of her as she looked over the pair of us. Her floral scent practically suffocated me as I tried to hold my breath for the moment. Her gaze locked on mine as she was followed by a short pink ghoul.

"Good. I thought I might find you in here." She hissed as she nodded to the ghoul. "I have something to show you both…"

I looked to Judas, brows furrowed as he began to walk towards his mother. He seemed just as lost as I was in the given moment. But as he drew near, the small ghoul hopped up onto the desk and produced a syringe. Before I could shout to Judas to look out, she turned to me and jabbed me in the neck. The plunger was pushed down as the contents flooded my system. Everything began to sway as I gasped, my hands finding the desk to keep myself propped up. Looking up, I watched as Lucille had done the same, Judas's body slumping against hers as his hands futilely pawed her away.

I attempted to scream, choking on my tongue as it felt like all my muscles were going limp. Our bodies hit the floor in unison with a heavy thud. Blackness consumed our vision...

All Things Must End

I wake up to someone carrying me across their shoulders like I was a sack of potatoes. My hands were bound in front of me with a tight rough rope, and my mouth gagged with a foul-tasting cotton rag that sucked the moisture from my mouth. I wriggled and struggled against the strong arm of whoever had ahold of me. The hand that held me tight was hot; it felt like a fire ghoul had a hold of me, their claws digging into my flesh. I kick and writhe fighting as much as I can but all it got me was a flick in the face from the ghoul's tail. My eyes dart about trying to figure out where I am, the stone floor though gives me nothing as I am stuck listening to his shoes clicking onwards.

Groaning, kicking, and writhing I fight back trying to get set down. The ghoul growls at me, the voice low and rumbling. My mind was racing as I continued to struggle, who the hell had me? Where were we going? Why was I tied up?

The sound of wooden doors being thrown open alerted me to where we were, that and the fact that I managed to whip my head around just enough to catch a glimpse of the doors before they were pushed open. The ghoul walks in further before throwing me hard to the ground, I land on my chest gasping and wheezing for air. The ritual chapel doors close and the footsteps return. I could hear someone else gasping for breath next to me, though they more sounded like they were crying. There was a rattle of chains and an eerie silence that then seeped into the room. I struggled to push myself upright when I felt someone's hands tangle in my long hair and rip my head up. I whimper with pain as I am forced up onto my knees, my eyes flickering up to see a familiar face. It was Phantom…

Well, it wasn't Phantom as I knew him, there was something wrong. He had around his neck an iron collar that seemed to burn against his skin, his face was covered in what looked like lashes. His beautiful fire-filled eyes were blackened out as if the flame were snuffed out and he was someone's puppet. Though he looked to be under someone's control, he still looked at me with morose as if he was not in control of any of his actions in this exact moment, but mentally he was still there. A single tear rolls down his ashen skin as he lets go of my hair and forces me to look to the right of me. On his knees with fearful tears running down his face was Judas. His hands were bound behind his back to his ankles, the rope cutting into his sensitive skin. His usually oh-so-perfect hair had been messed with like someone had been dragging him around by his scalp. He looked at me with terror on his face as he whimpered and cried, but he too was gagged.

Fear sunk into my bones and my blood ran cold. I looked around frantically as soon as Phantom let go of my face, he stalked up the ritual stage and stood like a puppet waiting for his strings to be pulled. Awaiting orders from some unknown source. My eyes flicker about the room, the alter was set up and there were two glass coffins in the room with what looked like bodies in them. My heart sank in my chest as I tried to catch a glimpse of who might be in those coffins. That's when it hit me, the pungent, acrid aroma of flowers.

"Ah, perfect. Everyone is all here…" I heard her voice croak out as she made herself known. Lucille stood up from her usual spot-on stage, hidden behind the stone altar. She had a cold smile painted across her face as she stepped up into view. Her body was clad in a long black dress reminiscent a mourning gown.

"You know, Arthur and Caesar were easy. They trusted me far too much to suspect anything. Arthur's face when he saw Phantom with that needle was so… satisfying." She chuckled, the tone as bitter as vinegar as she walked over to the coffins. With her hands resting on top of the glass cases, she gave a pause. "They went easy though... a little botulinum goes a long way, even with 'sons' of a great and powerful family..."

My eyes widened in fear as I looked upon those coffins. They were dead...? Arthur and Caesar? The two eldest of the family were dead? My body trembled as I gazed at those coffins, every ounce of my being, every nerve alight with sorrow and rage. I liked Arthur ... but at least he was with Mona now. Lucille smiled at me as she watched the tears roll down my cheeks, her gaze flickering to my beloved Phantom who stood waiting.

"It was so cute you sent your little Ghoul to hunt down Alessandro as well. It made it so much easier to take him from you too." Her hand gestured to Phantom. "Go fetch the last one." She hissed as she took a step back towards the altar.

"Judas, my little Cardinal... Don't you cry. Mommy is taking good care of you." Her smile turned sour, "I just want what is rightfully yours." She purred softly as we heard the rattling of chains again. Phantom emerges dragging someone across the ground, their face covered in a black bag. Their clothes were ripped and torn, and through the tattered white shirt seeped blood from residual wounds. Their hands and legs were chained together and they looked as if they had been prisoner for the last few days. Phantom's muscles rippled as he heaved the lithe body up onto the alter positioning it so that it laid face up. It groaned softly and

309

shifted on the alter as it was coming to. Phantom gripped the black sack to reveal the tattered beaten face and black hair underneath.

It was Alessandro, it had to be. He groaned as his eyes focused on the room around him, I watched as his chest rose and fell with panic as he recognized he was on the alter. He turned his head to look at us, a soft smile coming to his face for only a moment before it fell. His white and blue eyes flooded with fear as he realized Judas and I were both bound and gagged on the floor. His voice was raw as he opened his mouth to speak.

"Oh... my loves... Mi sei mancato..." he murmured softly. His lips were split and bloody, his gentle face was littered with gashes and he had a black eye. Lucille stepped up to him grabbed his black hair and pulled his head so he would stop looking at us.

I cried out through my gag, begging as my mind came round from the shock of the others. All that came out though were muffled screams. Judas stayed deathly silent, his eyes focused solely on Alessandro's body as he lay there beaten and bruised. This wasn't fair. I had been careful; she was supposed to be busy. River and Phantom weren't to be caught!

Fuck where was River...?

"Please... let me go I will step away no problem... please..." Alessandro whimpered as he was forced to stare at

310

Lucille. She grinned at him, her eyes showing no hint of mercy behind them.

"Oh now. I told you that if you kept messing with Judas, I would do something drastic no?" her claws grasped Alessandro's jaw as she yanked his face to stare at his brothers' bodies in their coffins. "They got it quick… I had no problems with them but all previous heirs must be gone if my little boy is to step into the role. A rule courtesy of fucking Cassian. Hah, he didn't want my bastard to take over, not when his 'sons' had so much potential."

"You bitch!" Alessandro cried out in anguish as he gazed at Arthur and Caesar laid peacefully inside their cases. Their papal robes were done up perfectly, their bodies lay as if only sleeping. He wrenched his face away from her as she cackled at his misery. His eyes quickly met mine again, as if begging for me to help him. I lunged forward only to fall onto my chest again unable to properly move with my limbs bound.

"Tch, go sit her up and if she moves again tie her wrists to her ankles," Lucille ordered. Phantom's body lurched as if he was controlled by a remote, his steps shambling as he drew closer. Once again, his hands grasped my hair as he ripped my body upwards. I cried in pain as I felt hairs snap from their place on my scalp.

"Stop it! Stop, please! Phantom please, Phantom get your hand off her!" Alessandro shouted; his voice was furious though it cracked with every word that left his lips. Phantom ripped my head back, forcing me to sit on my ankles before letting go and walking back to his position again. With tears streaming down my face, I looked to Judas who could not tear his eyes away from Alessandro. He was pulling at his ropes, the rough fibers digging into his skin more as he whimpered through the gag as if trying to plead with his mother.

"I'm sorry, I am so sorry…" Alessandro cried as his gaze stayed locked on mine as the tears rolled down his battered face. Lucille rolled her eyes, fed up with his simpering. From the altar she pulled out a rather small dagger, the blade crooked and jagged though even from where I was, I could tell it had a fine edge to it. With little hesitation, she sunk the blade into his upper thigh eliciting the most devastated cries from Alessandro's throat. His body practically arched off the altar as she twisted the dagger in further. Crimson leaked from the wound as she applied more pressure before ripping the blade from his body.

"You know, I would have left him alone. I mean the pretty boy who leads the band? He would have been fine to leave alone until he was a little older like his brothers. But no, he just had to mess around with my little boy, and his whore." Her words felt like razor blades as her cold gaze rested on me. "And now, that pretty little wench is knocked up with his child. Hah! After I dispose of one bad influence, I am going to cut that uterus out from your body. Judas can keep his whore, but if he wants children, it will be from a bitch I choose."

My stomach was doing summersaults, nausea bubbling up in my throat as I watched the blood run from Alessandro's thigh. My heart was racing in my chest as she threatened me, her words causing Judas to plead from behind his gag. He fought harder to get it out of his mouth, struggling until he finally pushed it free from his maw.

"Madre no please, please leave her be... let us go I will do whatever you ask just let us leave please." He begged his voice trembling with every syllable. "Please please I need them I nee-"

"Shut up. Good sons keep quiet while mommy is working." She snapped at him. "Now, I am going to make this as enjoyable for me as possible." She hummed as she fisted Alessandro's hair in her hand, yanking his head back as she exposed his throat. The world stopped for me, my heart pounding in my head as I watched her pluck the dagger from his thigh and bring it to his throat. With a swift motion, she slit his throat and I watched in horror as the blood ran down his skin. He cried and choked on his blood, gurgling as his throat was filled with it. Judas screamed out, the fearful voice turning to bitter rage as he lashed against his bindings harder. Alessandro's head fell to the side and I

313

watched as the light faded slowly from his eyes. He was still there, long enough for a small smile to creep across his face one last time as he looked into my eyes. A tear fell from his cheek. A deafening silence pounded in my head as I stared into his white and blue eyes watching his life drain from his body. The blood ran like a river down the stone altar, coursing across the red carpet. I was too focused on him to see Phantom approach the alter with a small wood axe. His superhuman strength swung the blade down hard removing Alessandro's head from his body.

My heart stopped in my chest as she gripped his hair and held up his head with a triumphant smile. She was clearly pleased with herself as she held the head of our lover in her claws. From Judas's throat left guttural growls and shouts as he jerked at his ropes, the bindings forcing his skin to bleed. Phantom's body crumpled in on itself as his blackened eyes stared at Alessandro's body. The blood leaked down the altar and snaked like a river across the stage where it dripped like a crimson waterfall from the edge towards us.

Lucille looked at me with a cryptic grin and chucked the head at me, a visceral splatter rung out as his severed head rolled to my knees. I felt sick to my stomach as my body forced me to dry heave at the head. Though painful tears streamed down my face, my eyes never leaving Alessandro's cold lifeless gaze as he lay at my knees. Between rib-shaking heaves my voice screamed out in horror, a blood-curdling sound muffled only slightly by the foul cotton in my mouth. Judas's voice fell silent as I heard his body hit with a thud. My eyes flicker to him for just a moment to see him rip his hands-free from his bindings. His wrist bleeding as he pulled at the ropes around his ankles. He threw himself forward and dragged his body towards the alter. Barely getting to his feet he dashes towards Alessandro's body. He shoved Phantom away, knocking the large ghoul to the ground as he clutched at his still-warm body.

As he grasped and begged for Satan or God to save his lover, his body became smeared in Alessandro's blood. Lucille planted her foot on his shoulder and kicked Judas to the ground. "I didn't raise a coward. I want you to watch as I cut his child from her stomach." She hissed as she started to walk towards me.

"No! NO!" he screamed out. "If you touch a single hair on her head so help me god, I will kill myself right here and now." His voice was full of conviction as from his cassock he produced a knife, placing the tip against his wrist. Lucille stopped in her tracks and leered at him.

"You wouldn't dare…"

"You took the one man in my life who meant the world to me… you took away my brothers and now you threaten to take my child." He growled low and full of rage as the tears carried black paint down his cheeks. "I will make sure I join them if you take one more step."

That seemed to be enough to stop her for a moment. Her path switched as she made a march towards her son.

"Oh, Judas. You were always meant to betray them... I mean, your name? But I could have never seen my son becoming some... floozy. I should have never told Cassian about your status as a bastard, mm all this blood was not needed in the end." She smiled as she grabbed his chin. "But you just do not ever listen... And you never grew out of that boyish crush of yours..."

She cackled as she let go, delivering a swift slap that sent him to the ground. His body curled up as she began to walk towards me. Rather than let me watch or fight, my body had other plans.

I felt my skin go numb as I continued to hyperventilate, my eyes filled with blinding tears as I watched for Judas. My world goes dark and my body falls forward, cradling the head in my lap as I pass out.

#

Judas and I sat in a dim chamber of the mausoleum, the room only lit with the candles scattered across the floor and window sills. In front of us were three glass coffins: Arthur,

316

Caesar, and Alessandro. Judas stayed silent his face to the floor as he stood there in his tight-fitting black suit, a bitter frown starched into his face. I stood alongside him staring at the coffins, not moving as I gazed at the three brothers.

Arthur looked the most peaceful, his hands clasped over his chest. His papal robes properly lain across his body; and his face painted perfectly as he lay in a sleep like death. A bouquet of roses had been tucked into his grasp; all clipped from his garden and stripped of their thorns. Caesar was a little less peaceful, his face rested in his forever frown. The once powerful mage was reduced to a cold lifeless statue, surrounded by gifts and trinkets left by those who adored him. His ferula lay across his body, hands clutching the staff so tight I swear it he was holding on for dear life and for a moment it felt as if he could rise from his coffin.

Alessandro's body was covered in his black papal robes, his hands clasped over his chest as his leather gloves with golden talons hid the wounds that had covered his hands and wrists. His neck was sewn together with a spool of golden thread, looped and embroidered beautifully. The mortician did a fine job of making sure he looked like he had died a peaceful death, but Judas and I knew better. While his body looked beautiful, a pit opened in our stomachs that felt empty and endless.

I stared at the coffins a bit more before pulling the little golden Satanic Cross from my neck. Carefully stalking over to

317

Arthur's coffin, I lay the necklace down on his case. It was the last part of Mona's soul on the surface; it belonged with him even if in the end he believed I would be the one taking her place.

I could no longer call Phantom, whatever spell Lucille had used to take control of him ripped him away from me. He was now forced to be a part of the Ghouls that Judas would use for his band for now, he had to learn to play his part. My feet carried my body to Alessandro's coffin next as I rested my hand on the glass, my vision fuzzy with tears as I gazed at his resting face. Judas cleared his throat and raised his head.

"Come on… we have to get going. The event starts soon, and we have to get to our plane…" he murmured. Resting my hand on my swollen stomach and frowned as I turned to him.

"I know… Come on, little dove…" he said as he held his hand out for me, patient and quiet as he waited.

I took one last look at Alessandro's body and shuffled to Judas, taking his hand. As the two of us were walking from the mausoleum, I was uncertain of what the future held for us now. Lucille lorded over Judas that she had won; his hands were tied on all actions unless he wanted to risk me. But she hadn't exactly beaten him either, especially knowing now that he would be willing to kill himself to stop her.

BETWEEN THE POWERS

Whatever else had happened when I was knocked out caused her to spare the life inside me, but that only meant she had a way to threaten him. Judas was her puppet; a puppet filled with gasoline and tinder, waiting for a match to be struck so that he could burn her down. I was determined not to stay under her rule, we had to think of something to throw her overboard.

Judas was now the only Papa Belladonna, he had the power over the congregation, the band and face of The Ministry. Cassian and Lucille ran in the background, convinced that they were invincible. I will change that...

Now, if only I could make my way to the top.

www.ingramcontent.com/pod-product-compliance
Lightning Source LLC
Chambersburg PA
CBHW050134120726
47903CB00002B/350